The

Colonel's

Cousin

A Pride & Prejudice Variation

by

Melissa Halcomb

Contents

Prologue

6 March 1810 ❧ Matlock House, London

itzwilliam Darcy ran a shaking hand through his hair, the letter he had just read fluttering unceremoniously onto the desk. He swallowed hard; it could not be true. How desperately did he not want to believe the cold, impersonal words on the cheap sheet of parchment.

10 February 1810

My Lord,

It is my regrettable duty to inform you that your son, the Honourable Colonel Richard Fitzwilliam has been gravely injured in service to his king. With few resources or able hands at our disposal, I am afraid there is little that can be done for the Colonel at this time.

As a courtesy to your rank and son's service, I will send word of his burial when the time comes.

Your servant,
Captain Samuel Billings

"Darcy, I—" Lord Matlock choked out.

"No. I do not accept this."

"Wha-what can we do? There is not the smallest hope. My son...my, my son is..."

"No! I do not accept this!" He picked up the letter and shoved it before his uncle. "He speaks of few resources or able hands. I have resources. I have hands. I will go and see to my cousin myself."

Lord Matlock stared at his nephew with a mixture of pity and awe. "Darcy, to what end? It will take weeks to get to the continent. By then...by then it will likely be too late."

"Then I will bring Richard home. He will not be buried in a lonely grave in a foreign land where his family cannot honour him. If, and I do not concede that he will, but *if* he..." He could not bring himself to say the words but saw in his uncle's eyes that there was no need. "Richard will be buried on English soil with his honoured ancestors like the hero he is." He walked to where his uncle sat and placed a hand on his shoulder. "Do not lose hope, Uncle. I am a Darcy, and a Darcy does not brook disappointment."

❧

*D*arcy looked around him in disgust. What the soldier who led him here had called a hospital was nothing more than several large tents pitched in close confederacy. The crude floors were slippery with mud, blood, and God knew what else. The stench of illness and death hung in the air like a bad omen. He would not wish this place on his worst enemy.

The young ensign, who himself had a bandage wrapped around his head and his right arm in a sling, spoke in low tones to a young woman in a grey gown and white cap who was holding a large bottle of some thick liquid.

"Sir, this way, if you please," the young man said to Darcy when he had finished questioning the nurse for the bed they sought.

Darcy followed the soldier through a maze of occupied cots. Each man they passed wore some form of bandage on some part of his body. Some men watched them pass with vacant looks, some mustered up a weak smile for the gentleman of obvious quality amongst them, some screamed and begged for aid. Some men slept, or at least Darcy hoped they were asleep. Some of them murmured incoherently, others were so still, Darcy wondered if they had passed unnoticed on to their eternal reward. One man reached out and snatched Darcy's arm, pleading for his mama in one breath and the sweet release of death in the next.

They passed from one tent to another, this one slightly less crowded, though barely. When they came to a stop beside a cot in the far back corner of the bivouac and the young soldier nodded towards the man lying within, it was on the tip of Darcy's tongue to demand the man quit dawdling and take him to Colonel Fitzwilliam. Not until Darcy looked again and recognised the signet ring on the injured man's right finger, which arm was bound in a sling, did he realise that he was looking upon the broken body of his most beloved cousin. There was a thick bandage wound around his head, covering his left eye and another tied about his neck.

"Dear God, Richard," he whispered thickly. To no one in particular, he asked, "He lives?"

"Aye, sir," a young nurse standing nearby answered. "Bu' on'y jest. I's a right miracle, tha'. We've been expectin' 'im ta go all th' time."

Once again, Darcy's frayed nerves nearly got the best of him. How dare this chit speak so callously of his most beloved cousin, a decorated war hero and the son of an earl? A glance around quickly softened his demeanour. It must be a matter of survival, he thought, to detach one's self from caring amongst so much death and suffering. He was humble enough to admit to himself that he would not have the fortitude to do what this young woman did every day. In that moment, he felt a surge of respect and gratitude for her and the others like her.

"Tell me about his injuries, please."

"Cer'ainly, sir. Th' Colonel took a blow ta th' 'ead when 'e fell from 'is 'orse. I's not serious, but it does bleed an awful lot, as 'ead wounds will. You see 'ere,"—she pointed to the bandage about his throat —"where a bullet grazed 'is neck. It, too, is jest a flesh wound. Th' arm is broke, jest below th' elbow. It's been set and bound, as you see."

Darcy listened in silence. Though her accent uncultured and her manners questionable, he was impressed with the succinct manner in which she answered him. There was no dissembling, no dramatic fluttering in the way of delicate females. Only precise, straightforward information which was invaluable to him.

"Th' real concern, sir, is 'is leg." She pulled back the thin blanket covering the patient. Darcy swallowed hard as he took in the blood-soaked bandage wrapped around his cousin's thigh. A putrid smell washed over him and he worried for a moment he would be sick. "Th' bullet wen' straight through and it might've been a'right 'ad we got to 'im quickly, but 'is 'orse was shot ou' from under 'im and fell on the Colonel. 'E was trapped underneath fer hours. 'Is leg took the brunt of th' weight. Infection set in quickly and we really thought 'e wouldn't last more'n a few days. But 'e's got a strong will, tha' one. You knew 'im?"

Darcy swallowed down the emotion fighting to surface. "Yes, I know him. He is my cousin." Clearing his throat, he straightened his shoulders and lifted his chin. A man of action, his fraught emotions would not deter him from what had to be done. "I have taken a house in the nearby town. I will be taking the Colonel to recover there."

"Oh, bu', sir, it cannot be wise ta move 'im?"

"Do you have any hope for his recovery here?"

"Erm, well, no, sir."

"If there is no hope, it can do no harm to move him. I have brought a doctor with me and men to see to his care. If you will excuse me, I will see to his immediate removal."

20. July 1810 ❧ At sea

"I owe you my life, Darcy," said Richard, looking over the side of the ship in the unfathomable inky depths below.

- 5 -

"You owe Dr Graham your life," replied Darcy, staring out across the watery horizon.

"And who brought Dr Graham? Who sat by my bedside for I am not even certain how long, spoon-feeding me water and broth and changing my putrid bandages and God knows what else?"

"Dr Graham, several nurses and servants, Adams at times."

"Darcy!"

"You make too much of it, Richard. I did what was necessary for my cousin who would have done the same for me. I am only sorry we could not do more for your leg."

Richard looked down at his leg and the stick he was now reliant upon to walk. "Nah. Now there I can readily believe you might have done more. Saw your chance to finally best me in the saddle and took it, I daresay." In a far more subdued tone, he added, "At least I still have it."

Darcy chuckled at his cousin's jest, in complete awe that he could still be the same jovial, light-hearted man after all he had endured. Just witnessing how Richard—and so many others like him—suffered had left Darcy a changed man. How petty and insignificant were his worries and cares when men were here on the continent giving their lives and limbs for king and country? Darcy, who had ever believed his name and fortune alone raised him above nearly all others, had met sons of butchers and farmers who were far more deserving of respect and honour than he ever would be. It was a humbling education, indeed.

"It was noble of you, you know, what you did for those men," said Richard, interrupting Darcy's thoughts and interpreting them correctly.

"Again, I could do nought else."

"Come now, Darce! You did not have to open your home to sick and wounded soldiers."

"Did I not? I should have considered myself very ungrateful otherwise. You and your comrades have sacrificed much to keep my country and her people safe. How could I stand by and let men who had a chance at life die if I could do anything about it? I had the space, it was quite literally the least I could do."

"No. The least you could have done was to read that letter and written me off as dead, as it seems the rest of my family did."

"Do not blame them, Richard."

"I do not, believe me. You say I would have done the same as you, but would I? Would I, upon receiving a letter telling me you were all but dead, waiting only to obligingly shuffle off this mortal coil that you might be buried and clear out the cot for another, have gathered a team of doctors, nurses, and staff, hopped a boat and crossed enemy-infested waters led only by the hope of a weeks' old letter stating nothing more than that you had not *yet* died, and come to nurse you back to health? I think not, Darce. I love you, Cousin, better even than my own brothers, but I think not. I should have drunk myself into a stupor, mourning my dearest friend in the world and one day name a child for you."

"Promise me you will not. Fitzwilliam Fitzwilliam seems almost cruel."

"*And then*," Richard continued, ignoring his cousin's jest, "to keep the lease on the house and turn it over to the army to continue caring for wounded soldiers. Do be careful, Darcy. It would not surprise me if there is a title waiting for you back home."

"God forbid."

"You are a good man, Darcy. Perhaps the very best. I will find a way to repay you. As much as I am able, in any case. I am certain there is not remuneration enough for a man's life. But I will do what I can."

Chapter One

Elizabeth Bennet could not remember a more enjoyable assembly. Every ball it was often the same; the same musicians, the same dance partners, the same refreshments, the same gossip being bandied about. Though she loved to dance and enjoyed the company of her neighbours, it had become rather tedious since her coming out some four years ago. The anticipated addition of the new residents of Netherfield Park, however, gave everyone something new to look forward to.

For weeks, the entire neighbourhood had been in a frenzy over the imminent arrival of the new master of Netherfield. Every mother in Meryton, most especially her own, had laid designs on the gentleman the moment it was learnt he was single and in possession of a large fortune. Gossiping matrons had flitted from house to house, collecting news as a hummingbird collects nectar; leaving behind bits of their own details to the story and taking away something new to spread elsewhere. No detail was too small to hash and rehash ten times over.

Mr Bingley, as it had been learnt was the young man's name, had been seen wearing a blue coat and it became of the utmost importance to determine the exact shade of blue it was. Certainly, it had not been the colour of the sky, but rather darker. Though not so dark as to be mistaken for black. Mrs Long was quite sure there was a striped pattern to it when he rode passed her parlour window, while Lady Lucas bet her life that Sir William had told her it was solid and it was his waistcoat which had stripes. Mrs Bennet—who could have no knowledge on the matter whatsoever, having never laid eyes on the gentleman but was certainly not going to be outdone by the likes of either Mrs Long or Lady Lucas—gave her very decided opinion that it was the exact shade of her eldest daughter, Jane's, eyes. Elizabeth found it all quite amusing.

Most entertaining had been the speculation caused by his returning to Town only a few days before the ball, ostensibly to fetch a large party of friends. When last she had heard, there was no doubt as to his returning with twelve ladies and seven gentlemen. No one could be pleased with the prospect of so many additional ladies with whom to compete for dance partners, but more than one mama was gratified by the idea of so many eligible gentlemen gracing the neighbourhood—because, of course, they must all be young, single, rich, and, most importantly, in want of wives.

In the end, however, Mr Bingley arrived at the assembly with only five others in his party; two elegant-looking ladies and three gentlemen entered the assembly room with Mr Bingley not long after the third set had begun.

Elizabeth watched with eagerness. A self-proclaimed studier of character, new neighbours came with the promise of much amusement. Her first impressions of Mr Bingley were favourable. He fulfilled all the young ladies' hopes of being good-looking and gentlemanlike.

Surveying the crowd as a glutton gazes upon a feast, his bright blue eyes bounced from person to person as if eager to partake, yet overwhelmed by choice and unsure where to begin. Indeed, he proved to be a most amiable young man. Having expressed a fondness for dancing, he took to the floor for every set. He proved Elizabeth's good opinion justified by being instantly taken with Jane the moment he laid eyes on her most beloved, and most lovely, sister, securing her hand for two dances.

Mr Bingley's sisters, the two ladies who accompanied the party, occupied little of Elizabeth's notice. It was clear by their pinched expressions and curled lips that they cared little for what they saw. She spent a moment noting that they shared their brother's tawny coloured hair, sharp nose, and weak chin—Miss Bingley's pumpkin coloured gown was horribly ill-suited to her colouring, and Mrs Hurst wore far too many feathers—then she put them from her mind. Elizabeth had not the patience to attempt to impress those who were unwilling to be impressed.

Of the gentlemen, more different specimens would be difficult to come by in one party. Mr Hurst, the husband of Mr Bingley's eldest sister, was a portly fellow with ruddy cheeks and little conversation. Upon arriving, he had scouted out a seat near the refreshment table and had not stirred since. If Mrs Hurst was injured by his neglect, she did not show it.

The final two gentlemen were, to Elizabeth's eyes, the most intriguing. Both stood a head taller than any other gentleman in the room and possessed very fine, noble bearings. This was, however, where the similarities ended. Colonel Richard Fitzwilliam was not particularly handsome despite his dashing red coat but very quickly proved himself to be exceedingly agreeable and everything friendly. There was, at first, a great murmur of disappointment when he entered the room limping and leaning heavily on an ornately carved walking stick. What was the purpose, many mamas whispered amongst themselves, of attending an assembly ball when one could not dance? Soon enough, this defect was quite forgotten in the glow of the Colonel's genial conversation and seemingly endless good humour.

In stark contrast, Mr Darcy, who was Colonel Fitzwilliam's cousin, turned every lady's eye upon first entering the assembly. Broad-shouldered and lean, with thick, dark hair falling across his brow most becomingly; there was no padding or planks in *his* well-fitted jacket. Even Elizabeth, who prided herself on being a rational, sensible creature, felt a swoop within her stomach when his rich coffee-coloured eyes swept the room and landed upon her for the very briefest of moments. The mamas of the congregation collectively fanned themselves at the whispered rumours that this fine, elegant gentleman enjoyed a fortune of ten thousand pounds per annum. Whatever his features, he was instantly considered the handsomest man ever to be seen.

Unfortunately, he did not have the handsome manners to match his appearance. Like Bingley's sisters, he seemed displeased with all he saw and wore a deep scowl as he stalked from one end of the ballroom to the other, speaking to no one outside his own party and deigning to dance only once each with Mr Bingley's sisters.

His cold manners could have no effect on Elizabeth. She allowed herself to be entertained by the thought of what a great pity it was that such a handsome man could not be more pleasant, then turned her thoughts to more enjoyable venues. She spent the evening dancing, laughing, and making a new friend.

"Pray, tell me, Colonel," she asked that gentleman when they had sat down with cups of punch to enjoy a "set" conversing together, "how are you enjoying Hertfordshire?"

"Though I have been here only a few days, I find myself quite overwhelmed by its charms."

"I am pleased to hear it. You hail from Derbyshire, do you not?"

"Indeed, I do."

"My aunt is from that county and has told me much of the beauties of the Peaks. I confess I long to see them."

"I have a great fondness for my home county and do not think I could ever consider another as superior, but I find Hertfordshire has many of its own spectacular beauties." He flashed her a bright smile as he said this and Elizabeth was obliged to stifle a laugh. Clearly, the Colonel was a practised flirt and she was flattered that he found her a worthy specimen upon whom to ply his trade. But it would take more than pretty words and cleverly veiled compliments to turn her head.

"Will you and your cousin stay long with Mr Bingley?"

This question made him chuckle and smile in a way that seemed to signal that he knew just what she was about—though she had meant nothing more than what she had asked. She raised a questioning brow and, after studying her face a moment, he mimicked her. She wondered for a moment if they were speaking at cross purposes

"Our plans are not firmly set," he answered at last. "I have been granted extended leave from my regiment to allow my leg to heal and am at something of a loss as to what I am meant to do with myself. So, I have left it up to Darcy. I know he will wish to spend the Christmas season with his sister at *Pemberley*." He put a strange sort of emphasis on the last word but Elizabeth could not fathom what he meant by it so simply moved on.

"And is his sister older or younger?"

"She is...younger," he said slowly, watching Elizabeth's face closely. "Georgiana has only just turned sixteen."

"Oh, what a terrible age! No longer a girl yet not quite a woman. I hope she does not give her family too much trouble."

"Trouble?" The Colonel's genial mien disappeared and his shoulders stiffened; he looked very much the battle-hardened soldier. "Why would you say that?"

Unsure where she had erred, Elizabeth answered warily, "I have three younger sisters of my own, Colonel. And the youngest is not yet sixteen. Lydia is a sweet girl, but in her eagerness to have her share of society, she gives our family no end of headaches."

"Oh. Oh, yes. Of course. No. I share guardianship of Georgie with Darcy and can attest that she is as sweet a girl as ever breathed."

A silence fell between them and Elizabeth looked away. In doing so, she noticed the Colonel's cousin standing not a few yards away, arms crossed over his chest with a deep frown on his face. "Your cousin does not appear to be as impressed by his surroundings as you seem to be."

Colonel Fitzwilliam twisted in his seat to observe his cousin. When he turned back to Elizabeth, his lips were turned up in an affectionate grin. She marvelled that two such dissimilar people could share such a bond. But then, she and Jane had little in common beyond their sisterly affection and there was no one in the world she loved better.

"Yours is not a unique impression. Darcy has never been easy in society. The scowl is merely a mask to hide his discomfort. I assure you, underneath that overly starched exterior, he is the best man I have ever known. I owe him my life, very literally."

"Well, I am glad you have such a good friend in your cousin, Colonel. Now, how long have you been acquainted with Mr Bingley?"

The Colonel started slightly at the change of topic and Elizabeth wondered if he were accustomed to ladies being far more interested in his very wealthy, very handsome cousin and digging for further information. Well, she had learnt all she wished to know about Mr Darcy until the gentleman gave her reason to inquire further.

"Ah, uh, only since I returned from the peninsula. Though I have known of him for much longer. He has been Darcy's close friend for, oh, the last five years, at least."

"Truly?" There must be some truly hidden depths to Mr Darcy if two such amiable gentlemen could hold him in such high esteem.

Elizabeth watched as Mr Bingley stepped away from the dance, leaving Jane standing awkwardly by herself at the top of the set, and approached his friend standing nearby. Torn between indignance on her sister's behalf and curiosity as to what could be so important that he would abandon her to speak to Mr Darcy, she watched with interest as Mr Bingley accosted the gentleman.

"Come Darcy," said he, not bothering to lower his voice. "You must dance. I hate to see you standing about in this stupid manner when there are plenty of pretty girls in want of a partner."

"Oh, dear," said the Colonel, pulling himself up with the aid of his cane. "Pray, excuse me, Miss Elizabeth."

Would this evening never end? Fitzwilliam Darcy thought peevishly as he hovered in the corner of the assembly room he had been dragged to. For two hours already he had been watching his friend and cousin make love to every girl in the room whilst he stalked the perimeter, avoiding Bingley's harridan of a sister. Already he had danced once with her to fulfil his duty to his hosts; he refused to encourage her delusional designs on him by capitulating to her hints for a second set. Were it not for a deep fondness for his friend, and his fear of Bingley getting himself sunk in over his head with his leased estate and weakness for a pretty face, Darcy would never have agreed to be in the lady's company for such an extended length of time. He knew very well her ambitions of becoming Mistress of Pemberley. He knew also Miss Bingley would never cease her attentions until he either informed her such hopes were in vain in a manner which would pain and offend her or he married another. His fondness for her brother prevented the first—for now; his having never yet met a lady with whom he felt he could share his life, the second.

It was not just Miss Bingley's unwanted and incessant attentions which attributed to his foul humour that evening. Darcy was never at ease in a ballroom. Whispered rumours of his wealth and prospects followed him about the room—how on earth people could presume to know his private financial affairs, he would never know. Scheming mamas thrust their daughters into his path, desperate fathers curried for his favour in hopes of replenishing the fortunes they had foolishly gambled away, shamelessly flirtatious debutantes flaunted their *assets*, dreaming of the prestige to be gained over their peers by achieving the status of Mrs Darcy.

He would never admit it aloud, but there were times often enough when Darcy wished he could be more like his cousin and friend. Both Richard and Bingley were of such unguarded, amiable tempers as to make friends everywhere they went. They could smile, flirt, and dance without second-guessing their every move or fearing that each word out of their mouths would either offend or raise a young lady's expectations. His friends seemed to thrive on being sociable whereas it near enough terrified him.

Scanning the crowd, he spotted Bingley. As usual, his friend had found the most beautiful girl in the room and was making himself agreeable to her. Darcy could admit that this month's angel was particularly lovely. Tall and slender, blonde-haired and blue-eyed; just Bingley's type. For the next fortnight, the man would become a besotted fool, making doe eyes at his latest obsession and sighing dreamily at odd moments—until another pretty face caught his eye and he moved on. Darcy would need to speak with his friend. It would not do to raise expectations he had no intentions of fulfilling; what might be tolerated as an idle flirtation in Town could be easily misconstrued as serious attentions to a country maiden.

Then there was Richard. With sandy blond hair, steel-grey eyes, and a slightly crooked nose from having been broken in a training exercise when he was a young lieutenant, no one would describe Colonel Richard Fitzwilliam as particularly handsome. As a second son, the Colonel had no fortune or estate and was required to make his own way in the world—to as much an extent as an earl's son might be made to do. Regardless, ladies flocked to him. Even now, leaning against his cane across the room, looking rather dashing in his scarlet coat, the Colonel was holding court, surrounded by no less than half a dozen ladies. His cousin had the entire group laughing and smiling adoringly up at him. Richard had pretty compliments tucked up his sleeves like handkerchiefs and was ever generous in handing them out. Ladies always accepted his smooth words with smiles, blushes, and flirtations of their own—then they turned around and latched on to Darcy's arm.

There was a flurry of activity as the set ended and a new began to form. The horde of ladies surrounding his cousin dispersed as they were claimed by their partners. Only one remained with Richard; a petite brunette who accompanied his cousin to the refreshment table for glasses of punch before taking seats against the back wall. For a lack of anything better to do, Darcy wandered near to where they sat. Likely the young lady was plying Richard with questions designed to determine whether it might be worth the effort to ensnare him. When he gave her the hint that he could not marry without consideration towards a lady's fortune, she would, no doubt, begin to angle for information on Darcy. It was a scenario the cousins had encountered countless times before.

It had, perhaps, become somewhat easier since he returned to England and politely refused the Crown's offer of a barony. Plenty of his acquaintances had thought him addled to deny himself a title and some even attempted to change his mind, particularly Miss Bingley. But he had never coveted a title. Even still, there were enough who still clamoured for his attention and society for no greater reason than his name having appeared in the papers for his supposed heroism towards his cousin and the mere nomination of a title. His newfound goodwill for his fellow man had nearly crumbled.

Unfortunately, Darcy could not hear their conversation over the music. He did note, however, Richard's strange reaction to something the lady said and wondered if her country manners made her far more brazen than the colonel was accustomed to. He had a thought to step in and perhaps pull his cousin away when Bingley approached.

"Come Darcy. You must dance. I hate to see you standing about in this stupid manner when there are plenty of pretty girls in want of a partner."

"I certainly shall not. You know I am not fond of dancing, particularly when I am unacquainted with my partner. There is not a woman in the room whom it would not be a punishment for me to stand up with."

Richard limped over, the thunk of his cane on the floor announcing his approach even over the music, and clapped Darcy on the back. "Gentlemen, shall we perhaps take this elsewhere?"

"I would not be so fastidious for a kingdom!" Bingley cried as if Richard had not spoken. "Never have I met with so many pleasant girls in my life. Several, I daresay, are rather uncommonly pretty."

Darcy shook his head. There seemed to be the prettiest and most pleasant girls everywhere Bingley went. "You are dancing with the only handsome girl in the room," he conceded to prevent his friend from running off on a paean of his latest obsession's imagined perfections.

"Is she not the most beautiful creature you ever beheld?" Darcy could recall at least half a dozen women Bingley had declared to be the most beautiful creature in just the last two months but refrained from commenting. "But, look! There is one of her sisters sitting just behind you. She is very pretty, as well. Were you not just speaking with her, Fitzwilliam? Will you not introduce Darcy to her?"

"Which do you mean?" Darcy knew very well who Bingley meant as he had observed Richard speaking to the lady himself. Thinking this might be a good opportunity to nip any hopes she might be forming for himself or his cousin in the bud, he turned and made a show of looking her over until she raised her eyes to his and gave him a flirtatious nod before looking away coyly. Pulling his gaze away, he said, "She is tolerable, but not handsome enough to tempt me. I am in no humour to give consequence to young ladies who are slighted by other men."

Beside him, Richard groaned and Darcy did feel a slight pang of remorse. His words were entirely ungentlemanly and his tone harsher than he had intended, but it was for the best. With any luck, she would accept the hint and spread the word that his cousin, his friend, and he himself were not gentlemen who could be easily ensnared.

"And here I had just been telling Miss Elizabeth what a good man you are," Richard lamented, rubbing a hand across his brow. "Bingley, return to your partner. You left the poor girl stranded on the dance floor." Bingley jumped and hastened away to return his angel. Richard turned to Darcy, pulling out a hipflask and pressing it into his hands. "You, take this and go sit down in some out of the way corner where you will not insult any more innocent ladies. We shall talk later."

Richard turned to leave but Darcy forestalled him. "What are you going to do?"

"I am going to attempt to persuade Miss Elizabeth that I am not a bald-faced liar."

Chapter Two

"Well, *that*," cried Miss Bingley the moment the party had entered the drawing-room at Netherfield after the assembly, "was an absolute waste of a new gown." She crossed to a small, gaudy red and gold brocade settee, eying Darcy pointedly. Studiously ignoring the lady's hint, Darcy walked purposefully past the sofa and, after accepting a desperately needed brandy from his cousin, stationed himself beside the fireplace, resting his elbow against the mantel.

"I do not know what you are talking of," responded her brother, falling gracelessly into another expensively hideous chair. "I have never met with more pleasant people or prettier girls in my life."

"Oh, Charles! You are in general too apt to be pleased. You must concede that you would be much better served to give up this pathetic house and take an estate in a more civilised county." She nonchalantly pulled off her gloves, one finger at a time. "Say, in Derbyshire, perhaps?"

"I must concede no such thing. I chose Netherfield on purpose of its being so close to Town. Derbyshire is much too far, pardon my saying so Darcy, Fitzwilliam." He nodded genially to the two gentlemen. Darcy returned the gesture while Richard held up his drink in a good humoured salute. "Two days journey, oftener three. I would not wish to give up the delights of London society. I should think you would not either."

"You are being silly, Charles. We may still spend as much time in London as we could wish. It is the owning of an estate which is important. The running of it may be left to your stewards. Is that not right, Mr Darcy?"

Darcy gritted his teeth and shot a glare at his cousin merely to avoid throwing it at Miss Bingley. He knew his expression would not be misinterpreted. Indeed, Richard looked as though he were desperately trying not to laugh at the whole exchange. Was the woman truly attempting to recommend herself to him with such statements? Quite contrary to her aim, it only served to highlight how little she knew him and why Miss Bingley was immeasurably unsuited for the role of mistress of his estate—or any estate for that matter.

There were gentlemen aplenty, Darcy knew, who behaved in the manner she alluded to. For many of the ton, a country estate was little more than a retreat from the heat and stench of London in the summer; a diversion until the parties, balls, and soirées of the season began again. They delighted in claiming the status of landowner, but very few were willing to spend any more time than was necessary on the estates for which they were responsible. The income garnered from the fields and pastures was freely spent, yet they knew not the pride of working the land.

To Darcy, there was no greater paradise than Pemberley. Were it not for his duties to his family and maintaining respectable connections so that his sister might one day make a good match, he would happily retire to his estate and never venture anywhere near London again. He loved the sensation of the wind on his face and in his hair as he thundered over his beloved fields and valleys on Sleipnir, gazing with pride over the lands cultivated by generation after generation of his predecessors. The smell of the fresh-turned earth, the feel of it in his hands, fed his soul and gave him to feel a deep, sacred connection with the lands over which he had stewardship.

Before he could form an answer which would not offend his hostess, Bingley sat up and made a surprisingly poignant observation as he slapped the arms of his chair with both hands. "Then why does it matter whether my estate is located in Hertfordshire, Derbyshire, or Cornwall? And what is wrong with Meryton society? Everyone was most kind and attentive this evening. There was no formality, no stiffness. It was as if I had been born here and a part of Meryton society all my life."

Tutting at her brother as though he were a small child in leading-strings rather than a man grown and in control of her fortune, Miss Bingley shook her head pityingly. "Charles, you astonish me. Only you could find merit in this community of country mushrooms. There was little beauty and no fashion at all outside our own party. Do you not agree, Mr Darcy?" she applied to him again, batting her eyelashes furiously in his direction. Darcy felt a shudder begin at the base of his shoulders and work its way down. Calling upon years of iron-willed self-mastery, he suppressed the worst of it.

He had certainly been unimpressed with the local society but he would be damned if he was going to admit as much out loud. To agree with Miss Bingley would only fuel her futile hopes. Thankfully, Bingley again forestalled any need to answer as he voiced his own incredulity.

"Little beauty? Come now, Caroline. I could not imagine an angel more beautiful than Miss Bennet! Confess it, Darcy. She is surely perfection itself."

Darcy shared a half-amused, half-exasperated glance with his cousin, who seemed content to listen as he nursed his glass of brandy, before allowing the eldest Miss Bennet to be very pretty. "Though she smiles too much."

"Oh, I absolutely agree," Miss Bingley simpered, flashing him a flirtatious gaze through her lashes. Then, as Bingley made a noise which indicated he meant to strenuously object to such a complaint, she turned a placating look on her brother. "However, I will confess that I found Miss Bennet to be rather...*sweet*."

"Yes, quite...*sweet*," Mrs Hurst agreed, though it was plain to Darcy, and Richard if his raised brow were any indication, that they had not meant any compliment at all.

"In fact, I should very much like to get to know her better," Caroline announced in overly saccharine tones.

"Do you know whose company I found rather agreeable?" Richard asked then provided the answer without bothering to allow anyone time to venture a guess. "Miss Elizabeth Bennet. If I have ever had a more enjoyable conversation with a woman, I cannot recall."

"Miss Eliza Bennet?" Miss Bingley sneered. "I heard Sir William lauding the girl as a famous local beauty. What say you to that, Mr Darcy?"

Feeling a tingle of discomfort in the pit of his stomach, Darcy took a sip of his drink to collect himself. He could sense Richard's hard gaze on him and resolutely kept his own eyes fixed on the dancing flames in the grate. "I cannot say I paid the lady enough attention as to be able to render an informed opinion."

"Well,"—Richard abruptly stood and threw back the last of his brandy—"I have finished my drink and think I shall retire. Join me for a nightcap, would you, Darcy?"

Darcy looked to his half-full glass and back at his cousin. Richard's lips were set in a firm line and his brows were furled. He looked less the jovial gentleman and more the hardened soldier Darcy had only seen a handful of times. Tossing back the remains of his own drink, Darcy nodded. "Of course. Bingley, shall you join us?"

Richard made a face at this invitation but Darcy gave him a look that declared it not to be questioned. He would warn his friend as soon as possible about the dangers of raising a country maiden's expectations.

"It would be my pleasure. Hurst? Will you—" Bingley looked around. "Where is Hurst?" But no one seemed concerned in the slightest as to the gentleman's whereabouts, his wife least of all. So, Bingley merely shrugged and, after bidding the ladies goodnight, followed his friends from the room.

The conversation regarding Bingley's tendency to flirt with the prettiest girl in the vicinity went as well as it ever had. Darcy did his best to stress the importance of tempering his enthusiasm for Miss Bennet—or any lady in the neighbourhood for that matter—lest she believe he felt more than a passing attraction. If the lady felt herself trifled with, Darcy tried to explain, his friend might very well find himself honour bound to offer for her. Though the Bennets were landed gentry and, therefore, above the Bingleys who hailed from trade, Mr Bennet was a minor country gentleman. Such a connection could not hope to fulfil Bingley's promise to his father to raise his family in society.

Darcy's efforts were met with the same results as they ever were; a good deal of blustering and whinging as Bingley petulantly declared that *this time* was different, "I can feel it!" There was nought Darcy could do but sigh and keep careful watch to ensure his friend did not entangle himself in a situation from which he could not be extracted. If Bingley appeared slightly chastised and a little more thoughtful as he sulked from the room, Darcy dismissed it. Such never lasted.

"You owe Miss Elizabeth an apology," Richard stated without preamble and without pouring Darcy another drink he sorely needed.

Already irritated by the last hour's discourse, Darcy bristled at his cousin's tone. He had been his own man and master of his own estate for five years; he did not appreciate being told what to do like he was an errant boy in short pants being scolded by his governess. "An apology? For what? Managing her expectations before she made a fool of herself?"

"Made a fool of herself? In what manner? Shamelessly throwing herself at you in a bid to coerce you to the altar? Pray, tell me, when do you intend to manage Miss Bingley's expectations? She has been making a fool of herself these last five years, at least."

"Do you think I have not tried to discourage Miss Bingley?" Darcy asked through clenched teeth. "Only unnecessary cruelty will ever convince her that I will never offer for her. I will not disrespect my friend in such a manner."

"Oh, but unnecessary cruelty towards a young lady with whom you had yet to even be properly introduced and had done nought more egregious but to simply exist in the room is perfectly acceptable?"

"I was not—"

Richard cut him off with raised tones. "You loudly declared the girl not pretty enough to suffer through even one dance! I daresay you have managed her expectations rather well. What makes you think she would be interested in you in any case?"

Darcy did not deign to answer that question; he only crossed his arms and fixed an expectant look on his cousin with one brow raised. Richard knew very well that Darcy had spent half his life dodging the advances of nearly every single young lady—and some married—who crossed his path.

"My God, when did you become so bloody arrogant?"

"I *beg* your pardon?" Darcy demanded, truly affronted.

Richard tilted his head to the side, looking upon his cousin as if seeing him for the first time. "You truly believe there is not a woman in the world who would dare refuse you."

"I know there is not."

Richard shook his head and Darcy did not like the look in his eye. It was something akin to disappointment tinged with pity.

"Shall I tell you what Miss Elizabeth said when I mentioned Pemberley?" Whether Darcy wished to hear it or not, he would as Richard gave him no opportunity to object. "Not a damned thing. She changed the subject, asked after Georgie."

"Georgiana?"

"Yes, lamented how odious it was to be a young girl of sixteen. When I attempted to apologise for my dear cousin's behaviour, she would not hear it as she said I had nothing for which to apologise. 'Twas not you who behaved in an ungentlemanlike manner,' said she. Then she wondered at two such charming, amiable gentlemen such as Bingley and myself,"—this was said with the most insufferable smirk and irritating wink aimed at Darcy—"being so intimate with such a proud, disagreeable man. Of course, *she* then apologised for speaking so against my relation who had just so harshly insulted her, which, of course, I then refused to accept as she was entirely correct.

"Pray, tell me, Darcy, beyond those first few minutes after our arrival, did anyone approach you? Did any mothers with single daughters step in your path and shove those daughters into your arms in a desperate attempt to force a marriage?"

"No, but—"

"No, they did not. Yes, there were whispers bandied about as to the state of your income and estate. But I can assure you, within a quarter of an hour, there was not one person in attendance who did not see your disdain and think you the most disagreeable man they had ever had the misfortune to meet. Well, perhaps not Miss Bennet. I have never met a lady so apt to find everyone agreeable. I daresay, she even liked Bingley's sisters."

To this, Darcy could think of nothing to say. It was true he had not found anything by which to be impressed at that evening's gathering and he was so far above these people it was almost laughable, but he had not disdained them for it. Had he? He had not spoken more than a few words to anyone, but then he had not been acquainted with anyone outside his party. Small talk was something he despised and was not accomplished at. He much preferred to be a silent observer, putting himself forward only when he felt he had something of true significance to say. That others might perceive his quiet, reserved nature as contempt had never occurred to him. His company was always sought in London.

Yet, it did not follow that the local ladies and matrons were not forming designs on him. He was likely the wealthiest man ever to set foot in this small market town. Even Bingley's wealth undoubtedly surpassed the leading family's income by a thousand pounds or more—and he would be surprised if anyone related to an earl had ever graced their presence. Any of the single gentlemen of their party would be quite the prize for these country bumpkins. Before Bingley had taken Netherfield, none of the local female population could have dreamt of catching anything greater than a moderately wealthy merchant or an insignificant country squire. He would not lower his guard, no matter his cousin's opinion.

"I know that look cousin," said Richard, standing to remove to his own chambers. "You are re-enforcing those damnable walls you have built around you to keep anyone from getting too close. But I spoke the truth to Miss Elizabeth. You *are* a good man. You will come to the correct conclusion ere long."

✤

hree miles away at Longbourn, two sisters were distractedly readying for bed as they similarly discussed the events of the evening—though with a good deal more enthusiasm and pleasure. Jane, in her serene manner, declared Mr Bingley to be everything a gentleman ought to be: sensible, good-humoured, and lively.

"And I never saw such happy manners. So much ease, with such perfect good breeding. He was so very obliging. He said he wished that there were more of him that he might dance with all the young ladies."

"You have said nothing as to his being handsome," Elizabeth teased sweet Jane, who blushed prettily. "A young man ought always to be handsome if he possibly can."

Jane sat upon Elizabeth's bed, plucking at the hem of her nightshift and cast her sister a sidelong glance. "You spent a good deal of time with Colonel Fitzwilliam."

To this, Elizabeth laughed. She knew she would not escape without accounting for her conversation with the good Colonel Her hand stilled in its occupation of brushing her thick, curly hair and she glared at Jane. "We spent the duration of one dance in conversation. It was no more than he afforded to any other young lady."

"Oh, but it was. For he sat with you for the span of an entire set."

"We had a very pleasant conversation," was all Elizabeth would say.

She spoke nothing but the truth. Conversing with the Colonel had been exceedingly enjoyable. But for when she had asked about Mr Darcy's sister—and she still could make neither heads nor tails of what had transpired there—there had been no awkwardness, no uncomfortable lulls. They discussed a wide variety of topics from London's diversions to the war; even canvassing the state of the roads as his party journeyed from Town had been made interesting by the gentleman's delightful way of speaking. After Mr Darcy's ungentlemanly insult, Colonel Fitzwilliam had returned to her, offering his deepest apologies. Having refused to accept an apology which he did not owe, they moved on, picking up as though they had not been so rudely interrupted. She marvelled at these two gentlemen being friends, let alone relations.

As if sensing where her sister's thoughts had wandered, Jane spoke again. "Mr Darcy was very handsome."

"Yes. Very handsome," Elizabeth agreed, turning with some annoyance to the mirror to plait her hair. "And rude, and arrogant, and insufferably proud."

"Perhaps he was having a difficult day?"

"Perhaps, but that would not excuse his being so uncivil."

"No, it does not. But we ought not to judge the man too harshly before we come to know him. I am sure he is sorry for what he said."

"Oh, Jane," Elizabeth lamented, standing from her dressing table and joining her sister on the bed. "Have you not even an unkind word for one who sorely deserves it?"

"No one deserves unkindness, Lizzy."

"As usual, you are correct. I shall have to learn to be more like you and think only well of people." A playful smile danced across her face. "Though I may not be handsome enough to tempt him, I shall be happy in spite of Mr Darcy. Surely, that is the best revenge."

"What Mr Darcy said was most assuredly inconsiderate and so wholly untrue as to be absurd but you must not allow it to disturb you."

"I will not, I promise you. Thankfully, I have vanity enough to comfort myself. But that does not mean that I must like him."

"You ought to endeavour to do so." A teasing glint shone in Jane's eye, one that few were ever fortunate enough to witness. "It is not well done to despise one's own cousin, after all."

"Oh, you!" cried Elizabeth as she snatched a pillow from the bed and lobbed it at her sister. They fell in a heap together, peals of laughter ringing into the night.

Chapter Three

An uncomfortable fortnight passed wherein Darcy made several distressing observations. The party from Netherfield received numerous invitations to dinners, parties, and outings—all of which were enthusiastically accepted by Bingley. They hunted with the local gentlemen and dined with the principal families. Bingley eagerly increased his acquaintance with all his new neighbours, dragging his household along.

The first of these observations concerned Mrs Bennet's improper and wholly unabashed practise of putting her daughters—all five of them—forward, especially in the company of gentlemen. It was patently obvious to Darcy that the lady had set her sights on Bingley and Richard for her two eldest. If Miss Bennet and Miss Elizabeth were refreshingly reluctant to acquiesce to their mother's vulgar machinations, it comforted him only slightly. Within a week of their introduction, Mrs Bennet was loudly crowing to anyone who stood near enough to hear of the inevitability of having two daughters so advantageously married and the boon this would be for her other daughters, as well. To all this Bingley seemed entirely blind, Richard amused, and the elder Bennet ladies highly embarrassed.

Strangely, Darcy was even more disturbed by the realisation that, since the night of the assembly, Mrs Bennet had not spoken so much as a word to him. She talked Bingley and Richard nearly to death—even as she was encouraging her daughters to speak to them; but with Darcy, she only glared at him as if he were a particularly filthy stableboy who had the audacity to set foot in her parlour. He had not heard one word of pairing *him* with any of her daughters. He might have been relieved had he not been so confused—and slightly mortified to realise that his cousin, perhaps, might just have been right.

In fact, few of Meryton's inhabitants made any effort to engage him. He caught many sidelong glances in his direction and more than once he had noticed conversations coming to an abrupt halt when he neared as he walked about the room. Some people even made excuses to walk away whenever he approached. When placed in a situation where one must speak or be rude, comments were always confined to such dull topics as the weather or inquiries after his health. He thought little of these occasions at the time but to be relieved he was seldom called upon to converse with strangers.

Dinner with the Gouldings at Haye Park three nights ago had given him the first reason to give sincere consideration to Richard's words. He had given little thought to the seating arrangements other than to stew silently in his annoyance at being denied a reprieve from Miss Bingley's cloying attentions for one evening as he had hoped. Seated between the pernicious sisters, his dinner conversation had consisted of listening to Miss Bingley's acid remarks on the pitiful company, whispered criticisms of every dish presented, and fawning comparisons to Pemberley on one side, and Mrs Hurst's parroted agreement on the other. It had not been until he had gained the blessed solitude of his chambers later that night that it had dawned on him.

He had been placed, along with Bingley's sisters, in the very centre of the table, as far from his hosts as it was possible to be. To Miss Bingley's right had sat Mrs Abbot, an ancient widow who was deaf on her left side, Richard had enlightened him, and nearly blind. Mrs Hurst had been seated beside her husband. Meanwhile, Richard had been placed beside their hostess with Miss Elizabeth Bennet to his left, looking as though he had never had a more enjoyable meal. Bingley sat near the head of the table beside Miss Jane Bennet, ignoring his other dinner companion entirely—as it had been Mrs Bennet, Darcy did not think the lady minded in the least.

Once, he had heard his aunt discussing how to make arrangements for a dinner party with his sister, Georgiana. *"Sometimes,"* Aunt Elaine had explained, *"one must invite those one would rather not."* Undesirables, she had said, were best seated together and, unless it was made unavoidable by rank, near the centre of the table. *"In doing so, one avoids importuning other guests with those who would otherwise dampen the atmosphere of the party."*

Was he, Fitzwilliam Alexander Ryan Darcy, an undesirable? Did he garner invitations not for the pleasure of his company but out of obligation? He thought back to dinners and parties he had attended in London. More often than not he was seated near the hostess who spent much of the dinner extolling the perfections of this single young lady or that. There was no denying, however, that he had eaten many a meal midway between the ends of the table.

But, here? Surely, these simple country folk would relish having one such as he grace their table. Rich, highly educated, and connected to nobility, he was descended from not one, but two old and respected families. It was likely these people would never dine with anyone more exalted. Of course, they desired his company; he had been invited, after all.

Yet, a voice in the back of his head which sounded uncomfortably like his cousin's whispered, an invitation could not very well be extended to Netherfield which would exclude members of the party. Such would be the height of incivility. Though they engendered rustic, countrified manners, no one in Meryton had been uncivil.

His final, and perhaps the most troubling, revelation was with what frequency his gaze landed upon a certain young lady with fine, sparkling eyes, a light and pleasing figure, and a musical laugh that somehow made his soul feel lighter; a lady who was very often in the company of his dearest cousin—a lady who he had insulted on his first night in town. Even more distressing was the difficulty with which he had in looking away.

When first he had looked upon Miss Elizabeth at the assembly, he had looked with the purpose of finding fault and had scarcely allowed her to have a good feature in her face. But the more she was thrust upon his notice, the more he recognised the way the beautiful expression of her dark eyes bore witness to an intelligence which intrigued him. Though she could not be considered a classic beauty, as was her sister, Darcy could not but notice with pleasure an uncommon delicacy in her features and her bright, sparkling eyes. Her manners were not those which he was accustomed to in the fashionable world; nevertheless, he was captivated by her easy playfulness and teasing nature and found he desired to know more of her.

Unfortunately, she seemed entirely unafflicted by the same curiosity and rarely looked in his direction or ventured near. She had no compunction, however, with spending a copious amount of time with his cousin. Richard was a man whom Darcy looked upon as a brother; other than Georgiana, there was no one he loved better. Yet, every time his eyes searched out that lovely countenance, something he had never felt towards the Colonel reared up within him as he watched Richard standing beside the bewitching creature, inspiring her radiant smiles—envy.

It was absurd. Richard could not marry without consideration to a lady's fortune and Miss Elizabeth had nothing. And it was not as if Darcy held any ambitions of taking a poor, country maiden to wife, in any case. Yet he could not stop himself from bristling internally every time he watched his cousin bask in the warmth of her magnificent eyes or her tinkling laugh reached his ears knowing Richard was the provocation.

Pushing aside this irrational jealousy, Darcy took a step towards becoming better acquainted with this intriguing young woman—for no reason other than that she *was* intriguing. He began hovering on the edge of her conversations, seeking an opportunity to speak with her himself. It was convenient, if mildly vexing, that Richard was often in Miss Elizabeth's presence as it gave Darcy a ready excuse to avail himself of her company as well. It was through Richard, in the end, that he was granted the privilege of conversing with the lady.

It was at a party at Lucas Lodge where he spent much of the evening standing stupidly about, feeling much too large for the room and never knowing what to do with his hands. As was often the case, Bingley was entranced by the eldest Miss Bennet to the point of neglecting all others, and Richard laughed and talked with her next younger sister.

"I say, Darcy!" cried Richard as Darcy ventured near. "Just the man to settle our dispute.

"I should hardly call it a dispute, Colonel," Elizabeth laughed.

"We disagree on the matter. 'Tis the very definition of a dispute." He turned back to Darcy. "Miss Elizabeth and I have been discussing the disparities between city living and quiet country retirement. I contend that the country can have no advantage over the delights of London with its balls and parties and all manner of diversion."

Darcy watched his cousin with narrowed eyes. Though Richard tolerated society far better than he and was a man to find enjoyment whatever his situation, Darcy knew the Colonel much preferred the quiet and simplicity of the country. No doubt, Richard was being contrary purely for the sake of the debate. The sparkle in her lovely eyes was certainly ample inducement.

"And I maintain," said Miss Elizabeth with a radiant smile that nearly knocked Darcy off his feet, even as it was not directed at him but rather his cousin, "that I have found great pleasure on my visits to Town, mostly in the bookshops and parks and visiting much beloved relations, but I should prefer the country any day. While you city dwellers may consider us country folk to be simple and rustic, I would argue that we are far more genuine and better pleased with our more humble pursuits."

"Londoners are nought but puffed-up peacocks, eh?"

"You said it, Colonel, not I."

"Ha! Hit, acknowledged, Miss Elizabeth. Very well, what say you, Darcy?"

"I wonder that you would call upon my opinion on the matter when you are well aware I cannot support your position, Cousin. As Miss Elizabeth says,"—he acknowledged the lady with a nod—"London certainly has its benefits. I, for one, take great pleasure in visiting museums, exhibits, and, like Miss Elizabeth, bookshops. However, you of all people must know, Richard, that were it not for social responsibilities to my sister and my family, I should happily retire to Pemberley and never leave."

"Ah!" Richard clutched at his chest theatrically. "Betrayed by my own kin!"

Taken aback, Darcy looked sharply at his cousin. "You know I would never—"

"Yes, yes! I jest, Cousin!" Richard barked out a laugh and turned to Miss Elizabeth. "Madam, you may have my word that there is no more loyal or trustworthy man in all the kingdom than my very dear cousin, Mr Fitzwilliam Darcy. That, I would stake my life on."

The lady turned to Darcy and raised a rather expressive brow, causing his breath to catch in his chest. "Then he is the consummate gentleman."

It was subtle, but it was no doubt a barb and Darcy knew she was thinking of his insult at the assembly. Now was his chance. He would offer the apology she so richly deserved.

"Miss Elizabeth, please allow me—"

"Oh, Lizzy! There you are." someone called from behind him. A moment later Miss Lucas was at her friend's side, pressing her to sit down at the instrument.

Surprisingly, Elizabeth demurred, but Miss Lucas would not relent. Soon, with added urgings from Richard, she was convinced to take up her place at the pianoforte. Darcy had said not a word but felt a strong desire to hear the lady play.

He was not in the least disappointed. Her liveliness and sparkle carried over into her playing, drawing the listener in and holding them spellbound. There were missed notes and slurred passages, to be sure, but there was such depth of feeling and warmth in her exquisite voice as to render those fortunate enough to hear uncaring for such slight imperfections and she was entreated to play again. She obliged her audience only insofar as to play a second song, then relinquished the instrument to her next younger sister whose performance was technically flawless, yet lacked the heart and emotion of Miss Elizabeth's.

After several songs which provided dubious enjoyment, Miss Mary was prevailed upon by the youngest Misses Bennet to play something to which they could dance. Darcy shifted uncomfortably. Dancing was an activity which he did not enjoy. In his experience, it was nothing more than a torturous half hour of focusing his attention on one woman whilst simultaneously ensuring not to convey too much interest. Conversation was superficial and stilted, requiring him to feign interest in topics which interested him not at all. Were it acceptable, he would gratefully pass every dance in silence; or, better yet, avoid the activity altogether. More often than not, he dodged poorly veiled hints at a lady's willingness to accept his addresses—and more than once, a boldly stated offer for a tryst on a darkened terrace.

A familiar dread settled in his stomach and he fought the urge to loosen his cravat. By habit, his eyes began searching the quickest path to an out of the way corner or the nearest exit from the room when his gaze landed on Elizabeth, gracefully drifting once more towards the spot where he and Richard stood. The unease which had been tightening his neckcloth and dampening his palms dissipated only to be replaced by something equally unsettling; for the first time in as long as he could remember, and for reasons he could not explain, Darcy felt a strong desire for a dance. In that moment, he cared not for the unfamiliar persons standing around him nor the relative inferiority of her position. No, in that moment he knew only a hunger for one woman's undivided attention for the space of a song.

"Miss Elizabeth," Richard, leaning heavily on his cane, addressed the lady, and Darcy went cold. Occupied by his observation of the mesmerising way her hips swayed as she approached, he had forgotten not only the gathered company but his cousin's presence, as well. "I should very much like to stand up with you for a dance, but I fear I have been standing in one attitude for too long and I am sure I would do neither of us any credit." Darcy turned his head sharply to stare at his cousin. He had shown no signs of discomfort, but then, Darcy had hardly been paying strict attention. As if he had just been struck by a grand epiphany, Richard took up Miss Elizabeth's hand and turned to him. "Darcy, allow me to present this delightful young lady to you as a most desirable partner. You cannot disappoint her and refuse to stand up when I am unable."

Darcy reached out to accept her hand with readiness when she unexpectedly drew back. "Indeed, Colonel, I have not the least intention of dancing. You must not suppose I moved this way as part of some underhanded scheme to beg a partner."

"I should be very happy if you would honour me with a dance, Miss Elizabeth," Darcy applied in earnest.

"That is very kind of you, sir. But I am not inclined towards dancing this evening. I should be just as pleased to continue our conversation, Colonel."

"I could not ask you to curtail your enjoyment for my sake, madam," Richard entreated. "Already you sacrificed a whole set at the assembly for my poor company. And Darcy, though he is not fond of the activity, is very accomplished. I am sure he can have no objection. Eh, Darcy?"

Peals of raucous laughter rang over the crowd and all three looked towards the source of the gaiety. In the centre of the impromptu dance floor, the youngest Bennet daughter, grasping the hands of an officer of the militia, was spinning wildly about. Though undoubtedly ashamed of her sister's antics, Darcy did not miss the look of relief which crossed her features.

"I beg you would excuse me." Elizabeth dipped a hurried curtsey and hastened away.

"Singular girl, that Miss Elizabeth Bennet," Richard remarked, clapping his cousin on the back before turning away to find a seat.

Though disappointed, Darcy was in no wise any less charmed by the lady. It was clear that she had not only heard his boorish remarks at the assembly but that she meant hold him accountable for them—as she ought, of course. Yet, never before had he met a lady who would challenge his objectionable behaviour. It was true that he had never been so blatantly insulting, yet he was only ever barely civil in the face of persistent hopefuls and never had any one of them done anything less than simper and smirk before him regardless. Miss Elizabeth was singular, indeed.

"Yes, I quite agree," a most unwelcome voice intruded on his reflections. "I am very much in agreement with your thoughts."

"I should imagine not."

Miss Bingley released a throaty chuckle as she brushed her shoulder against his and Darcy shifted away. "But of course, you are considering what a waste of an evening this has been, forced to mingle with such savage society. I am entirely of your opinion. I cannot comprehend their gaiety. About what have they to be merry? Such insipidity, such self-importance, yet such nothingness! Not an ounce of culture in the whole room that we did not bring with us. What I would not give to hear your strictures on them."

"You are entirely mistaken. I had no thoughts of the kind." In truth, he had been considering the great pleasure which a pair of fine eyes in the face of a pretty woman can bestow, but kept his counsel. He watched as Elizabeth, having spoken to her sisters, moved across to the room to where Richard had taken a seat and fell easily into cheerful conversation again. She was a unique young woman, lovely in an unconventional way and intelligent. But he could not ignore her lack of fortune and the impropriety of her family. Therefore, nothing could ever come of such an attraction. He would be best served to put the lady from his mind and focus on his purpose for coming to Hertfordshire.

"Your cousin seems to have made an interesting conquest," Miss Bingley scoffed. Whether she had noticed where his own attention was fixed or her comment was mere coincidence, he could not say. Tittering behind a gloved hand, she continued, "What a splendid match that will be. Think you the earl will approve? Perhaps he might gift the lovely couple a neat little cottage on his estate where they might live. Or they could take up a tenant farm at Pemberley. Have you one available?"

In this vein did she continue for some minutes until Darcy abruptly excused himself and walked away. How she tolerated his incivility, he hardly knew and cared less. There was no denying Elizabeth and Richard enjoyed one another's company. Yet, it was equally undeniable that Richard could not afford to marry such a lady, not if he wished to maintain the lifestyle to which he had become accustomed—and that which such a lady deserved. Beyond these considerations, however, was further reason to forget Miss Elizabeth; Darcy would never compete against his most beloved cousin for a woman, magnificent eyes and refreshing wit be damned.

Chapter Four

*B*reakfast at Longbourn was often a noisy affair but today there was a thrum of excitement hanging in the air. The recent arrival of a regiment of militia soldiers to be wintered at Meryton, and the subsequent inclusion of the officers at last evening's gathering, had left room for little else in the minds of Kitty and Lydia Bennet. They chattered over each other—and everyone else—of regimentals, officers, which of these most distinguished of gentlemen had been danced with last night, which were already great favourites, and, of greatest importance, which of the two youngest sisters had been most favoured by the dashing soldiers.

Longbourn was only a mile removed from Meryton where Mrs Bennet's sister, Mrs Phillips lived. That lady, being the wife of the town's solicitor and most conveniently situated right along the main thoroughfare, was a veritable fount of useful knowledge such as who came and went from which shop, what officers passed down the street, and where said officers were lodged. Mrs Phillips considered it her duty to know the goings-on in the neighbourhood and Kitty and Lydia had taken to visiting their aunt as often as they were able to learn all they could of each new officer. They soon came to know many of the officers themselves as Mrs Phillips was quite happy to host small gatherings in her home, always including her dear nieces and any officers which could be tempted. With such delights to be had, the youngest Bennets were exposed to a felicity wholly unknown before.

At the foot of the table, Mrs Bennet kept up an endless recitation of Mr Bingley's every interaction with Jane from the night previous and continuous raptures over his five thousand a year or the wonders of the son of an earl paying such decided attentions to Elizabeth. In her mind, there was no doubt that at least one wedding was in Longbourn's very near future. Jane was the loveliest girl in the neighbourhood, if not the entire county, and surely Mr Bingley could not resist such beauty. Colonel Fitzwilliam, she mused, seemed immune to her second daughter's wild ways and impertinent manners. No amount of Elizabeth's imparting the Colonel's earliest hints that he could not marry without consideration to a lady's fortune would dissuade her mother from her fantasies. For her own part, Elizabeth was not much disappointed. The Colonel was an amiable, gentlemanly man and she greatly enjoyed his company, but she was not a woman to cast hopes where there was none to be had. She was always pleased to make a new friend.

Though she was the very picture of serenity, the pretty blush that dusted Jane's ivory cheeks at every mention of Mr Bingley could not escape Elizabeth's notice, who knew her most beloved sister so well. The most beautiful Bennet daughter had oft been admired and there had been one or two gentlemen who had brought a smile to Jane's lovely lips but Elizabeth had never seen her sister so quickly or strongly affected. She could only hope Mr Bingley was earnest in his attentions.

"This just come from Netherfield, Ma'am," Hill announced as she entered the dining room with a missive held out. "For Miss Bennet."

"Oh!" cried Mrs Bennet, fluttering her napkin about her face. "What does he say? Is he to call upon you? Has he requested a private audience? Does he ask to speak with Mr Bennet?"

"Mama, Mr Bingley could hardly write to Jane," Elizabeth pointed out.

"It is from Miss Bingley," Jane confirmed, her eyes scanning the note. "She has invited Lizzy and me to dine with her and Mrs Hurst. The gentlemen will be dining out with the officers."

At the mention of officers, Lydia burst into speech again, wondering aloud that her aunt had not told her of such an occasion. Nobody paid any mind to her effusions, but that could hardly stop her.

"Dining out?" Mrs Bennet frowned. "Oh, that is most unlucky. But, still, you must go and make what you can of it."

"May we have the carriage, Father?" Jane asked.

Mrs Bennet cried out, "The carriage? No, indeed! You must go on horseback, for it looks like rain and then you must both spend the night."

"Mother!" both girls chorused.

"Do not look at me so. If you are not to see the gentlemen, why bother going at all?"

"Mama, you forget I do not ride," Elizabeth reminded her mother.

"Oh, posh," scoffed Mrs Bennet with a wave of her napkin. "You can sit atop the horse for the three-mile ride to Netherfield well enough."

"I have not been on horseback since I was seven years old, Mama. I am certainly not getting on one now."

The disagreement continued for several more minutes until Elizabeth insisted that they would go by carriage or she would refuse to go at all. At this, Jane began to wonder if it might not be best to refuse the invitation until such a time as the weather might be better. Mrs Bennet would not hear of it and, at last, relented, though with little grace. Her every waking thought was of promoting advantageous marriages for her five daughters and she was not a little put out that her most stubborn child seemed determined to thwart her every scheme.

The girls readied themselves and were soon off in the carriage. They had only just turned out of Longbourn's drive when a great clap of thunder announced the commencement of the storm and sheets of rain began to fall. Elizabeth could not help the smile that tugged at her lips as she pictured her mother watching crossly out the window, lamenting the waste of a perfectly good shower.

Her good humour was of short duration. The rain was falling in a steady torrent and she worried for Jonesy, the Bennet's faithful coachman, seated atop the carriage, taking the brunt of the deluge. There was also no denying that the road was rapidly deteriorating beneath their wheels. She could not help but fear that her mother might gain her end after all.

When they reached Netherfield at long last, Jonesy handed the sisters out and they made a dash through the rain to the stairs and up to the covered portico. Shaking out their cloaks and bonnets, they turned back to look out at the storm.

"Thank you, Lizzy," Jane said earnestly, "for standing up to Mama. I do not think I could have done it. I shudder to think what might have happened if Mama had not been persuaded."

"I can easily imagine it. You would have arrived soaked through and well on your way to a violent cold."

"And you?"

A laugh bubbled up from Elizabeth's throat. "I should still be at Longbourn's stables, shaking in my boots while Peter attempted in vain to persuade me onto poor Nelly!"

Their relief at being off the treacherous roads increased their merriment and they shared a laugh before Jane reached forth and lifted the knocker. A tall, lanky butler with more hair on the sides of his cheeks than the top of his head opened the door and bid them enter, taking their damp cloaks, gloves, and bonnets. When they were divested of their outer gear—and Elizabeth had spent a moment groaning over the mud splatters on her hems from the sprint from the carriage—Mr Galloway, as he had introduced himself, bade them follow and led them down the hall to a large, richly furnished drawing-room where Miss Bingley and Mrs Hurst sat.

"Miss Bennet and Miss Bennet," he announced before bowing them into the room.

"Oh, dear Jane! Miss Eliza," Miss Bingley cried as she and Mrs Hurst stood to receive them. "We had nearly despaired of you! We thought for certain the weather would frighten you away. But here you are and we are just delighted."

"Thank you, Miss Bingley," said Jane. "We are very grateful for your kind invitation."

"Come, come. Do be seated."

For the few minutes before dinner was served, conversation revolved around the squall outside and Miss Bingley insisted they admire the furnishing she had chosen for her brother. Jane paid all the proper compliments while Elizabeth remained mostly silent, offering only smiles and nods. She could not help but feel as her hostess prattled on of the extravagance and elegance of each piece, that she sat in the parlour of a wealthy eccentric who could not see colour properly.

The chair upon which she rested her posterior—rather uncomfortably—was a stiff gilded armchair in the Egyptian style, the arms adorned with sharply pointed dogs' heads. Jane perched beside her on a cream and puce striped wing-backed chair. Elizabeth wondered, as Miss Bingley enthused at length over the latest London fashions she had utilised, if the lady understood that just because one could afford such luxuries did not necessarily mean they ought all to be combined in one room.

Thankfully they were summoned to dinner before Elizabeth was called upon to give her opinion and what followed could only be described as an interrogation. Miss Bingley and Mrs Hurst expressed a wish to know *everything* about their guests and questioned them as to their accomplishments, favoured activities, and whether either sister had ever enjoyed a London season. The questions became steadily more intrusive and Elizabeth wished she could somehow prevent her sister from answering each and every one. Jane, who could not imagine that everyone was not as kind and well-meaning as she, provided Mr Bingley's sisters with her father's income, the state of their dowries, and even the general details regarding the entail upon Longbourn. Though Elizabeth could never be ashamed of her most excellent relations who resided in London, she did not miss the look of triumph which passed between her hosts when they learnt of her Uncle Gardiner's being in trade. It was quite rich, she thought, as it was not unknown that the late Mr Bingley had been a very successful tradesman in the north and it was through the very means which they scorned that the Bingleys had gained their fortune.

"Now," said Elizabeth, fixing an innocent smile on her face when she was unable to remain silent any longer, "we must know more of you. Pray, tell me, where was your father's estate located and for how many generations has your family been seated there?"

A violent flush flashed across Miss Bingley's face and Mrs Hurst's jaw flew open. Before either could sputter a response, however, a commotion was heard in the hall outside the dining room. Elizabeth heard raucous laughter and the thunking sound of what she thought was Colonel Fitzwilliam's stick. A moment later her conjecture was confirmed when the two men burst through the doors, both splattered in mud from the tip of their boots to the knees of their trousers and quite soaked through.

"Miss Bennet!" exclaimed Mr Bingley and Elizabeth suspected he had perhaps indulged a little too freely in spirits at dinner with the officers. "What a marvellous surprise! I did not expect to see your lovely face today."

"Miss Bennet, Miss Elizabeth," Colonel Fitzwilliam bowed to both ladies.

"Miss Elizabeth!" Mr Bingley cried as if he had only just noticed her. "What a marvellous surprise—again!"

"But where is Mr Darcy?" Miss Bingley demanded in her shrill tones.

Gesturing vaguely behind him, Mr Bingley said, "Out there."

"What?!"

"Our carriage," explained the Colonel, "became mired in the muddy lane just as we gained Netherfield's drive. Darcy remained to assist the coachmen in freeing the wheels." He made a wry gesture towards his injured leg. "I was unfortunately rather useless just standing about and Bingley, here,"—he cast an amused glance at his companion who was grinning stupidly at Jane—"is in no fit state to be of any service to anyone. Mrs Hurst, Mr Hurst made directly for his rooms to change."

Mrs Hurst received this information with a wave of her hand, clearly unable to bring herself to muster any concern for the whereabouts of her husband. Elizabeth wondered if she would have reacted any differently had the Colonel announced that her husband had met with a terrible accident and was laying insensible in a ditch somewhere between Netherfield and Meryton.

Realising the implication of the Colonel's words, Elizabeth turned to her sister. "Jane, we ought to return to Longbourn while we are still able."

"I am afraid it is too late for that," replied Colonel Fitzwilliam. "We left Colonel Forster's quarters early for fear of being marooned and it was nearly too late then. Even were the lanes not entirely impassable, our carriage is blocking the exit from the park."

"You shall have to stay the night!" Mr Bingley cried, sounding every bit as thrilled by the idea as Elizabeth was certain her mother would be.

Jane and Elizabeth exchanged looks. Elizabeth was prepared to protest, but the words died on the tip of her tongue at the hopeful look in her sister's cerulean eyes. "I suppose if it must be, but we would not wish to impose."

"'Tis no imposition at all," answered Mr Bingley, bouncing on the balls of his feet like a child who had just been granted a sweet. The expressions on his sister's faces did not support his claim in the least but there was little to be done about it.

"Let us not settle on anything just yet," said Miss Bingley. "Why do not you gentlemen go change out of those wet clothes while we ladies adjourn to the parlour. It is early yet and the rain may let up soon."

"I would not—" began the Colonel before Miss Bingley cut him off with a wagging finger.

"Pah-pah-pah! Run along now, Colonel. You would not wish to catch your death."

With a roll of his eyes and a tug at Mr Bingley's sleeve to tear his gaze away from Jane, the gentlemen excused themselves while the ladies followed Miss Bingley to the parlour. Jane and Elizabeth sat together on a small, fashionably ugly settée as silence settled around them. Miss Bingley and Mrs Hurst sat a little way removed, huddled together in close confederation. The former was whispering and gesturing energetically as the latter nodded along with enthusiasm, their guests seemingly forgotten. Elizabeth did not particularly mind; she had had enough of the superior sisters' attention for one evening to last her a lifetime. She could not help watching the falling rain outside, hoping against all logic that Miss Bingley might be proven correct and the weather would turn, the roads miraculously drying with unprecedented swiftness, and they might be able to return home.

They sat in this attitude for nearly a quarter of an hour before footsteps were heard outside the parlour. Elizabeth would not have been bothered had it been bandits come to carry them away if only it would end the tedium of the evening. She was only marginally disappointed when the door opened and Mr Darcy entered, stopping just inside the threshold, in a terribly dishevelled state. His boots were entirely caked in mud, as were the greater part of his trousers. There was dirt and filth spattered up the left sleeve of his coat while the right sported a large tear. A smear of mud marred his chiselled jaw and his dripping hair was slicked back away from his face.

Jane gasped and even Elizabeth had a difficult time concealing her astonishment at the sight of such a sombre, proud gentleman in such disarray. When Colonel Fitzwilliam had said that Mr Darcy had remained with the carriage to assist, she had naturally assumed that meant he would stand to the side under an umbrella and bark commands at the coachmen. To look at him, one might have been justified in thinking Mr Darcy had told all the servants to stand aside and attended to the task himself. Despite anything else she might feel towards this man, she could not help but acknowledge a slight increase in her respect for him. She might also have been forgiven for the unseemly thought that dishevelment rather became him.

"Oh!" shrieked Miss Bingley, leaping to her feet and crossing the room to stop a few feet short of Mr Darcy. By the look on her face, she was struggling between wanting to press herself against him while at the same time wishing to remain as far away from the filth as possible. "Oh, Mr Darcy! You poor thing! Come, sit by the fire and warm yourself."

"No, I thank you. I would not wish to ruin the, ah, furniture." His eyes roved over the odd collection of expensively mismatched decor. Elizabeth looked up and their eyes met. The slightest smile played at his lips as he twitched his right eyebrow and rolled his eyes, finishing it off with a wink. She clapped a hand over her mouth to stifle the laugh that bubbled forth at this unexpectedly sardonic display. "I only came this way seeking Bingley and my cousin to inform them that I had returned. If you would be so kind, I must now go and subject myself to a severe scolding from my valet." He indicated his soiled clothing with a wave of his hand.

This time, Elizabeth laughed freely at his obvious jest, as did Jane beside her. Miss Bingley, however, was not in the least amused.

"I do not see what is so funny?" she said with a glare directed towards her guests. Turning back to the gentleman, she reached for his arm but pulled back after thinking better of it. "Mr Darcy, you must not tolerate such disrespect from your servants!"

"Do not make yourself uneasy, Miss Bingley. It was merely a joke. I assure you my man is adequately respectful and proper. Though, I should be quite lost without him, I am sure."

"What you need, sir, is a wife," Miss Bingley purred, sidling a little closer to the gentleman, "to keep you out of trouble."

"And I shall do all in my power to procure one," he agreed with a solemn nod, "whenever I should meet the right lady. Excuse me."

With a swift bow, Mr Darcy turned and left them. Miss Bingley huffed and returned to her sister, arms folded tightly across her chest. Elizabeth turned to gaze out the window at the storm, which was still raging as fiercely as ever. It seemed increasingly likely she and Jane would be unable to leave Netherfield this night. It would not, perhaps, be wholly unpleasant, she mused. Colonel Fitzwilliam was delightful company and, though her sister would never admit such aloud, Jane was obviously pleased to be given the opportunity to further her acquaintance with Mr Bingley. *And who would have ever thought that the proud, disagreeable Mr Darcy would have a sense of humour?!*

Chapter Five

espite the steady trickle of icy rainwater dripping from his hair down under his collar, the squelching of his sodden boots, and being filthier than he could recall having been since Richard had tipped their boat in the lake when he was nine years of age , Darcy trod the path to his chambers in jubilant spirits. He had made Miss Elizabeth laugh, not once but twice. The musical sound echoed around in his mind as he presented himself to a thoroughly displeased Adams.

He had not been entirely untruthful downstairs. His valet was nearly as fastidious as he, and doubly so about Darcy's wardrobe. The man would never presume to scold his master, but the tightness about his mouth and the furl in his brow as he helped Darcy to disrobe from his ruined dinner jacket—one of his best, no less—was evidence enough of Adams' feelings on the matter.

But even his valet's obvious pique could not lessen Darcy's triumph. He had been the cause of the genuine smile that graced a beautiful woman's lovely lips and he had not even needed Richard's support or aid. It had not been awkward or embarrassing and he felt neither the impulse to apologise nor offer his hand. He wondered idly, as he soaked in the hot bath Adams had readied for him, if this was how Richard felt all the time. If so, he could understand, at least to a degree, his cousin's enjoyment in engaging with pretty ladies. It was a shame, he mused, that dragons were nought but fiction; buoyed by the memory of a pair of fine eyes made brighter by laughter, he felt capable of slaying an entire horde of beasts.

Darcy had not been enthusiastic about this jaunt into the country, but mayhap it was just what was needed. He would never be so cavalier as Richard or Bingley, but an innocent flirtation with an intelligent woman could surely have no dangers. He did need a wife; Miss Bingley had not been wrong about that. This, he thought, might be considered something like practise. He would smile and flirt with Miss Elizabeth, enjoying her sharp wit, intelligent conversation, and magnificent eyes— all the while being careful not to raise her expectations—then take his newfound confidence to London and seek out a proper wife.

Patiently submitting to Adams' ministrations, Darcy thanked his faithful servant for his excellence and care before making his way downstairs with almost indecent eagerness. He had never been so keen to be in the company of a woman before. Stopping just outside the drawing room doors, he tugged at the hem of his waistcoat and sleeves and straightened his lapels, prepared to indulge, for once, in the delightful attentions of a beautiful woman. Miss Elizabeth's tinkling laughter drifted out the open doors and tipped the corners of his mouth upwards with very little effort. This was going to be a most enjoyable endeavour.

With a final breath to steady his nerves, Darcy stepped through the doors, his eyes seeking her out, when his expectations and exultant spirits shattered to the ground. She was seated on a sofa beside his cousin, her body angled fully towards Richard, a bright smile plastered on her lovely face as she laughed at some—no doubt exaggerated—story his far too charming cousin was relating. In all his enthusiasm, Darcy had entirely forgotten the presence of Richard "Much too Popular with the Ladies" Fitzwilliam. There would be no competing with his cousin, who was far more practised and adept at being pleasing, nor would he ever wish to. The two men enjoyed plenty of friendly competition, from fencing to horse racing, but he would never go up against his cousin over a lady. No woman could ever be worth risking his relationship with a man he looked upon as a brother.

Darcy crossed the room, his mettle now greatly wounded, and took up a book in a chair nearby where the pair were absorbed in lively conversation. It was likely for the best, he thought as he covertly watched the way her eyes danced with merriment and her lovely lips turned up at the corners in a mischievous grin. His advice to Bingley had been sound. Bestowing his attentions upon a young country maiden with no fortune could only set the lady up for disappointment—and potentially engage his honour in an imprudent situation.

It was a foolish notion, he convinced himself, somewhat peevishly. He might be as careful as possible and still find himself trapped. Miss Elizabeth did not seem a woman with mercenary tendencies; her embarrassment at Mrs Bennet's vulgar pronouncements on seeking wealthy husbands for her daughters seemed genuine, but he had met with talented actresses before.

Her sweet laughter tickled his ears again and he tightened his grip on his book, crumpling the page.

"I do not think your cousin is enjoying his book," Elizabeth said to Richard in an exaggerated whisper meant to carry and he realised he had not turned a single page. "Perhaps it is merely tolerable and not interesting enough to tempt him."

Richard snickered and Darcy stiffened at having his ungentlemanly words thrown back at him. He ought to apologise for the slight, and now would be an opportune time to do so but he was smarting. He had been thwarted in his ambitions to bask in the attentions of the lovely Miss Elizabeth and was now awakened to the unlikelihood that she would even have welcomed his regard; he was being laughed at and, while he might have welcomed some sweet-natured teasing not half an hour ago, he was in no humour at present to endure it.

Setting his book aside and standing, he mumbled a stiff "Excuse me," and fled the room, deaf to Miss Bingley's protests.

A quarter of an hour later, Richard found him in the billiards room in his shirtsleeves, sending balls scattering across the felt with more force than was necessary. Darcy spared only a glance for his cousin before returning his attention to the table, though he had little enough interest in the game.

"Ah, yes, I see," said Richard in the manner of a man who had solved a great puzzle. "You will freely hand out insults and slights, but will not stand to be on the receiving end of them."

Not bothering to look at Richard, Darcy lined up another shot. "When do the ladies leave? Should not they have returned to Longbourn by now?"

"You are joking?"

Darcy cast a glare at his cousin who nodded towards the window. The rain was still coming down in relentless sheets. A groan escaped his lips. How could he have forgotten the blasted rain? A vision of Miss Elizabeth's bright smile as she laughed at his earlier comments flashed across his mind's eye. Grimacing, he shoved it away. The vexing temptress would not be leaving this night.

"There is something the matter with you," Richard said, leaning his cane against a chair and picking up another cue, dusting the end with chalk. "It is not like you to behave in such a petulant manner."

"I am perfectly well, thank you."

"Have you some objection to Miss Elizabeth,"—the Colonel leant over the table and sent a ball sailing into a corner pocket—"other than mistakenly believing her to be anything less than absolutely lovely?"

Gripping his cue tightly, Darcy held his tongue until he was more master of himself, for it was not his cousin with whom he was angry nor even Miss Elizabeth, but himself. He had behaved poorly at the assembly and knew that he deserved every word of the lady's censure. He could only wish she had not looked so pretty with that eyebrow arched so mischievously when she delivered his well-earned set down. It made it far more difficult to ignore the strange pull he should not feel towards her, yet which tugged at him all the same. Could she not have been a terrible shrew about the whole ordeal?

He silently reminded himself that her fine eyes and pleasing figure hardly mattered; she was not an appropriate candidate for his wife, therefore he could not entertain any serious intentions where she was concerned. Not that he did. She was pretty and interesting, nothing more.

"I find no fault with her person," he answered when he could trust in the steadiness of his voice.

"You disapprove of her manners?"

"Not in the least. She is lively and intelligent. 'Tis refreshing, if anything."

Richard regarded him for several moments, the billiards game forgotten by both men. "Then you are interested in the lady?"

"Of course, not," he answered, perhaps with a mite too much conviction.

"Of course, not? You say that as though it were perfectly obvious why any man should not wish to take such a bright, vivacious, lovely thing to wife."

"It ought to be." Darcy turned away from his cousin and returned his cue to the rack, trying not to think of all the ways Miss Elizabeth would make a charming wife; reasons which had nothing to do with fortune or duty—reasons which made the more ungentlemanly side of him come alive. Shaking his head against such thoughts, he simply added over his shoulder, as much to remind to himself as to answer his cousin, "She is not suitable."

When Richard said nothing, Darcy turned around and found his cousin still leaning against the edge of the table, staring at him with a contemplative look on his face. His eyes were narrowed and his head tilted slightly to the side as if he were attempting to decipher some deep, hidden meaning to his words. But there was no such message, his words were genuine; even if he wished things could be different.

Darcy suppressed the urge to fidget under Richard's scrutinising gaze. His cousin knew him better than any other person and would no doubt discern his inconvenient attraction to Miss Elizabeth. Such a discovery could only have two results: either Richard would tease him mercilessly or encourage him to throw duty to himself and his family to the side and court the girl—neither of which he could countenance at the moment.

"Then you would not mind if another were to pursue her?"

This was not at all what Darcy had anticipated and stumbled over his answer. "I—well, I did not—what? No. Not at all." Even as he said the words, his gut clenched with irrational envy at some unknown man being so fortunate as to be free to enjoy the lively attentions of Miss Elizabeth Bennet.

"Good," Richard positively beamed. "Then I should like to inquire as to the offer you made some years ago. To part with one of the Darcy estates if ever I should feel the need to sell my commission."

"Wait, what?" He could not mean...

"You once said that should I ever find the life of a soldier no longer palatable, you would be pleased to gift me one of the estates in your possession. I could not fathom such a thing at the time—you know how I feel about charity—but then, I had never yet met a woman worth giving up my life as a soldier." As if a candle had been snuffed, the jovial expression so profoundly characteristic of Richard Fitzwilliam suddenly dimmed as he glanced down towards his injured leg. "I am increasingly fearful that my leg will never fully heal. It has been above a year and I am scarce better off now than I was as I lay trapped beneath my horse on that battlefield in Spain."

Darcy flinched at this reminder of how close his family had come to losing this dear man. Pushing past the melancholy, he said with more bravado than he felt, "You have managed to ride again."

"Yes, but only for short bouts. I have not the strength to remain saddled for any great length of time." He took a deep breath and shook away the dark look that had clouded his eyes. With a smile, he continued. "I unexpectedly find myself in the position of wishing to hang up my red coat and take up the mantle of gentleman. If I were to wait until I have saved enough, I might never marry!" Richard chuckled light-heartedly at this but Darcy could see no humour in the matter. "Come, man. I shall do what I can to compensate you. Perhaps name a son after you. Or a daughter. Fitzwilhelmina." He shook his head in distaste. "Very well, a son. Oh, wait. We spoke of this once before, did we not? Ah, yes. Fitzwilliam Fitzwilliam! You were entirely correct. Far too cruel."

"You cannot mean to seriously pursue Miss Elizabeth."

"Whyever not? As you say, she is lively and intelligent. Beautiful, whatever you say about her. I think she will make a charming wife."

"She has no fortune."

"We shall never be rich, to be sure, but I should think we would be happy. And is that not more important? I have no desire for a marriage such as my parents and brother enjoy. I should very much like to at least esteem my wife."

"What of her kin? Her mother and sisters? Even Mr Bennet is hardly a credit to the family."

"And that is why I would request Grünerberg, if I may be so bold. I think placing a few counties between us and the Bennets ought to make things easier. I cannot imagine Mr Bennet rousing himself to travel to Derbyshire more than once or twice a year, even for his favourite daughter. Though, with your blessing, I should like to rebrand the estate. *Grünerberg* is so harsh sounding."

"It means 'green mountain,'" said Darcy distractedly.

"I know, but the German language is so aggressive, do you not think? And I am still unwilling to accept charity. I will insist upon paying you rent. You ought to think of me as any other tenant."

Darcy did not answer, having hardly listened to his cousin. He was struggling to comprehend the conversation. Richard wished to court Elizabeth? It was enough of a distasteful notion thinking of some nameless, faceless stranger one day taking her to wife—taking her to bed—but Richard? Must he be subjected to being witness to her falling in love with his dearest cousin? Watching her carrying his children and ply him with adoring looks?

Of course, he must. Darcy mentally shook himself. It was not as if he were in love with Elizabeth. 'Twas nought more than an infatuation. What better cure than to see her attached to the man he esteemed as no other?

"So, truly?" Richard's voice pierced his contemplations. "You have no desire whatsoever to court Miss Elizabeth yourself? Because I would not compete with you, Cousin."

"I assure you I have no intentions in that quarter," Darcy answered honestly.

"Then I have your blessing?"

"Do you need it?"

"Not at all, but I should like to know I have it all the same. Lord knows I shall need you in my corner when my parents learn of this."

"Then be assured, you have my blessing and my support."

"Thank you, Darcy." The two men stood in silent confederation for several moments, each lost in their own thoughts, until Richard spoke again, reviving some of their natural ease. "Bingley does not seem to have heeded your warnings."

"No, he has not. But I am not unduly concerned."

"Oh?"

"I have observed Miss Bennet a little. She receives his attentions with pleasure, but I have not seen any particular sign of regard. She does not smile any brighter at him than any other gentleman as far as I have noticed. I do not think Miss Bennet's heart likely to be touched. Therefore, she will not be injured when his attentions stray. If I have any concerns, it is that there is little in this neighbourhood to turn his head and he will offer his hand before he knows what he is about. Should it come to that, I do fear the lady would accept him for the sake of her family. I shall keep watch and interfere if necessary."

"Then I shall leave you to it and devote my attention to my own affairs."

Darcy smiled at his cousin's cheerful optimism. He refused to allow the sliver of jealousy which had taken up space in his gut any further allowance. He *would* get the better of this, and no doubt soon enough. There was no acceptable alternative.

Chapter Six

Unsympathetic to Elizabeth's desire to return home, the rain persisted all through the night and into the next day. The Colonel's enjoyable company and Jane's happiness in Mr Bingley's attentions aside, she did not like being an imposition and was quite sure at least three of Netherfield's residents wished the Bennet sisters miles away. Miss Bingley and Mrs Hurst spent the rest of the previous evening sitting together in whispered conversation, casting glares upon the interlopers. The words "overstaying their welcome" had reached Elizabeth's ears—no doubt by design.

Mr Darcy did not return to the drawing room after so abruptly quitting it and, despite the Colonel's assurances to the contrary, she was sure she had offended him with her teasing. Mr Hurst, she was quite certain, was indifferent to who came or went, so long as he had good food and drink enough.

Waking at her usual hour, Elizabeth dressed in the gown she had worn the previous day, but which had been brushed and pressed by some diligent maid, and made her way downstairs for breakfast. In a house occupied by those who routinely kept Town hours, she held every expectation of breaking her fast alone and did not regret the idea. It was looking increasingly likely that she would not be afforded her usual daily walk and would need the solitude to fortify her equanimity if she was to be forced to remain at Netherfield another day.

Her surprise, therefore, was great upon entering the breakfast parlour and finding none other than Mr Darcy seated at the table, a plate of eggs and rashers and a steaming cup of coffee before him. He raised his eyes from the letter he was reading when she entered and stood with a bow.

"Miss Elizabeth, good morning."

"Good morning, sir," she replied before turning towards the sideboard.

"May I fix you a plate?" he offered, which she declined.

A silence fell between them as Elizabeth filled her plate then turned back to the table. Choosing a seat proved, for a moment, to be a more arduous task than it ought to have been. She felt no desire to sit near Mr Darcy, nor did she believe he would wish it. However, neither did she wish to be rude and ignore him. The decision was taken from her when, unexpectedly, Mr Darcy rose once more and moved to pull out the chair beside his own with a look of invitation. Stifling a resigned sigh, she accepted the seat with polite thanks.

Several minutes passed wherein the only sound was the occasional clinking of flatware on their plates. Mr Darcy did not resume the perusal of his letter but sat beside her with an air of agitation. Elizabeth wondered whether it was her presence which had discomposed him so and was on the point of offering to change seats—though it had been only at his instigation that she had sat here at all, she thought with some indignation—when he spoke.

"Miss Elizabeth, I would like to apologise for the rude manner of my departure last evening."

With a sideways glance, she saw such a look of true contrition as to still any sarcastic or teasing remark which had been forming on her tongue. Such had done her no favours last evening, after all.

"Do not make yourself uneasy, sir. I provoked you for no better reason than the gratification of my own wounded pride. I offer my own apologies, as well."

"You could not have provoked me had I not provided the provocation in the first place. Besides, it was not your words which disturbed me but rather the remembrance of my own boorish behaviour and the enlightenment of what must be your own justifiably poor opinion of me. My words at the assembly were not only ungenerous and ungentlemanly, but also unequivocally untrue. I was in a foul humour that evening and determined to be displeased. I wished only to stop my friend's pestering. Such is no excuse, I know, but there it is. Please accept my most humble apologies for having spoken in such an uncivil manner."

Cocking her head to one side, Elizabeth contemplated this almost overwhelmingly mercurial man. Just when she felt she had him figured out, Mr Darcy said or did something to throw all her assumptions to the wind. Was he the proud, haughty gentleman who had insulted her at the assembly without even the benefit of a proper introduction? Or the hard-working man who was unafraid of dirtying his hands—or his very fine clothing—doing the work of servants whilst still being able to produce a joke as easily as a breath even as he stood in the doorway covered in mud? What of this gentleman who sat beside her? The sincere, contrite, perhaps even slightly diffident man who looked for all the world as if he would not be happy again unless she absolved him of that which she held against him.

There was only one way to find out. She held her hand out to him. "I forgive you, Mr Darcy. Let us quarrel no more over the past and agree to begin anew."

Taking her hand in his own, rather large, one, Mr Darcy smiled. "Agreed. Thank you, Miss Elizabeth."

They each turned back to their plates and Elizabeth, in an effort to dissipate the awkwardness of the past few minutes and follow through on her resolve to gain a better understanding of the man seated beside her, broached the subject of books. After his hasty exit of the drawing-room last evening, and his cousin's subsequent chase, she had taken up the volume Mr Darcy had left behind, surprised to discover it to be a copy of Shakespeare's *Much Ado About Nothing*, a favourite of hers.

They soon were deeply engaged in a lively discussion on the intricacies of the relationship between the principal characters, Beatrice and Benedick.

"You will forgive me, but I disagree, sir," said she. "It is my opinion that Benedick and Beatrice were in love with one another all along. Two rational people will hardly fall in love simply because others suggest that they ought."

"Why, then, does he antagonise her so? What man would behave in such a manner towards the object of his affection?"

"We know there is a history between the couple, and that Beatrice, by her own admission, once loved Benedick. Whatever happened between them was such that it destroyed her affection for him, or so she wished others to believe— perhaps was even convinced of it herself. I choose to believe that whatever caused Benedick to break Beatrice's heart was done for good cause. Perhaps he feared he would not return from the war, perhaps he felt she was too young, or that he was not worthy of her. Whatever the cause, he loves her still but receives no encouragement from her, blinded as she is by her own heartache, obstinance, and pride, and so endeavours to disguise his own, apparently unrequited, feelings."

"With what evidence do you support your argument?"

"The very vehemence of his proclamation of hatred. They dance together, though Beatrice is unaware of his identity, masked as they are, and describes Benedick to her partner as the prince's jester, a very dull fool. Until this point, Benedick's wit is rather benign, he even declares to Claudio his opinion that Beatrice is far more lovely than her cousin, Hero. But, having been wounded by the lady he loves, he cannot even bear to be in her presence and departs. I daresay, I should feel the sting of injury far more acutely coming from a man whose good opinion I craved rather than a man for whom I cared nothing."

She turned to him then, intent on hearing his opinion on the matter. When her eyes met his, there was an expression therein which sent a shiver down her spine and, for reasons she could not even begin to understand, her tongue reached out impulsively to moisten her lips. Drawn by the movement, his eyes lingered on her lips for a long moment before slowly rising to meet her gaze, seeming to search hers, seeking something, though she knew not what.

"This is, of course," she said in a voice scarcely above a whisper, strangely incapable of tearing her eyes away from his, "merely conjecture."

"I am of Miss Elizabeth's opinion," the Colonel's voice announced from somewhere behind her and both she and Mr Darcy jumped. "Of what are we speaking?"

Mr Darcy hastily stood and pushed back his chair. "Richard, good morning. Here, take my place. I am finished."

"I can just as easily sit to Miss Elizabeth's other side, Cousin. You need not run away."

A silent conversation seemed to take place between the cousins as she watched. Colonel Fitzwilliam glanced at herself then raised a brow in question at Mr Darcy. That gentleman's reply was to square his shoulders, raise his chin, and offer the slightest shake of his head. Whatever they could be about, she could not guess, but it was over as quickly as it had begun.

Taking a step back, Mr Darcy bowed to her. "Thank you, Miss Elizabeth, for the rousing debate. I shall need time to consider the matter, but I believe you may have convinced me. Now if you would both excuse me."

The Colonel took his cousin's place as Mr Darcy left the room and inquired as to the quality of Elizabeth's sleep and the pleasantness of her morning thus far. She reciprocated his inquiries and they spoke of pleasant nothings for some time before those less inclined for early mornings began to drift into the breakfast parlour.

"Miss Elizabeth," the Colonel addressed her, pushing himself to stand with the aid of his cane, "I have heard you speak often enough of your delight in a country walk to know that you must be in need of a good ramble."

"You have taken the measure of me, Colonel," replied Elizabeth with a smile.

"I cannot improve the weather, but perhaps a turn about the gallery in my poor company might tide you over until this bothersome rain stops."

"That sounds lovely, Colonel. I thank you."

"Should anyone care to join us?" he made a general invitation to the party gathered around the table, but no one paid him any heed. Jane and Mr Bingley were seated at the far end, the gentleman leaning towards her sister, their plates completely disregarded; Miss Bingley sat beside her sister, lamenting having missed Mr Darcy at breakfast yet again while

Mrs Hurst nodded absently and patted her arm half-heartedly. Mr Hurst had yet to appear. When no reply was received, the Colonel held out an arm for Elizabeth and led her from the room.

They climbed the stairs and traversed down the hall to where the gallery was located at the back of the house. Their pace was much slower than Elizabeth would ordinarily have preferred for her morning exercise owing to the Colonel's injured leg, but she endured it with good grace.

Ambling about the room, the pair stopped here and there before a portrait of the owner of Netherfield's ancestors. They amused one another by concocting details of the subject's life or what had transpired to affect such an expression upon a particularly dour-looking individual. It could not replace Elizabeth's customary morning constitutional, but she laughed a good deal and that was an activity she dearly loved.

When they had made two circuits and begun a third, Colonel Fitzwilliam cleared his throat and tapped his cane against the floor.

"Miss Elizabeth," he said, "it has been a true pleasure making your acquaintance."

"I thank you, Colonel. I feel the same."

"I should very much like to continue getting to know you and wondered, well. I wondered if you would be so good as to consent to enter into a courtship with me?"

"Courtship?" Elizabeth asked in surprise, stopping their progress and stepping away to look up at him properly. "I am flattered, Colonel. Flattered and confused. Did you not mention during the earliest moments of our acquaintance the need for you to marry advantageously?"

"I did."

"Then I do not understand. My situation has not altered, sir."

"Perhaps not, but mine has. Or, rather, it shall." It was rather endearing the way he shyly avoided her gaze. She had never considered with what courage a man must pursue a woman. A lady's part was only to accept or decline; the risk was nearly entirely on the gentleman's side. She gave him a look of encouragement and he continued. "Darcy, excellent man that he is, has long extended the offer of an estate to me if ever I should wish to leave off the life of a soldier. To own the truth, I had never expected to accept his kindness. It has of late, however, become a more appealing prospect to me."

Consulting her feelings, Elizabeth contemplated the man before her. Colonel Fitzwilliam was not what many ladies would consider handsome. His steel-grey eyes were set a touch too far apart and there was a distinctive crook in the bridge of his nose, indicative of having been broken some time in the past. He possessed a strong jaw—a trait shared with his much handsomer cousin—and a prominent brow. While Elizabeth certainly hoped she might be physically attracted to her future husband, she was of the opinion that a man's good character added much to a lacking countenance.

There was no denying the Colonel was a good man. He displayed his amiability in his patience with her younger sisters who had been enthralled by his scarlet coat and his kind manners towards her neighbours who had fawned over the son of an earl. He was loyal to his cousin, even when Elizabeth had felt such loyalty misplaced, and, though he did not excuse Mr Darcy's uncivil behaviour, he had, from the earliest moments, worked to convince Elizabeth of his excellence.

She hesitated only with the matter of her own heart. Long since made to recognise the defects in her own parent's dismal marriage, Elizabeth had determined that nothing but the very deepest love would ever induce her into matrimony. The

Colonel's early hints as to his need to marry a lady with at least a modest fortune had effectively instigated the guarding of her heart. She had no desire to fall in love where there was no hope. There was little doubt they might do well together, both being of such open, lively temperaments, but could love ever grow between them?

Looking upon the Colonel now, she did not detect any particular display of deep affection. That he admired her was obvious, that he was hopeful of an affirmative answer equally so, but she did not believe him to be in love with her. It would be absurd if he were; they had been acquainted only a little under a fortnight. Was she willing to take the chance and enter into a courtship where she could not be sure of ever receiving or returning love? What if he fell in love with her, but she found she could not reciprocate? What if she gave him her heart, but his remained within his possession? There was great potential for injury on both sides.

But was that not true with so many aspects of life? Did not the dark days of winter make the summer sun shine that much brighter? Was a sweet morsel not made more delicious following the taste of bitterness? Could one who had never experienced grief truly appreciate joy?

"Colonel, I must be honest with you." He nodded and she pressed forward. "Our acquaintance is of such brevity, at this moment, sir, I do not love you."

"I should consider you suspect if you claimed otherwise, madam."

"Furthermore, I will not marry where I do not love. I feel there is potential for a happy match between us, but if I cannot give you my heart, if you cannot give me yours, I shall not accept an offer of marriage. If, after my words you are still inclined to make your offer of courtship, then I accept."

A broad grin stretched across his face. "I have said it once and I shall say it again, you are a singular woman, Miss Elizabeth Bennet."

"Thank you, Colonel. How so?"

"There are few women of my acquaintance who would not accept my hand on the hope alone that my brother will meet with an untimely end and she shall gain a title."

Pressing a hand to her chest theatrically, she cried, "Me, a countess? Heaven forbid!"

"Do not fret," he chuckled. "My brother's wife is currently with child and, if the Fitzwilliam legacy holds strong, he shall have his heir and I shall be safe from the earldom." The Colonel flashed her a sly look. "I am, after all, the second of four brothers."

Elizabeth laughed at his jovial manner before sobering slightly. "I hope, Colonel, you will understand when I ask that, with the exception of your cousin and my sister, I would rather suspend any announcement until you have spoken with my father."

"Of course. I am relieved you approve of informing our dearest relations as I have already apprised Darcy of my intentions."

"Then he approves?"

He held his arm out to her and she took it, allowing him to lead her down the room again. "Wholeheartedly. You and my cousin seem to have put your differences aside and come to an accord. I must say, I am glad to see it. He is the dearest man in the world to me. I should not like it if you and he were at odds."

"We have agreed to put the past behind us and start afresh."

"I am glad to hear it. Though I shall be on my guard. Darcy is truly the best man I have ever known and you may not be so keen on accepting my suit once you have come to know him better."

"I am not so fickle, sir," Elizabeth laughed. "I require more than a handsome face and a vast fortune to turn my head."

"Oh?"

"Indeed." She quirked her lips in an impish smile. "A man must also show a superiority of mind to win my heart."

"I am doomed!"

Chapter Seven

or the remainder of the day, the newly courting couple continued to enjoy one another's company as ever they had, but took care to include others in their activities or spend time apart so as not to ignite the suspicions of the others in the house. To anyone none-the-wiser, there was very little difference in their behaviour.

Darcy's first inclination was avoidance. When his cousin returned from his escapade in the gallery with Elizabeth on his arm, both sporting winsome smiles, his gut had twisted and writhed within him. Each time he witnessed Elizabeth sending secret smiles across the room to Richard, Darcy was overcome with a desire to mangle whatever he happened to be holding. If his hands were empty, he was forced to tamp down the urge to search for some nearby object which to destroy.

To think, if things were only slightly different, if she had only a modest fortune, it might be to himself that she aimed those radiant smiles. Had she but five or ten thousand pounds he could overlook the discrepancies in their stations and justify taking her to wife. It was well and good for Richard to disregard the want of fortune; he had not the responsibilities Darcy shouldered. Richard was the second son born to a family of four brothers. The continuation of his family name was not in question. But Darcy and his sister were the last of their line. As head of his family, it was his duty to ensure not only the promise of future generations but to maintain the legacy he had been entrusted with.

Such duties had ever given Darcy a sense of purpose and pride. He had ever felt honoured to be entrusted with the faith and confidence of those who had come before him and those who would follow. Never before had such responsibilities felt so much like a burden. One day, he had always known, he would need to choose a wife who would assist him in ushering in the future for Pemberley and the Darcy family. It had never felt a pressing matter, rather something to be dealt with at some future date when he met a woman who met all his requirements. In all his life, he had never imagined that he could not have any wife of his choosing.

Much of the day was spent sequestered in the library when he could no longer vouch for his equanimity. The pleasure he felt in his cousin's happiness was warring terribly with the envy he felt at Richard's freedom to marry where he wished. Until he got the better of these feelings—but no. There were no feelings. He did not love Elizabeth—Miss Elizabeth. This was nothing more than an infatuation, a passing attraction. This was not the first time he had experienced such a phenomenon. There had been pretty ladies aplenty in London who had caught his eye since he came out in society. Inevitably, the death of his fancy was brought about by a deeper knowledge of the lady. What a handsome face and a pleasing figure could not disguise for long was an ugly character or an insipid mind. He had been going about the whole matter all wrong. He need not avoid Miss Elizabeth, but rather increase his intimacy with the lady. No doubt, in short order, she would reveal some glaring error in her character and he would be cured of his unfortunate attraction.

Wherefore, it was with a renewed determination that Darcy girded his hypothetical loins and returned to the drawing-room, resolved to put an end to this strange fascination with the woman his cousin intended to marry.

✦

"Oh, good Lord," Elizabeth murmured in horror at the vision laid out before her on the bed.

"Lizzy, be kind," Jane admonished, though Elizabeth could see the dubious look on her sister's face.

"Jane, just look at this!" She held up a peach-coloured monstrosity covered in enough lace to cross even Mrs Bennet's eyes. "Why on earth does Miss Bingley even own such a gown? And why would she travel with it?"

Jane reached down and picked up another, equally revolting dress. "It was very kind of Miss Bingley and Mrs Hurst to lend us something to wear."

"This," replied Elizabeth, pulling at the large, frilly bow covering the entire bust of the gown, "is not kindness, Jane." She held the dress against herself and was relieved to see the hem falling several inches beyond the toe of her slippers. Tossing the hideous gown back upon the bed, she heaved a sigh of relief. "Never again shall I lament being the shortest of my sisters."

"Lizzy, you must!" It was more a desperate plea than stern admonishment. "We have been wearing the same gowns for two days."

"And I shall wear mine for another. It may shock Miss Bingley's sensibilities, but I am sure I shall survive the indignity. The rain has let up and I am sure the roads will be dry enough that we may return home tomorrow."

"And what will the Colonel think?" Jane asked with a sly look in her eye. Laying down an equally vile gown with much more care than Elizabeth had done, she turned to her sister with a look of innocence, but there was an air of mischief in her angelic face. "You seem to be enjoying his company."

Elizabeth felt the flush creep across her cheeks. "I confess, I am, Jane. I do not see how anyone could not like Colonel Fitzwilliam. He is open and amiable and everything gentlemanly."

"He is a good man. Perhaps not so handsome as Mr Bingley. Or Mr Darcy."

"No, but a good character can go a long way in compensating for a lack of good looks, I believe. And he is not so very plain." Feeling uncharacteristically shy, she sat down on the edge of the bed. "Jane, Colonel Fitzwilliam has asked me for a courtship. And I have accepted."

"Oh, Lizzy!" Jane sat beside her sister and took up her hands, her eyes glistening with emotion.

Looking upon her sister's blatant joy on her behalf, Elizabeth laughed. "Dear Jane! Do not go supposing me to be in love already! 'Tis but a courtship! Our acquaintance is of such short duration. What is it?" Jane had quickly pressed her lips together and averted her gaze, suddenly inordinately interested in the nail of her left thumb. "Jane?"

Jane stood and crossed the floor to the dressing table, where she began absently picking up various objects only to replace them an inch or two from where they had been. "You say it is too soon to have such strong feelings, and I am sure you are correct. But, Lizzy...oh, I do not know!" She sat heavily on the dressing table stool. "I have met gentlemen aplenty in Town when I have stayed with Aunt and Uncle Gardiner. They are always pleasing and attentive. They flatter and flirt but not one has ever made me feel the way Mr Bingley does. When he looks at me, I feel as if I am the only woman in the whole world. Do you think...is it possible to feel real love so soon?"

Elizabeth contemplated her sister. Jane was of such a tender-hearted disposition, inclined to think well of everybody and their motives and never judged anyone too harshly. It was a wonder she had never fancied herself in love before, what with all the male attention Jane received for being so beautiful.

"I do not believe it to be impossible," she answered. "You ought not to judge your feelings by my opinions, dearest. You are far more likely to give your heart freedom to guide you. I shall probably question and doubt every feeling and never come to any conclusion on the matter at all. I shall only marry for love, and I shall likely only fall in love quite by accident!"

"What of the Colonel? Do you think you could love him?"

"I do not see why I could not. He is intelligent and sensible, good-humoured and lively. I imagine he is just the kind of husband to suit me. If I can prevent myself from thinking too much on the matter, I believe all that is wanting is time."

"Can he afford to marry? Did he not imply that he must marry with consideration to a lady's fortune?"

"He did. He told me his cousin has long offered the gift of an estate in his possession as inducement to give up the life of a soldier. He says he had never thought to accept until he met me," Elizabeth told her sister with a good deal of blushing.

"That is very kind of Mr Darcy."

"Indeed, it is. I do not think he is quite the terrible ogre we all imagined him to be when first he came to Hertfordshire. I believe Mr Darcy is simply a man who takes a little more effort to come to know. Colonel Fitzwilliam speaks so highly of him and I believe the Colonel to be sensible enough not to allow familial regard to blind him to a bad character. He has said more than once that he prefers Mr Darcy even to some of his brothers."

Elizabeth shared with her sister the pleasant conversation she had with Mr Darcy that morning at breakfast and confessed to beginning to come to like the gentleman. "He is not so open and amiable as his cousin or his friend, but I believe he is, at his heart, a good man. I should not be opposed to coming to know him better."

"Then help me change my gown and we shall go down so that you may begin to become acquainted with your future cousin." Jane stood and turned her back to a laughing Elizabeth to undo the buttons.

"Jane, do not do this! I am sure there was some malicious intent behind the lending of these gowns."

"I must, Lizzy. I have not so reasonable an excuse as you do. It would be terribly rude not to wear it."

"It was rude of those superior sisters to lend such awful gowns!"

They gently argued over the matter for several more minutes until, not wishing to distress her sister, Elizabeth yielded and helped Jane into the vile article. She won her point in the end, however, when the gown could not be stretched, pulled, or buttoned over her sister's generous bust. Sighing with relief, though she would voice no such emotion, Jane redonned her own clothing and the sisters walked arm-in-arm downstairs.

The rest of the party was already gathered and Jane and Elizabeth were accosted by Miss Bingley the moment they entered the drawing-room.

"Dear Jane! Miss Eliza! Were the gowns we so kindly offered not to your liking?"

The Bennet sisters shared a look before Jane answered for them. "The gowns you provided were, um, lovely, Miss Bingley. It was very kind of you to offer. Unfortunately, they did not fit either of us. But we thank you for the consideration."

With a curling of her lip, Miss Bingley turned away and before anything else could be said, dinner was announced. Colonel Fitzwilliam shot Elizabeth a quick wink before presenting himself to Miss Bingley to, as the highest-ranking gentleman in the room, escort his hostess to dinner. Mr Bingley bounded to Jane's side, arm held aloft, while Mr Hurst took his wife by the elbow with a look of a man resigned to his fate. When the others had preceded them, Mr Darcy held out his arm to Elizabeth.

"Miss Elizabeth, may I?"

"Of course, Mr Darcy. Have you given any more thought to our earlier discussion?" she asked as she gently wrapped her hand around his sleeve.

"I have and I have come to the conclusion that you are mostly correct."

"Oh? Only mostly?"

They entered the dining room and Mr Darcy paused their conversation to pull out the lady's chair and seated himself beside her. He helped her to fill her plate before returning to the topic at hand.

"I agree that Benedick had likely long harboured tender feelings for Beatrice. And, having looked at the situation with the insight you presented, can even accept that he was wounded by her callous words at the masquerade."

"I am glad to hear it, sir."

"However, I will contend that Benedick himself was unaware of the depths of his own feelings, as you argued Beatrice may have been similarly in the dark as to the state of her heart. He likely could not explain, even to himself, why her insults should be so painful."

They continued in this vein, veering into the subjects of the Bard's other works when their discourse on *Much Ado About Nothing* had been exhausted, for the whole of dinner. Elizabeth was rather surprised to find that their tastes aligned almost perfectly, even if their feelings and interpretations were, in some instances, at odds. She was delighted when Mr Darcy pressed her on her opinion when it differed from his, rather than dismiss her ideas outright as many a gentleman had done in the past. A strange thrill ran the course of her spine when she coaxed a smile from him as they debated the bizarre romantic entanglement of *Twelfth Night*.

So absorbed were both parties in their lively conversation, the looks they garnered from Miss Bingley and Colonel Fitzwilliam at the foot of the table went entirely unnoticed. When the ladies rose to leave the gentlemen to their port, the Colonel caught Elizabeth's eye. She sent him a warm smile, tamping down the mortifying realisation that she had not once during the meal regretted not being seated next to the man who was courting her.

The gentlemen joined the ladies soon enough, Mr Bingley looking upon Jane as though their separation had been absolutely unendurable. The Colonel sat beside Elizabeth, and they engaged in light banter. It was enjoyable and entertaining, though could not excite Elizabeth's enthusiasm as had Mr Darcy's intelligent debate.

"Should we not have some music?" Miss Bingley suggested when multiple bids to draw Mr Darcy's attention away from his book did not yield the desired results. No one objected, though there were some in the room who paid her little heed, so she took herself to the pianoforte where Mrs Hurst joined her in singing some lovely Italian songs. When those had finished, Miss Bingley fell into a lively Scottish air. Mr Bingley led Jane to the centre of the room where they began to dance a reel.

"I have yet to enjoy a dance with you, Miss Elizabeth," lamented the Colonel. "And I do not think I am equal to it now. If you are inclined to dance, I will call upon my cousin to do the job."

Elizabeth looked to where Mr Darcy sat on the other side of Colonel Fitzwilliam, his eyes fixed on the page, yet she had the distinct impression he had caught every word and was awaiting her reply. Whether he hoped she would demure or not, she was uncertain. "I would not wish to disturb Mr Darcy if he is engrossed in his book. I am perfectly content as I am."

Putting his book aside, and making no pretension to any kind of shame for having overheard, Mr Darcy stood and bowed before her. "Tell me, Miss Elizabeth, that you do not feel a great inclination to seize this opportunity to dance a reel?" He looked pointedly towards her tapping toe on the carpet.

Stilling her traitorous foot, she raised an arch brow at him. "I am always ready, Mr Darcy. I only wonder that you do not tire of standing proxy for your cousin."

"Be assured, if I were not willing, I should not have set down my book." He held out a hand to her which, with a smile and a strange fluttering in her chest, she accepted. They joined his friend and her sister in the most dignified reel she had ever taken part in.

When Elizabeth laid her head down that night, it was with very confused feelings. She had, just that day, accepted an offer of courtship from Colonel Fitzwilliam. He was an excellent man and she enjoyed her time with him immensely. Yet, when he was not in her presence—and even sometimes when he was—she found her thoughts straying to his taller, more handsome, and quieter cousin. She often wondered what Mr Darcy's opinion would be on whatever she happened to be speaking of with the Colonel. When he was not in the room, her mind questioned where he might be. Even now, as she lay in bed, when her thoughts ought to have been for Colonel Fitzwilliam, the gentleman by whom she was being courted, she was remembering the dance she had shared with Mr Darcy and how right it had felt every time his large, gentle hand had enveloped her own.

Turning over in the large bed in the room she had been given at Netherfield, she castigated herself. Her tumultuous thoughts meant nothing. Mr Darcy was an interesting man whom she had misjudged. It was only natural that she should be curious about him. She enjoyed puzzles and was simply intrigued by the gentleman's deep, intricate character. Besides, he was the Colonel's cousin; she ought to get to know him. The two men were as close as she and Jane. It was likely, if this courtship came to its natural conclusion, she would oft find herself in Mr Darcy's company. Yes, that was all. She certainly did not care that he was incredibly handsome and challenged her mind and respected her opinions like no other man ever had. Such a quiet, reticent gentleman could hardly suit her in any case.

She was pleased to be courted by the Colonel. Truly. He was a delightful man and far more suited to her. On the morrow, before they left Netherfield, she would give all her attention to Colonel Fitzwilliam. Interesting though Mr Darcy may be, he was not courting her and she did not regret it. If she tossed and turned for several more hours, it was certainly *not* because she could not get the vision of Mr Darcy's dark, soulful eyes and that mysterious, elusive smile of his out of her head.

Chapter Eight

The Bennet's carriage rolled away and Darcy released the breath he felt he had been holding all morning. His plan had failed monstrously. Not only had he not discovered any ghastly quirks in Miss Elizabeth's character except that she had a strong aversion to mushrooms— for which he could hardly blame her—and sometimes hummed when she read—which was, frankly, rather adorable—but their discussion over dinner had highlighted several new delightful qualities he had not yet been made aware of.

She was intelligent—and not only for a woman. He doubted not that she could debate some of his former masters at Cambridge and come out the victor. When he had briefly explained his worries over his sister suffering her first heartache in London—though he had not gone into specifics—Miss Elizabeth displayed such concern and compassion for this young woman she had never met, he was momentarily speechless. Throughout it all, she was genuine. Not once did she simper or bat her eyelashes at him. When their opinions were in alignment, he could see that she was in earnest, not simply parroting his own views back at him in order to gain his favour as did so many ladies of the ton. What was more, she was unafraid to disagree with him. No unmarried lady unrelated to him had ever disagreed with him. He had long believed he could declare up to be down and left to be right and any number of women within hearing would go blue in the face demanding compasses to be altered.

This was not a welcome development. That she had not fortune nor connections no longer concerned him so grievously. She was such a marvellous creature, he would willingly face the displeasure of his family and the disapprobation of society for the privilege of calling her his own. No, her position in life was the least of his worries. He could not, nay *would not* fall in love with his cousin's lady.

"Well," said Richard with an impish grin as the three gentlemen who had accompanied the Misses Bennet out returned to the house, "if one is to be shut in on account of rain, one ought to always strive to do so with a few pretty ladies in company."

"Here, here!" agreed Bingley. "If I had known such loveliness existed in the country, I should have ventured to take an estate far sooner!"

"I daresay that is true enough," Richard laughed. "If ever persuasion is needed to lure you out, one need only announce that pretty ladies will attend and Bingley shall come bounding."

"It is a shame we shall never have the chance to test your theory, Cousin," said Darcy, allowing his friends to precede him into the house. "One need only say to Bingley 'come' and he will be at your disposal."

At this characterisation of himself, Bingley only laughed. "I ought to be offended, but I cannot deny the truth of your words. I am afraid I am shamefully complying."

"It only makes you a valuable friend," said Richard with a clap on the young man's back as they entered the library. Bingley crossed to the sideboard and poured out a measure of brandy for each man.

"I thank you, Colonel. I will not deny that I enjoy the company of a pretty woman. And Jane Bennet is as pretty a girl as I have ever seen."

The cousins shared a look of amusement as they accepted their drinks before Richard answered. "Aye, she is uncommonly lovely."

"Very much like, oh, what was her name? In London. Miss, oh, Price? Prince? Pincer! That was it. Miss Eloise Pincer. Phew. Now *there* was a diamond of the first water." He held up his drink in salute then fell back into a deep, comfortable armchair. Miss Bingley had been given no say in the arrangement of the library, much to Darcy's relief.

Richard nodded. "Indeed. Though now she is Lady Linder."

"What?" a scandalised looking Bingley asked, sitting bolt upright.

"Had you not heard? She was introduced to the viscount at a ball at Almacks. I understand he took quite a fancy to her and arranged the whole thing with her father. The whole affair was accomplished within a fortnight."

"But he must be fifty at least!"

"Nearer sixty. But now she has a title, a handsome fortune, and two step-children who are both her senior. Her family has been raised in society and is quite pleased with the match. I only wonder if she is as content or if she patiently awaits widowhood."

"Bloody hell," Bingley murmured. "Well, what about Miss Alice Barton? She is not yet married, is she? Or Miss Sally Deen?"

Bingley continued on, drifting through the memories of his past angels, for some time. Richard indulged him and antagonised him a fair amount. Darcy had heard it all before and simply listened, enjoying the pleasant comradery.

"You are not so different yourself, Colonel," said Bingley, responding to Richard's teasing. "You, too, have a weakness for a pretty face. I say, you seemed rather pleased with Miss Elizabeth Bennet's company these last two days."

Darcy stifled a groan. He had only just gotten the lady out of his head; must he be reminded of Miss Elizabeth's perfections so soon? Could they not give him a few moments of peace to get a handle on his inconvenient feelings? He ought to have known it was a futile hope when he took into consideration his companions but, nonetheless, hoped he had.

"I confess," said Richard, "she is a remarkable woman. Did you know, Darce, she began visiting her father's tenants when she was just seven years old? And learnt to keep the estate books when she was eleven?"

Clenching his fists at this further proof of his grave error in not choosing to pursue Elizabeth himself, Darcy inhaled deeply before answering his cousin. "I was not aware of that information, Cousin."

"'Tis true." Richard raised his glass to his lips but did not drink, rather he gazed thoughtfully over its rim. "I think a woman like that would make a fine mistress of any estate, large or small."

"I am certain you are correct," Darcy agreed through gritted teeth.

"Who could ever have imagined that such a beautiful woman could also be in possession of such a keen mind. If she has her equal, I am certain I have never come across her."

Darcy slammed his glass down and jumped from his seat. "I am going for a ride."

"Oh," said a bemused Richard. "Very well. Would you like some company?"

"No," he answered, a little too quickly. "I thank you, but Sleipnir has not been out in days and I intend to take a good, long ride."

"I understand. I had thought to call on the Bennets later. You know, to ensure the ladies arrived home safely and all." Richard cast his cousin a significant look and Darcy knew he meant to call upon Mr Bennet to receive consent for his courtship. "Shall I wait for you?"

"That will not be necessary. Enjoy your visit."

Before another word could be said, Darcy turned and hastened from the room. In short order, he was dressed in his riding clothes and mounting his favourite stallion. He could not listen to one more word about Elizabeth Bennet. Everything he learnt of the woman only increased his admiration and regard. She was everything he had never even imagined he would want in a wife; it was just his luck that Richard had seen from the first what he had wilfully ignored.

Kicking his horse into motion, they tore off down the drive, cutting through the trees into a nearby field. He allowed his horse to have his head. Darcy had no destination in mind, he simply needed to outrun the terrible truth; he *was* falling in love with Elizabeth, the woman his dearest cousin was courting and would likely marry. And he was falling fast.

They flew across fields and over fences. Sleipnir dashed through a small creek and around large oak trees as he carried his rider from the fields into the woods. His horse slowed to a trot through the underbrush and Darcy sighed in resignation as thoughts of Elizabeth caught up to him. Clearly, there would be no outrunning this. Like every other difficult task he had ever faced, this particular dilemma would need to be dealt with, in one way or another.

To his own benefit, he could speak to his cousin and confess his feelings for Elizabeth. In all likelihood, Richard would bow out gracefully if only Darcy would deign to ask. He would gain the woman of his dreams, but at what cost? It was almost certain his relationship with his dearest cousin would never be the same again. That was something Darcy was not willing to risk.

He could leave; put distance and time between himself and the object of his desire. Surely, in time, his feelings would abate and he would one day be able to meet with Elizabeth as common and indifferent acquaintances. If this courtship came to its natural conclusion, she would become his cousin and he must learn to look upon her in the same light he beheld Cousin Anne.

But how to accomplish such a thing? He had come to Hertfordshire to give Bingley advice and support in learning to run his own estate. If he left now, he would be going back on his word—something he had never done before and he certainly did not intend to begin now. Richard would unquestionably wish to remain. How would he even begin to explain why he must go? There was nothing pressing he must address in Town or at Pemberley, and Richard knew him well enough that he could never dissemble with any degree of success.

Then he must consider the possibility that he may never get the better of his regard for Elizabeth. Would he simply never see Richard again? Avoid his favourite cousin for the remainder of his life; a man whom he held in the highest esteem, looked upon as not only a dear cousin, but as the very best of friends and the nearest thing he had ever had to a brother? Impossible.

The only true solution was to reconcile himself to the match. Inure himself to the idea that he would never have the first woman he had ever thought he could love; that she would bestow her attentions and affection upon his cousin, share his bed, and bear his children. He would remain where he was, assisting the couple in their courtship, watching them fall in love and build a strong foundation for a joyful marriage. Perhaps, as their bond grew stronger, her hold on his heart would weaken.

As he was coming to this dreary conclusion, he looked around at where his horse had brought him. The trees had thinned and, up ahead, he could see the beginnings of a gentle rise in a clearing. When Sleipnir broke through the trees, they came to a stop at the base of a large hill. It brought a feeble smile to his lips, this vague reminder of the foothills surrounding Pemberley. Hertfordshire was a lovely county, but in his mind, it could not compare to the wild, untamed ruggedness of Derbyshire.

Elizabeth would love Derbyshire, his traitorous heart declared. In the short time they had been acquainted, he had come to see plainly that she was an active lady who took great pleasure in the out of doors. More than once, her love for a good walk had come up during the Misses Bennet's stay at Netherfield. She had been noticeably restless at being made to remain within the house whilst the rain persisted. He could just picture her at Pemberley, exploring its miles of walking paths, acres of forests, and extensive grounds. It would take her years to fully breach them all. He could not stop his mind from thinking of all his favourite places on the estate he would love to show her, if only it could be his privilege to do so.

Reining Sleipnir to a stop, he surveyed the hill rising before him. His eyes followed the well-established trail up its side until it disappeared around a large boulder. Something about this place cried out 'Elizabeth' to him. The way this patch of land rose above its surroundings, quiet in its undeniable superiority; a gem hidden amongst mediocrity. The exquisite array of wildflowers growing confidently along the hillside; so very different from the cultivated and carefully shaped rose gardens and hothouse blooms those of his set preferred, yet strangely far more appealing to his eyes in their understated and carefree beauty.

Movement caught his attention as the subject of his thoughts burst into view from the trees only a few yards away. She wore the same gown she had been wearing for the past three days, covered by the cloak that had sheltered her when she left Netherfield. The only change from the last time he had laid eyes on her was the position of the bonnet which swung lazily from her hand rather than covering her head. It was not fashionable, certainly, but he could not bring himself to find fault. The way the afternoon sun highlighted the honey-coloured tones of her chestnut curls and illuminated her lovely face nearly took his breath away.

She did not notice him at first, looking down towards the ground as she was. As she approached, however, Sleipnir huffed and pawed at the ground, causing her to look up and stop in her tracks.

"Oh, Mr Darcy," said she, dipping a polite curtsey. As she did, she glanced down at the hem of her gown which, as his own eyes followed her gaze, he noted was stained with several inches of dirt, mud, and grass stains. Far from putting him off as it ought to have done, he was only further intrigued by the perfect picture of a playful woodland nymph she presented. When she looked back at him, he was hopelessly mesmerised by the bright sparkle of her eyes and the youthful glow of her cheeks brought on by exercise. "I did not see you there."

"I surmised as much, Miss Elizabeth. Have you...forgive me, have you been to Longbourn?" She had left Netherfield not more than an hour ago.

She gave an impish smile, biting down on her lower lip and consequently driving him mad. "I have, sir. At least, I have been to the estate. As much as I enjoyed my stay at Netherfield, I could not go another minute indoors without taking a little time to reacquaint myself with nature. I am an awful creature when I cannot get my exercise. I set off on my walk straight from the carriage. Mama will not be well pleased but I am afraid it could not be helped."

"I sincerely doubt you could ever be considered anything remotely awful." The words tumbled out of his mouth before he had a chance to think better of them. She was kind enough to reply with only a smile and move on.

"What brings you to Oakham Mount, Mr Darcy?"

"I did not know that was where I was. I am quite often an awful creature—as you are well aware—but I, too, do not fare well when sequestered inside for too long." He reached down and patted his horse's neck. "And Sleipnir here becomes positively ghastly without regular exercise. It was he who chose our course."

"Would you like to join me?" She gestured towards the path that led up the side of the mount.

He knew he ought not to remain in her presence any longer. To be alone with her felt both wonderful and terribly wrong. Had things been different, he might have viewed this chance meeting as delightful happenstance, an opportunity to further bask in her radiance. As it was, it felt like a betrayal to his cousin. He ought to take pains to only be in her company when Richard was also present so that he might become accustomed to the notion of them as a couple; to begin the numbing of his heart against her. It was imperative that he return to Netherfield at once and opened his mouth to tell her so.

"It would be my pleasure."

Chapter Nine

*P*ulling away from Netherfield Park, Elizabeth settled into the threadbare cushions of her father's carriage. Beside her, Jane gazed dreamily out the window, a serene but radiant smile on her face. Her sister had been most reluctant to agree to Elizabeth's suggestion that they return home today rather than wait for the morrow. But the rain had ceased and the grounds were drying quickly in the bright sunshine that had succeeded it. There was little reason to remain and, if she were completely honest, Elizabeth was ready to be home and away from that place which facilitated so many conflicting feelings.

Watching her sister, she wondered at the juxtaposition of their situations. Mr Bingley, as far as Elizabeth was aware— and she truly believed Jane would have told her—had made no declarations or any formal addresses. He had been excessively attentive towards her sister, nearly to the exclusion of all others, and certainly seemed a man smitten and well on his way to being in love. Yet, he had taken no steps to officially further his relationship with Jane. Even so, Jane was in a state of pure bliss. Contented sighs escaped her lips and she had not responded to more than one out of every three things Elizabeth said to her on their short journey home.

In direct contrast, here she sat, one half of a courting couple, feeling very little different than she had before they had made this same journey in the opposite direction. She liked the Colonel—a great deal, in fact. Yet, he inspired no great burst of feeling from her. She did not perceive that he was greatly moved by his own feelings either. That he liked her was plain, and she could see that he found her attractive. Still, something was lacking.

The carriage rolled to a stop in Longbourn's drive and the ladies climbed out, assisted by Jonesy. Jane made for the front door, but Elizabeth could not yet bring herself to go inside. Looking longingly towards her beloved Longbourn woods, she called to her sister.

"Please tell Papa I shall be along in a while, if you would be so kind. I have not had a true walk in days and am in no humour to face Mama's inquisition without some fortification."

Having received Jane's assurances, she turned away from the house and crossed the park to her favourite path which led to Oakham Mount. That was where she preferred to go when she had weighty matters to consider. The Mount was just a little over two miles distant and anything which could not be sorted out on the walk was often put into perspective as she gazed out over miles of Hertfordshire countryside from its summit.

Turning her mind back to the matter at hand, she wondered at the absence of giddiness she had always imagined she would feel when a suitor presented himself. It was early yet, she reminded herself. They had only entered into this courtship yesterday, and it had been most unexpected. Perhaps that was the crux of the matter. She had already accepted that they could be nothing more than friends when the Colonel had decided to explore the possibility that they might be more. Certainly, their feelings would now catch up.

Furthermore, there was such a vast disparity between Elizabeth and her sister; it was hardly fair to compare them. Jane, with her tender heart and easy temper, felt quickly and deeply. She was cautious, having met with many gentlemen in the past who had proved less than constant but, at two-and-twenty, she was ready to fall in love. It was little surprise that she would so readily give her heart when she met a most worthy man.

Elizabeth, on the other hand, was in many ways much too exacting. Oh, she needed not a breathtakingly handsome man or a man with great fortune. His physical qualities mattered far less to her than his intellectual capabilities. She need look no further than her own parents for the dangers of what came from marrying for nought but a handsome face. If she could not respect a man's character, she could never accept him as her husband. She had no objections to a handsome man, certainly, but she could never abide a man who was stupid or ignorant or someone who devalued her intelligence.

It was fortunate then, she mused, that Colonel Fitzwilliam was both intelligent and appreciative of her keen mind. Surely, with time and as they grew to know one another better, stronger emotions would develop and she would discover the excitement of falling in love which she had long anticipated and it would feel all the sweeter for being confident in her choice.

Reaching the edge of the clearing where woods met the base of Oakham Mount, with very little notion of the journey, she was torn from her reverie by the sound of a huffing horse much nearer than she ordinarily preferred such creatures to be. Looking up from the path before her, she was met by the sight of an enormous grey beast with a long, silky black mane, stamping its hoof on the ground and eyeing her with what she thought looked like distrust. She ceased her steps immediately, having no desire to increase her proximity with the creature and only noticed its rider a second later.

"Oh, Mr Darcy," said she, glancing down and noticing the filth attached to the hem of the gown she had been wearing for three days now. They had reached a tentative truce at Netherfield but, surely, her appearance would do nothing to improve his opinion of her. "I did not see you there."

A small smile played on his lips and there was a look in his eye which she could not quite interpret. He kindly did not comment on her untidy appearance and only seemed slightly confused at coming upon her so soon after having just parted company. Shrugging internally, she decided she could only be what she was and gave her explanation.

"I am an awful creature when I cannot get my exercise. I set off on my walk straight from the carriage. Mama will not be well pleased but I am afraid it could not be helped."

"I sincerely doubt you could ever be considered anything remotely awful."

A slight, and entirely endearing, blush crossed his face and he quickly turned his gaze away. Unable to discern the meaning of his nearly flirtatious words, she decided it would be best to let the matter drop and press forward. She asked after his presence at the mount and learnt that he was nought more than a victim of his horse's meanderings.

Knowing not what else she ought to say, she gestured towards the path up the mount to excuse herself to continue her walk. The words which left her mouth, however, were not those she had intended. "Would you like to join me?"

He hesitated a moment, looking very much as though he would refuse. Strangely, the thought of his going away left a hollow feeling in her chest. She was surprised and unaccountably pleased when he accepted, gracefully slipping off his horse. There was a look on his face as he turned to tie off his horse to a tree at the edge of the clearing that was difficult to interpret. She could not call it displeasure; rather, it was more akin to panic.

Just that morning, Colonel Fitzwilliam had made a vague comment regarding his cousin. His words had implied that, while seeming excessively haughty and uncivil, Mr Darcy was in truth most uncomfortable amongst strangers and especially in crowds. In short, the gentleman before her was quite shy. She wondered if he was nervous to be in her presence since, despite a few pleasant conversations in the past days, they did not know one another well and she determined to do what she could to put him at ease.

He turned back to her and held a hand out towards the path, inviting her to precede him. They walked in silence for several minutes while she considered what topics would be best canvassed without disturbing his sensibilities. Thinking his favourite cousin to be a safe subject, she asked after him.

"Colonel Fitzwilliam did not wish to accompany you?"

Immediately, she knew she had said the wrong thing, though she could not think why. He flinched at her words as if she had physically taken a swing at him. He composed himself quickly, however, and gave his reply.

"No, though he often does. Richard is an avid horseman but has been prevented of late from enjoying long rides due to his injury. As I knew I would be some time, he declined to join me."

"Oh, I see." They carried on for several more minutes, not a word passing between them.

"Do you take this path often?" he asked at last, almost startling her with his unexpected question.

"Yes, very often. It is a favourite walk of mine. The views from the top are lovely."

He nodded at this and swallowed before speaking again. "Then you must bring Richard. I am certain he would be pleased to enjoy the views with you."

She looked at him askance. "Do you think the Colonel could make the trek, sir?"

His lips twisted into a grimace and he shook his head, though she did not think it was in answer to her question, rather the sudden recollection of his dear cousin's newly acquired limitations. "No, I do not suppose he could," he said rather stiffly before they fell into silence once again.

Hesitant to raise another subject that might cause him discomfort, she took a breath and asked, "Your horse? You called him Sleep Near, I think? Is he an excessively lethargic beast?"

In direct contrast to his previous response, this made him chuckle and she triumphed. She was also struck once again by how handsome he was when he smiled and thought it truly a shame that he did not do so more often.

"No, quite the opposite, I assure you. His name is Sleipnir. The eight-legged horse ridden by the Scandinavian god Odin. He is described as the best and fastest of horses."

"Scandinavian god? I am familiar with Greek and Roman mythology, sir, but I confess I am in complete ignorance of such lore."

"I cannot say I am surprised. It is not a common area of study. Modern scholars tend to focus their teachings on Greek and Roman philosophy. I was fortunate enough to have a master at Cambridge who had spent his grand tour in the Scandinavian countries. He formed a club at university to impart his knowledge of this obscure branch of study. I would wager, however, that you have at least heard of some Norse mythology, though you may be unaware of it."

Intrigued, she looked up at him with eager eyes. She was always interested in gaining new knowledge and suspected Mr Darcy might turn out to be a fine teacher. "How so, sir?"

"The days of the week. You have likely been taught that the names which designate each four- and twenty-hour period are derived from the gods of Greek and Roman origin." Entirely enraptured by his narrative, Elizabeth nodded in response as she eagerly anticipated being edified by his superior knowledge on the subject. "But have you ever wondered how 'Tuesday' had been derived from Mars or Ares, the gods of war? Or 'Wednesday' from Mercury or his counterpart, Hermes? 'Thursday' does not sound remotely like Jupiter or Zeus. Nor does 'Friday' resemble Venus or Aphrodite in any way."

"I am ashamed to confess that I have not. It seems odd as I am an incurably curious woman, yet I fear I have taken something so commonplace as the days of the week for granted. I beg you would enlighten me."

"Just as each Greek god has its Roman counterpart, there is also a Scandinavian correspondent. Sunday and Monday refer to the sun and moon personified in the sister gods, *Sunna* and *Mani*—or 'Sunna's day' and 'Mani's day.' Tuesday is derived from *Tīwesdæg*, or 'Tiw's day.' Wednesday, or *'Woden's day*,' is named for the allfather, Odin, Thursday for the god of thunder, Thor. Friday honours the goddess of love and fertility, Freya. Saturday...well, that day has retained its Romanic influence. In the old Norse tradition, it is *'laugardagr,'* or 'washing day.' Not terribly romantic, I am afraid."

"Fascinating," Elizabeth breathed, hardly paying attention to where she walked as she gazed up at the gentleman beside her in awe. As a result, she forgot to avoid the root protruding from the ground in her path. The toe of her slipper caught the nuisance and she pitched forward with a cry of, "Oh!"

Before she could find herself in an ungraceful heap on the ground as she might have expected, a large, strong hand shot out and captured her by the upper arm, pulling back to counter her forward motion. Everything happened so quickly, she could not account for how she next found herself flat against a broad, muscular chest, her hands burning as they discovered the hard planes of a tight, strong stomach beneath a fine, silk waistcoat. Struggling to find her bearings, she inhaled deeply, only to be intoxicated by the rich, manly scent of citrus, sandalwood, and leather emanating off the body which supported her.

A throat being cleared somewhere above her awakened her other senses and she looked up to find Mr Darcy staring intensely back. His deep, dark eyes bore into hers leaving her feeling exposed and bare in a way she had never experienced. It was not a humiliating feeling, but rather she felt as if he was searching to discover who she truly was and she had no power to block his scrutiny. Furthermore, she felt as if she did not even wish to.

Only when she noticed the movement of his chest against her breast did she realise that her own breath was heavy and ragged, but she could not explain why.

"Are...are you well, Miss, Miss Elizabeth?" he asked, his voice thick and deep.

She swallowed down the tightness in her throat and offered a tiny nod, or at least that was what she intended. Whether her body cooperated, she could not be certain. "Um, yes. I...I thank you."

"Shall we continue our walk?" he asked in that gravelly tone that was driving her to distraction.

"Oh, um, yes. Certainly." But neither made any attempt to move, only continuing to stand there, gazing upon one another. At last, however, movement against her back brought her to herself and she realised the impropriety of their position. His right hand still grasped her upper left arm while his left arm was wrapped around her waist, pressed against her back, holding her to him. "Um, you—you will need to release me, sir."

As if she had suddenly burst into flames, he let go, pushing her away, and stepped hastily back, nearly stumbling himself. "Forgive me."

"Not at all, sir. I thank you for your speedy actions. I might otherwise have ended in a pile on the ground, even more dirt-covered than I already am," she responded, taking a stab at humour to distract herself from the tumultuous sensations coursing through her body.

She smiled and turned back towards the path, desirous of putting the episode, and the barrage of feelings which had accosted her, behind them. Glancing at the man beside her from the corner of her eye, he seemed excessively agitated. His gloved hands were clenched in tight fists and his lips were drawn down in a deep scowl. A muscle in his cheek twitched and his eyes were fixed on a point directly ahead of him.

Cautiously, she returned to the subject they had been canvassing before her untimely clumsiness interrupted them and asked him to tell her more of the mythology of which she had never heard. He complied, though somewhat apprehensively at first. But as they walked on and he was drawn deeper into his narrative, he seemed to relax. When they reached the top of the mount, they sat together on the large boulder where Elizabeth often perched to ponder her life and troubles and talked with ease for more than an hour. The time passed them by with very little fanfare and they were both surprised when Mr Darcy consulted his watch. He suggested that they descend and, with reluctance, Elizabeth agreed.

Their return down Oakham Mount's side was completed mostly in silence which Elizabeth made no attempt to disturb this time. Her thoughts were a confused jumble and she knew not what to make of them. She felt as though she could sit and listen to this gentleman speak all day. Every word which came out of his mouth was interesting and enthralling. She was hungry to discover what more he might teach her. Yet, there was something...intimidating about him. No. Intimidating was too strong a word but she could find no other to describe how she felt, so unfamiliar were these sensations.

He was large and possessed a commanding presence. He was so handsome, it was almost difficult to look upon him, much like looking upon the sun. Yet, to look away was even more arduous. He was an exceedingly intelligent man and listening to him made her feel doltish, though he was in no way condescending or belittling. He was simply so knowledgeable she was made to feel her inferiority keenly. She felt no fear of him, but neither was she completely at ease. Her time with him had overwhelmed her senses, and yet, she was by no means ready to be rid of him. Never had one person inspired so many competing feelings within her and she was deeply unsettled by it.

Tumultuous thoughts followed her home, having declined Mr Darcy's offer of escort. His company was welcome and enjoyable, but so befuddled did his presence render her, it was a relief to be free of him.

As it was, she could not seem to settle on just one path of thought. With excitement, she ruminated on all he had taught her about the gods of the Viking cultures. It was a fascinating branch of study and she was already wondering if her father had any books which might be of use in learning more. But as she pondered this new information, she could not help but remember the pleasing way his mouth moved when he talked, the light in his eyes when he spoke on a subject which he was passionate about. Each word he uttered was caressed as it crossed over his lips and his deep, soothing timbre danced on her ears.

Though more than an hour had passed, she could still feel how powerful his hand felt against her back and the strength of his arms as he held her. She knew it was wrong, but at that moment she felt as though there was little she would not give to be pressed so securely against his hard chest once again. In Mr Darcy's embrace, she had never felt so safe, so protected, so *womanly*.

Dashing these thoughts away with a swipe of her hand across a low hanging branch, she scolded herself to cease immediately. These were imaginings no proper young lady ought to indulge in. She was simply affected by having stood nearer an unrelated man than ever she had before. It was novel and foreign and exciting, but could only cause mischief. So, crossing Longbourn park once again, she pushed such thoughts from her mind and entered the house, determined to behave as a young lady ought.

Not until she had removed her cloak and joined her mother and sisters in the drawing-room did she realise that, but for her one inquiry to Mr Darcy, at no point during the last several hours had the gentleman who was paying her court crossed her mind. She was made aware of this mortifying revelation when she was informed by a very excited Mrs Bennet and two giddy younger sisters that Colonel Fitzwilliam was, even now, in the house and having a private interview with her father.

Chapter Ten

"*L*izzy!" cried Mrs Bennet when her second daughter entered the room. "Gracious, where have you been? Oh, look at you! Covered in filth! : fit to be seen! Oh, but it hardly matters. What have you to do with it? Oh, but I shall go distracted!" The lady waved her hands excitedly back and forth in front of her, one hand tightly clutching a lace handkerchief.

"Whatever is the matter, Mama?" Elizabeth asked, looking around at her sisters for some clue as to what had caused her mother's agitated spirits this time. Kitty and Lydia covered their faces and giggled madly; Mary only shrugged and excused herself to go practise the pianoforte. From Jane, she received a look filled with meaning but before her dearest sister could open her mouth to explain, Mrs Bennet provided the answer.

"The Colonel is here, of course!"

"The Colonel?" Elizabeth asked, momentarily bemused. When clarity dawned, she felt her face flush with shame. "The Colonel! Oh, dear."

"He has come to have a private interview with your father. Whatever it is about, I am sure I do not know! Jane will not say a word, though I am sure he has come to ask your father for her hand. Oh, but what about Mr Bingley?" she fretted, obviously having forgotten all about her previous schemes for Elizabeth. In her mother's mind, there could be no possibility for a man to overlook Jane for Elizabeth. "He is far richer than the Colonel but Colonel Fitzwilliam is the son of an earl! Jane might one day be a countess! Perhaps Mr Bingley can be persuaded towards Lydia. She is just as pretty as you, Jane, but ever so much more lively."

"Mama," Elizabeth tried, but her mother paid her no heed.

"Even if his brother never dies, to be related to an earl! Oh, Jane! I always knew you could not be so beautiful for nothing!"

"Mama," tried Elizabeth again, but her mother was in full stride so she contented herself with a sigh and sat beside Jane to wait it out, picking up a piece of embroidery.

"Oh, Lady Lucas will be so jealous! I cannot wait to tell her! How grand you shall be! Surely his father will settle a vast fortune upon his son. A house in Town for certain, and two carriages, at least. Oh, what a wedding it will be! To think, an earl in my home!"

"Ahem," a masculine voice from the doorway, at last, interrupted Mrs Bennet's mortifying effusions. All the ladies looked up to find Colonel Fitzwilliam standing just inside the room, clearly trying to disguise his amusement. Kitty and Lydia began their wild giggling again, whispering behind their hands at the sight of him. "I beg your pardon, madam, but Mr Bennet would like a word with Miss Elizabeth."

"Elizabeth?" Mrs Bennet questioned with bewilderment. "Whyever would he need Lizzy? Surely, you meant Jane?"

"Not at all, madam. It was assuredly Miss Elizabeth for whom Mr Bennet asked."

"Oh, well. I am sure he has something of estate business to discuss with her or some old dusty book. Go, Lizzy. Go on. Colonel, why do you not sit here next to Jane? I am sure she will be vastly pleased to entertain you."

Exchanging looks of exasperation with Jane, Elizabeth stood and crossed the room to where Colonel Fitzwilliam still stood. She cast him a look of deep apology, which he acknowledged with a wink, before dipping a hasty curtsey and hurrying out of the room. Her mother's shrill voice encouraging her suitor to converse with Jane followed her from the room and down the hall; though how Mama expected anyone to speak at all when she would not close her mouth was beyond even Elizabeth's comprehension.

Reaching her father's study, she quickly knocked on the door before letting herself in. "Papa?"

"Come in, my child. I am sure you know what it is I wish to speak to you about."

"I am sure I do, Papa." She went to her father and pressed a kiss to his cheek before taking her usual seat before his desk. He sat in his old leather chair, looking older and wearier than she had ever seen.

"I confess, my dear, I had always imagined that when this day arrived, it would be Jane some young dandy had come to court. In fact, I had depended upon it. Then I would be more prepared when another such came believing himself to be worthy of you. If I am to be entirely honest, I will admit I had hoped even Mary, or perhaps all your sisters, would be married first. I do not know what I will do without you, my Lizzy."

"Papa, 'tis only a courtship."

"What is a courtship but a precursor to marriage? Oh, do not worry, my dear. I have given the young man my consent, though I will confess I have my doubts."

Elizabeth reached across the desk and took one of his wizened hands in her own. "Tell me, Papa."

The gentleman took a deep breath and looked fondly at his daughter. "Is this what you wish?"

That was a question she did not know quite how to answer. Only the day before, when the Colonel had offered her this courtship, she had accepted with the confidence that, in time, they would grow to know one another better and develop the affection she deemed necessary for marriage. Why, then, was she suddenly so unsure? "I believe it is, Papa."

He leant back in his chair, crossing his arms over his chest and raising one disbelieving eyebrow at her. "You forget, my dear, that I have known you since the day you were born. Tell me what troubles you. Did he coerce you into this courtship?"

"Oh, no, Papa! Nothing of the sort. Colonel Fitzwilliam, and Mr Bingley and Mr Darcy for that matter, behaved in the utmost gentlemanly manner whilst Jane and I were at Netherfield." She heaved a great sigh and leant back in her own chair. "I wish I could explain it. I have always imagined the kind of man I would one day marry and Colonel Fitzwilliam fits that model in almost every particular."

"Then why are you not leaping about as I expect Kitty or Lydia will do when their suitors come calling?"

"What if...oh, Papa. What if what I had always imagined I would wish for, is not what I find myself wanting now?" She looked pleadingly at her father who had always given her sound advice, even to her silliest problems. That he would not have the answer now did not even cross her mind.

"Do you wish for me to withdraw my consent? I have no qualms in doing so."

"No, Papa. Not at all. I like the Colonel. He is a good man and I am sure will make a fine husband." She smiled, as much to reassure her father as herself. If it was rather brittle and fled her lips as quickly as it came, there was nothing to be done for it. "I am sure it is nothing more than nerves. Every young lady grows up knowing she will one day marry and leave her father's house for her husband's. Even still, it always felt like an event for the distant future. Even as recently as yestermorn, 'someday' seemed so very far away. Now that it is before me, I find I am both excited and frightened of it. But do not worry. You know me, Papa. My courage always rises to the occasion. I shall soon laugh myself into better humour and then all will be well, I am certain of it."

Mr Bennet looked upon his favourite daughter and she could see that he was by no means comforted but there was little more to say on the matter. He sniffed and twitched his lips but said nothing further. Standing, he gave her a feeble smile and said, "Well, then. Shall we go and ease your mother's curiosity? If she has not frightened your young man away, that is."

"Papa!" she laughed and came around the desk to wrap her arms around his waist. "I love you."

"Very well, very well." He patted her head affectionately. "Let us get on with it."

"Oh, wait. Do you have any books on the lore and mythology of the Scandinavian countries in this old library of yours, Papa?"

"Scandinavia?" He patted his pockets as if he often stored old books on ancient, foreign lore there as he looked around at his vast array of bookshelves. "I cannot say that I do. Why this sudden interest?"

"Oh." She pressed her lips together and looked around as well. Confessing to having met with Mr Darcy and spending so much time alone with the gentleman could certainly lead nowhere good, yet she did not like to lie to her beloved father. "I recently heard something about the subject and thought I might like to learn more. It is of no great importance. Come, Mama is convinced Colonel Fitzwilliam has come to offer for Jane. We must rescue them both before Mama coerces a proposal from my suitor for my sister!"

They walked arm in arm down the hallway to the drawing-room where Mrs Bennet's voice was still the principal sound, detailing all of Jane's best qualities. Elizabeth squeezed her father's arm and briefly leant her head against his sleeve. They nodded to one another and Mr Bennet opened the door.

"Mrs Bennet," said he, "I hope you have not ordered Jane's trousseau just yet."

Elizabeth looked from one person to the next. Colonel Fitzwilliam stood on their entry, looking vastly relieved that she had returned. She marvelled at her mother's talents; she had managed to discomfit even the valiant Colonel. Jane was as red as a ripe tomato and looked as if she would never raise her eyes from the floor again. Kitty and Lydia had gotten over their amusement and were looking excessively bored now that there was little chance of gaining the dashing officer's attention for themselves. Mrs Bennet had the good sense to look embarrassed by her husband's astute remark.

"What are you talking of, Mr Bennet? You are always teasing me."

"I confess, I am. I am certain you will forgive me when I tell you that I have come to announce that I have given my consent for a courtship between Colonel Fitzwilliam,"—he paused dramatically—"and our dear Lizzy."

"Oh, Jane!" cried her mother, jumping from her seat and rushing to embrace her eldest daughter. "I knew how it would be! I knew how it wou—Lizzy?" She stopped dead and turned a suspicious look on her husband, waiting for the punchline of his joke she would not understand.

Colonel Fitzwilliam stepped to Elizabeth's side and offered his elbow, which she wrapped her hand around. "Indeed, Mrs Bennet. I mean no slight against Miss Bennet,"—he nodded respectfully at Jane—"but it is Miss Elizabeth who has captured my attention with her wit and charms."

Almost as if she were reading words in a book, Elizabeth could easily see the thoughts that raced across her mother's features. Mrs Bennet was weighing the benefits of protesting in Jane's favour against those of biting her tongue. In her mind, there was no comparison between her eldest, sweetest, and most beautiful daughter and her next most obstinate child. Of the two of them, Jane was far and away more deserving of gaining such exalted relations as an earl and a countess. However, she had long bemoaned Elizabeth's headstrong and wild ways and despaired of the girl ever finding a husband at all. Who was she to question if the Colonel was charmed by the girl's sharp tongue and hoydenish manners?

"Of course, you have taken a fancy to our Lizzy! Such a clever girl and, though she is not so pretty as her sister, Jane, quite lovely, as well!"

"Indeed, madam," replied the Colonel and Elizabeth fought the urge to hide her mortification in her hands.

"And Jane feels no slight at all," the lady answered for her daughter. "Mr Bingley has, after all, been paying her every attention. Oh, why did not he accompany you? Surely, he will wish to speak to Mr Bennet, as well?" She looked hopefully at Jane.

"Mrs Bennet," her husband said admonishingly. "As much as you would like to, it is not for you to determine the timeline by which these things happen."

"Oh, but you must stay for dinner!" cried Mrs Bennet, neatly ignoring her husband.

"I am afraid," said Mr Bennet, "tonight will not do for we shall already have a guest for dinner this evening." Every eye turned to him in question and Mr Bennet made a show of pulling his spectacles from his pocket and wiping them on a cloth. He held them up to the light and was apparently dissatisfied with the results, for he scrubbed them again. When he was pleased with his work and his eyeglasses were carefully replaced—and Mrs Bennet looked as though she might faint if he did not soon reveal the mystery guest—he spoke again. "I have received a letter from my cousin, Mr Collins, who will arrive this afternoon to stay with us for a short duration."

The effect on Mrs Bennet was instantaneous. "Oh, Mr Bennet! How can you mention that odious man?!"

"Ahem," Colonel Fitzwilliam turned to Elizabeth. "I wonder if you would care to join me on a ramble in the gardens if one of your sisters would be so good as to join us as chaperone."

Elizabeth voiced her approbation for the plan, if for no other reason than to remove her gentleman from the spectacle playing out in the drawing-room, and solicited Jane to join them. The ladies excused themselves to gather their outdoor things and met the Colonel by the front door. After allowing the sisters to precede him, he held out an elbow for Elizabeth. Jane trailed behind them and a little way to the side. Ordinarily, Elizabeth might have easily outstripped her older sister who was not as accustomed to the exercise as she, but she constrained herself to a pace more comfortable for the Colonel's injury.

"I must apologise for my mother's behaviour, sir. And my father's." She tried to contain her grimace at the thought of her parent's impropriety, though she could not be sure of her success.

"Your mother seemed rather incredulous that any gentleman would wish to court you."

Elizabeth sighed and turned her gaze down towards her shoes. "Mama is a simple creature. Her greatest ambition in life is to find husbands for her daughters, particularly before Lady Lucas can find husbands for hers. But she has very nearly despaired of me. She thinks I am too clever, too outspoken, and too wild to ever turn any gentleman's head. It is surely the only reason she did not defend Jane's right to lay claim to an earl's son. She will not look this gift horse in the mouth."

"Does she imagine a man wants only a silent bonnet rack to parade about on his arm?"

"That," Elizabeth laughed, "is precisely what she imagines!" Mostly to herself she mumbled, "How she imagines she shall ever marry off Kitty or Lydia, I cannot guess."

"Well,"—he hooked his cane over his arm and patted her hand where it rested on his sleeve before taking up his walking stick again—"I know plenty of gentlemen who would disagree. I have no desire for such a wife, and I know Darcy does not wish that either. He has been fighting the ton and even his own family against such a fate for years."

"Has he some lofty requirements for the lady who would become his wife? I imagine a man of his station and consequence would insist any candidate be an accomplished musician, artist, and dancer as well as fluent in several languages. He will expect his wife to speak and carry herself with unadulterated grace and betray nothing in her expressions." Even as the words left her tongue, they left a sour taste in her mouth she could not account for. Why ought she to care for what kind of woman Mr Darcy would marry?

The Colonel laughed at this representation of his cousin. "You are too harsh on the man. He is a rather fastidious fellow, I cannot deny, but he has no such expectations. He does, I suppose, wish for a wife whom he will be proud to bestow his name upon, but do not most men? Above all, my cousin desires a wife he can love. His parents, my excellent uncle and aunt, were a love a match and I know Darcy strives for a marriage such as they enjoyed."

A shiver coursed through her body which had very little to do with the crisp fall breeze causing the fallen leaves on their path to dance. "Oh," was all she could manage to say as she fought to push the memory of being held in that gentleman's strong arms from her mind.

"Tell me...well, perhaps it is not my place." Colonel Fitzwilliam turned his gaze up into the treetops.

"You have begun, you may as well continue." She squeezed his arm playfully.

"Your younger sisters?" He looked down into her face uncertainly and she nodded with an encouraging smile. "They are...quite young to be out in society."

Elizabeth inhaled deeply, puffing her cheeks as she slowly released her breath. "Kitty and Lydia are full young. Would you be shocked to know that Mama brought all of us out at fifteen? Well, except Lydia who made such a fuss at Kitty's turn that Kitty was made to share her debut with our youngest sister who was then only just fourteen."

"You are joking?"

"I sincerely wish I was, Colonel. Perhaps you have heard that Longbourn is entailed upon my father's cousin whom we have never met?"

"I had heard something to that effect. That was the gentleman of whom he was just referring, was it not?"

"It was. Mama is so fixed in her belief that this unknown relation will throw us all into the hedgerows the moment my father has quit this mortal sphere that she is, as I have already told you, quite preoccupied with marrying as many of her daughters off as quickly as she is able. She lives in mortal fear of the day she must make way for another to stand as mistress of Longbourn."

"Surely you have family who will give their support?"

"Oh, yes. My uncles would never allow us to starve, but Mama is rarely so rational as to consider that. Her heart is in the right place, I only wish sometimes that she could realise the effect her actions have upon her children. I am afraid she has often done more harm than good."

"I see," was all he said before turning the subject to other matters.

Chapter Eleven

Mr William Collins was, without a doubt, the strangest gentleman Elizabeth had ever had the dubious pleasure of meeting. It had not been well done of her father to keep the coming of his cousin and heir from his family, springing it upon them at the last possible moment, but Mr Bennet rarely concerned himself for the comforts of his wife and daughters if it meant disturbing his precious peace. No doubt he anticipated his wife's hysterics at the news of the man who would take over Longbourn at Mr Bennet's demise coming to visit and wished to endure the commotion as little as possible.

The letter which preceded Mr Collins went a long way in mollifying Mrs Bennet's concerns, whereas it only served to heighten Elizabeth's. He spoke a good deal on the beneficence of his patroness, a Lady Catherine de Bourgh, and the condescension he received from that great lady. But it was the allusion to the injury to Mr Bennet's daughters caused by Mr Collins being next to inherit and his intentions of making amends that gave her the greatest unease. It was precisely this which made Mrs Bennet amenable to tolerating his visit.

"If he is disposed to make our girls any amends, I shall not be one to discourage him," said she.

Mr Collins was true to his stated time and arrived promptly at four o'clock. Elizabeth could not have said what she expected exactly, yet when the gentleman presented himself, she was not in the least surprised. He was a tall, heavy-looking man with long, thin legs and drooping cheeks dressed in the garb of a clergyman. His manners were very formal and he spoke with an air of gravity and self-importance. As they entered the house, everything was to be remarked upon and complimented; the hallway was excellent, being neither too long nor too short; the artwork on the walls was perfectly to his taste; the chair he sat upon in the parlour positioned just right. There was no shortage of the gentleman's conversation.

His gallantry extended beyond the furniture and house, as well. He gratified Mrs Bennet's vanity by heaping much praise on the fineness of her daughters. Of their superior beauty, he had been informed and was eager to assure his hostess that their charms far surpassed what had reached his ears.

"I have no doubts that, in due time, each of your amiable daughters will be satisfactorily disposed of in marriage." As he paid this dubious compliment, he turned an admiring gaze upon Jane, making no effort to disguise the way his eyes roamed her figure from head to toe.

Jane, swallowing audibly, reached for Elizabeth's hand and squeezed tightly, which her sister returned in solidarity. Thankfully, Mrs Bennet watched over these proceedings with a keen eye. Though she was anxious for Mr Collins to turn his attentions towards one of her daughters that her place at Longbourn might be secured, her two eldest were, as far as she was concerned, already spoken for. She wasted no time in informing her guest so.

"You are very kind, Mr Collins, and astute. My two eldest daughters have lately been on the receiving end of the attentions of two very fine gentlemen lately residing in the neighbourhood. Just this morning, Mr Bennet gave his consent for Lizzy's courtship with Colonel Fitzwilliam, who hails from the north. And we are every day in anticipation of Mr Bingley paying his addresses to Jane, as well."

The fulsome smile dropped from Mr Collins' face as he took in this information and Elizabeth felt free to inhale a breath of relief. Until, that was, Jane modestly made to protest this claim. Before she could do more than hail her mother, Elizabeth surreptitiously reached over and pressed her heel down on the toe of Jane's slipper. Mrs Bennet's continued efforts to promote her other daughters covered the resulting gasp.

"But as for my younger daughters, I know of no prior attachments at all."

Looking over the remaining daughters with an air of disappointment, Mr Collins sniffed. "Well, we shall see."

To nearly everyone's relief, dinner was soon called. But if anyone held hopes that eating would occupy the parson's mouth and prevent his plentiful speech, they were to be disappointed. The room was declared most comfortable, the place settings were perfectly serviceable, every dish was praised to excess; never had Mr Collins had such an excellent boiled potato— except, of course, at Lady Catherine's table. Elizabeth had ever enjoyed her place at the table beside her father, but she felt that night that she had never appreciated it fully as she watched Mr Collins at the other end shovel heaping forkfuls into his mouth even as he continued to speak. Her heart went out to Mary who looked as though she would cast up her accounts when he turned in her direction and bits of food flew out of his flapping maw and landed on her plate.

When he seemed to run out of compliments to pay the meal, Mr Collins' conversation turned to his noble patroness, of whom he seemed to be in complete awe. He spoke her name with a reverent adoration and developed a certain gleam in his eye as he spoke of the lady. To hear Mr Collins speak of it, her home, Rosings Park, rivalled even that of the royal family. Even Lady Catherine's daughter, who Mr Collins explained was of a low, sickly constitution, could be considered nothing less than the brightest jewel in the kingdom. Elizabeth was forced to cover a laugh with her napkin as she wondered if Mr Collins was not a little in love with his patroness by the way he extolled her endless virtues.

After dinner, Mr Collins produced a copy of Fordyce's sermons which he offered to read from, looking very much as though he were bestowing upon them the greatest favour. With no polite way to decline, the ladies sat around the parlour in the final hour before bed listening to the droning on of the oblivious parson as he lectured them on the proper comportment of young ladies from an archaic volume while Mr Bennet escaped to his library. Unprecedentedly, Kitty and Lydia were the first to bid the family goodnight that evening as they eagerly escaped to their shared chamber.

⚜

Pacing the great hall while he waited for his cousin to descend, Darcy cursed himself for not having conjured a valid excuse to remain behind rather than dining at Longbourn. He had not slept well last night, filled as his mind was with the remembrance of holding Elizabeth

Bennet in his arms. Each time he closed his eyes, the vision of that divine creature perched in the bright sunshine, radiating loveliness smothered every other thought.

What had he been thinking? He had known his weakness yet, against his better judgement, had indulged it anyway. Already he had admitted to himself that he felt her pull far too fiercely; that he was in great danger of falling in love with Elizabeth, the woman his cousin was courting. His plan to find any glaring faults by coming to know her better had backfired monumentally. The risks were blatant and yet he had ignored the warnings screaming in his head and spent the afternoon with the magnificent creature anyway.

He ought to have made his excuses and left her presence the moment she had appeared in the clearing. He ought to have declined to join her on her climb. He ought not to have revelled in the bright expression of her beautiful eyes as she eagerly drank in tale after tale he imparted.

That had possibly been the most grievous mistake. Had they simply walked on in silence, taken in the view and kept conversation light and superficial, he might have better ignored her charms. But she was so earnest in her interest, he had been utterly captivated; intoxicated by the heady exhilaration of being the sole object of that woman's attention. He had continued to share his knowledge, eager for each smile she bestowed upon him. She had not given half an ear to his narratives only to indulge a rich man as so many ladies of the ton did. Elizabeth absorbed the information like a sponge, asked insightful questions, and made him feel as the only man in existence.

It had been delicious, heady, and dangerous. He vowed to himself after he had returned to Netherfield that he would not allow any such occasion to happen again. When next he found himself in Eliz—no, *Miss* Elizabeth's company, he would be civil, but no more. There would be no more unchaperoned walks—no walks at all if he could help it. He would greet her then step away, leaving her to Richard's company and attentions.

The moment Richard returned from his call at Longbourn, successful in his bid to Miss Elizabeth's father for their courtship if that detestable grin on his face was any indication, Darcy was resolved. He confessed to the encounter with Elizabeth, which his cousin accepted with a strange light-heartedness having already heard the tale from his lady; the man actually thanked Darcy for his timely assistance to Miss Elizabeth and saving her from indignity and possible injury had she, indeed, fallen.

Darcy had been dumbfounded. If Richard had witnessed what had transpired between himself and Miss Elizabeth, brief though it was, Darcy could not believe he would have been so charitable. He wondered what of the encounter the lady had told him. "But...I held her, in my arms, for, well, more than a moment."

"Yes, as she said," Richard had replied. "She tripped on a root and you caught her before she could end a heap in the dirt."

While that was, essentially, the gist of the matter, it certainly had been much more significant than simply reaching out to prevent a fall. Had Miss Elizabeth undervalued what had happened to ease her own conscience? The stinging thought had then occurred to him. *What if I am overestimating the event?*

He had thought, as they had stood on the hillside, his arms around her, holding her so deliciously close to his body, that she had been as affected by their embrace as he had been. The breathless, husky quality of her voice, the impassioned look in her magnificent eyes, the trembling of her fingers as they pressed against the fabric of his waistcoat, the heat seeping into his body even through so many layers—had he imagined all that? Or had it been nothing more than her stressed maidenly sensibilities reacting to being held in such an improper manner by a gentleman—and not the one by whom she was being courted?

Going over every moment, he analysed her every look, her every move. She had seemed to grow easier as they walked on, asking him to explain more of the Scandinavian traditions. Had she simply been trying valiantly to move beyond an awkward encounter? Their descent, he recalled with some mortification, had been entirely silent. He had been wholly occupied committing her every inquisitive response, the smiles she had bestowed, and, yes, the feel of her in his arms to memory. What if she had been much less rapturous? She had, after all, refused his escort home—a circumstance he had only been prevented from arguing against for feeling the danger of remaining in her presence any longer. Had she simply wished to be away from him, afraid he might attempt more liberties? Dear God! Had he imposed himself upon her? What she must think of him!

He was relieved, certainly, that his cousin did not feel ill-used by him. Yet there were other, unpleasant emotions clawing at his insides. Holding Elizabeth Bennet in his arms, no matter what little right he had to do so, was almost magical. His very existence seemed to hinge to that one moment. He knew, beyond any doubt, that he would cherish that experience for the rest of his life. But to learn she had seen his actions as merely helpful, or worse, overly familiar, left him feeling hollow and disappointed, though he knew he had no right.

Stop this! he chastised himself. *This is not to be borne!* Already he had decided his course and he would not alter it. He would distance himself from Miss Elizabeth and put an end to these deucedly frustrating feelings.

"Punctual, as always!" Richard's teasing voice broke through Darcy's self-castigating thoughts as the Colonel limped down the stairs. "I should have been down ages ago but for this damned leg. Makes even the most mundane tasks, such as putting on one's trousers, twice as difficult as it ought to be."

"Perhaps it would be best if I were to remain behind, Cousin," Darcy blurted out, cursing himself for his awkwardness. If he could not keep himself under good regulation, Richard would see through him for certain and discern the feelings he harboured for Elizabeth.

"But of course, you must come. Why would you not?"

Composing his features to the best of his abilities, Darcy rummaged his mind for a plausible reason why he ought not to attend dinner. "The Bennets have already a guest this evening. I should not like to be in the way."

"Nonsense. Mrs Bennet loves to entertain. She was telling me only just yesterday how she is looking forward to hosting the entire neighbourhood in the near future."

Of course, she was...

"Mrs Bennet herself, I am sure, would not wish me there. Even I can perceive she does not care for me."

"Only because she does not know you. And then there is that small matter of your having insulted her daughter your first night in town." Richard flashed his cousin a sardonic grin. "But come tonight and charm the Bennets. Let them come to know the good man I know you to be. Besides, I should like you and Miss Elizabeth to become better acquainted."

Stifling a groan and the urge to run away, Darcy took a slow, deep breath. "Richard—"

"Come. I defy you to give me one good reason why you ought not to attend."

How about how the way I frightened your lady yesterday after taking her in my arms? Darcy thought. *Or that I cannot cease thinking about it and would give my entire fortune to repeat that moment for but an instant? What of the fact that, no matter how I try to prevent it, I am rapidly falling in love with the woman you shall marry? Or that if you only knew the improper thoughts I have entertained for that delightful creature, you would have just cause to run me through?*

"I can think of nothing."

Chapter Twelve

Judging by the look on Mr Collins' face, he was not best pleased at the notion of sharing his fair cousins' attention with other gentlemen. Though not the cleverest of men, he was, at least, shrewd enough to constrain his complaints about intruders on his visit and the injustice of limited choice to mumbled grumblings at quiet moments and lulls in conversations. He may as well have remained silent, for all the notice he was paid.

For her own part, Elizabeth could not quite decide how she felt about tonight's company. Had it been only Colonel Fitzwilliam, she might have been easier. For Jane's sake, she was pleased with the prospect of Mr Bingley's society, though his sisters she could, perhaps, do without. Even Mr Hurst gave her no pause as it was likely he would be in his cups by the second course and insensible by the end of the meal.

It was the final member of the Netherfield party that had her pacing her bedchamber and worrying the curl that always slipped out of her pins no matter how she tried to contain it. Mr

Darcy had hardly left her thoughts since their parting at the base of Oakham Mount yesterday. Even as she walked with Colonel Fitzwilliam in the garden and tried to put his cousin from her mind, he seemed intent on keeping that gentleman foremost in her thoughts by extolling on Mr Darcy's virtues. He told of how his cousin had crossed to sea to be at the Colonel's side at his hour of greatest need and the months spent nursing him back to health. It was endearing, really, how fond of his cousin the Colonel was, and understandable; but it did not help to untangle any of Elizabeth's terribly confused feelings.

That moment on the mount, when Mr Darcy had saved her from her own clumsiness, was replayed in her mind over and over again. When she recalled how it had felt to have his strong, protective arms wrapped around her, she felt a rush of heat course through her body even as a shiver ran down her spine. As she had lain in bed last night, she remembered the look in his eyes as he had gazed down upon her and all at once her mouth went dry as her heart began to beat faster and the pit of her stomach tingled and hummed. Never had she experienced such sensations. These contemplations were not for young maidens to consider, but she could not help but feel that she wanted to experience whatever Mr Darcy had done to her again.

She did not know what she would do tonight when she saw him. How would he react to seeing her? Had he noticed the way she had responded to his touch on the mount? What did he think of her now? Did he even think of her at all? Was she overreacting to simply having been saved from certain humiliation when he had not given it a second thought? Had she imagined the look of heated desire in his eyes as he held her close to his body?

Most of all, what did she *want*? She liked the Colonel. They were very similar in temperament and she thought that to be an advantage in a union between them. Or, at least, she had once thought so. They laughed together, and teased one another...surely there must be more to love? She had never been in love, so she could not say for sure what it ought to entail, but she imagined something more than the easy friendliness she felt for the Colonel. In truth, she had ever dreamt that love would feel something akin to what she had felt in Mr Darcy's arms.

When she had been walking with the Colonel yesterday, she had attempted to recreate the feelings she had experienced with Mr Darcy by standing a little closer to her suitor than she might normally have done. She focused on the feel of his strong arm beneath her hand as it rested in the crook of his elbow, looking for that heat that had verily scorched her back where Mr Darcy's hand had touched her. For a few uncomfortable moments, she had gazed deeply into his eyes, trying to find the searing depths his cousin's possessed.

Alas, she had felt nothing but the awkwardness of the moment. Colonel Fitzwilliam had inspired nothing in her but laughter when he had tried to alleviate the strange tension with a well-timed joke. For one desperate moment, she had considered pretending to trip so that the Colonel might be made to catch her as Mr Darcy had done, holding her close to his body. In the end, however, her courage failed her and she resigned herself to these frustrating feelings.

Was it foolish to continue a courtship which, at even so early a juncture, showed little potential of ending successfully? Even more to the point, was it foolish to continue a courtship when her thoughts were constantly straying to another man?!

"Lizzy," Jane's sweet voice called to her from the stairs. "Our guests will be here soon."

"I am coming," she answered and turned to inspect her reflection in the mirror.

She need decide nothing at present. Her courtship with Colonel Fitzwilliam was still in its infancy. That she had not fallen madly in love with the gentleman in the space of *two days* was hardly reason to despair. The foolishness would be to put him off now. It was something of a miracle that a man of his station should take an interest in a poor, simple, country maiden. Her mother was not entirely wrong; Elizabeth was fortunate any man was willing to overlook her lack of dowry, silly family members, and a preference for rambling about the out of doors, muddying her hems, to more ladylike pursuits, let alone the son of an earl.

Besides, she had never been in love; she could not know that what she felt towards Mr Darcy was love or anything like it. Or that he had felt anything at all. What were the chances that two such illustrious gentlemen could consider her a worthy choice for a wife? No, she would decide nothing for the moment. She would go down to dinner and allow the behaviour of the two gentlemen guide her.

Despite her resolve and frequent reminders to herself to remain calm, her heart nearly beat its way out of her chest when the sound of a carriage was heard on the drive. Thankfully, the members of her family who might have noticed her disquiet were quite consumed with their own concerns. Jane reached for her hand and squeezed; a beatific smile stretched across her lovely face in anticipation of meeting again with Mr Bingley. Papa was standing beside Mr Collins, a pained grimace displaying his displeasure as the loquacious parson exhibited his singular talent of speaking endlessly without the need to draw breath.

At long last, yet still too soon for her fragile equanimity, the guests were announced into the parlour by Mrs Hill. Colonel Fitzwilliam preceded his cousin into the room and properly greeted his hostess with a bow and warm expressions of his gratitude for having been invited. Kitty and Lydia tittered beside Elizabeth behind their hands over his scarlet coat. Jane shifted beside her and her hand went limp in Elizabeth's.

All of this happened somewhere in Elizabeth's periphery. She heard the sounds as a distant echo and was aware of the others as they moved about and spoke, though she could not discern their words or give any account as to what occurred around her. The moment Mr Darcy entered the room, her eyes found his of their own volition and were held captive. The heat of his gaze seeped into her body and settled in the centre of her chest, filling her with warmth and causing her stays to feel far too tight.

"Miss Elizabeth." Colonel Fitzwilliam turned away from her mother and greeted her warmly, bowing over her hand. "You look positively radiant this evening."

Releasing the breath she had not even been aware she had been holding, Elizabeth tore her gaze away from Mr Darcy, yet remained entirely cognisant of his every move as he bowed his greetings to her mother and father. "Thank you, Colonel. I am happy to see you."

"Oh, but where is Mr Bingley?" cried Mrs Bennet, awakening Elizabeth's awareness for the first time that Colonel Fitzwilliam and Mr Darcy were the only guests to have been announced. She also noticed Jane's brave attempt to cover her disappointment.

"Forgive me, Mrs Bennet," answered the Colonel. "Mr Bingley had already accepted an invitation for his family to dine with Colonel Forster and his new bride this evening,"—Kitty and Lydia gasped and began whinging at the cruelty of not having been invited to dine with the officers, as well—"when I extended your kind invitation. He did ask that we extend to you his deepest regrets and hopes to be remembered on your next invitation."

"Of course! Of course!" Mrs Bennet babbled on about not being the least offended and how delighted they would be to have all their friends from Netherfield to join them soon.

Elizabeth paid her mother little heed as she turned to quietly comfort her disappointed sister. With a gentle smile and press of the hand, Jane signalled to Elizabeth that she was well and moved to sit beside Mary. To anyone else, Jane might very well have appeared entirely unaffected, but Elizabeth saw the disappointment in her lovely eyes. Knowing there was nought she could do for her sister at present, Elizabeth gathered her courage to approach Mr Darcy. Taking a deep breath in a fruitless attempt to still her pounding heart, she stepped before him.

"Mr Darcy, I have scoured my father's library and have had no success in locating any literature pertaining to the lore of the Scandinavian countries. I wondered if you might have some recommendations that I may write to my aunt in London to beg her to procure some for me."

Mr Darcy's shoulders visibly stiffened and she noticed his jaw tensing. He did not look her in the eye as he answered her. "I am afraid I can offer no useful suggestions. If you would excuse me." He gave her a curt bow and took himself to the other side of the room where he stationed himself before the window, looking grimly out into the darkening night.

Taken entirely aback, Elizabeth could do nought for several minutes but stand where he had left her, staring after the gentleman. Never had she met a more changeable man! Quite clearly, he felt nothing for her and she felt foolish for having imagined that he might. What she had experienced on Oakham Mount had obviously been nothing more than the novelty of being in such proximity to a man as she had never before been. It was a relief, truly, to come to this conclusion. There was no need to disrupt her courtship with the Colonel who, no doubt, was much better suited to her than his mercurial and taciturn cousin. Surely, the disappointment she now felt would quickly dissipate. Hopefully.

tepping away from Elizabeth was nothing short of a Herculean task. From the moment Darcy set foot in the room, his entire being was attuned to her presence. His eyes instantly sought her out and he felt a thrill of joy course through him to find her attention fixed on him already. She was so lovely in her pale yellow gown, one dark, playful curl hanging seductively down her neck, nothing but his long-practised, iron-clad discipline had prevented his feet from carrying him to her, taking her in his arms, and kissing her senseless, propriety and family loyalty be damned.

"Ahem." Darcy turned at the sound that was loud enough to attract everyone's attention and noticed a tall, portly man in clergyman's garb he had not noticed before standing beside Mr Bennet, his chin held high and eying Richard's red coat with undisguised disdain. "Might I be introduced to these gentlemen?"

For one tense moment, no one spoke as no one was quite sure how to proceed. Even the youngest Misses Bennet seemed aware that it was not this parson's place to request an introduction to the son and nephew of an earl. Darcy glared his indignation while Richard only chuckled lightly and nodded his approbation to Mr Bennet.

Clearing his throat, Elizabeth's father stepped forward, making a point to do the thing properly, which Darcy could only approve. Of course, one could not be certain Mr Bennet did not act for his own amusement and the enjoyment of watching the parson recognise his mistake. "Gentlemen, may I introduce my cousin, Mr Collins. Mr Collins, it is my pleasure to introduce the Honourable Colonel Fitzwilliam, second son of the earl of Matlock,"—Mr Collins' face fell a little at the revelation of

Richard's station—"and his cousin, Mr Darcy of Pemberley in Derbyshire."

Before the introduction was even complete, Mr Collins dropped his supercilious demeanour and began bouncing in a manner which made Darcy wonder if he might urgently need a chamber pot; and he was not alone in that concern if the giggles from the younger girls and the looks of disgust on the faces of all the others were any indication.

"Oh! Oh! Mr Darcy! Mr Darcy of Pemberley? In Derbyshire?"

"As I said, Cousin," Mr Bennet said wryly, but Mr Collins paid him no mind. Instead, he rushed to stand before Darcy and bent double in an absurdly low bow.

"It is such a pleasure, indeed, an honour, sir! I am Mr William Collins, sir—"

"Also, as I said."

"—and it is my very great honour to serve as humble rector to her most illustrious ladyship, your own aunt, Lady Catherine de Bourgh!" As the name of his patroness rolled off his tongue, Mr Collins fell forward in another deep bow as if he were paying obeisance to the lady herself.

Darcy exchanged looks with his cousin, who looked to be fighting back the urge to laugh.

"Well," said Richard, "Lady Catherine has certainly outdone herself this time."

"Oh, you are also familiar with her ladysh—the earl of Matlock? You are the Honourable Colonel Fitzwilliam? Son of Lord Matlock, brother to her most beneficent Lady Catherine de Bourgh?"

Mr Bennet rolled his eyes at his cousin's ridiculousness and cast a resigned look towards his other guests.

"You know," said Richard, crossing one arm over his chest and rubbing his chin, "that does sound vaguely familiar." He turned and raised his brows comically at Mr Bennet, who shot him back a crooked grin.

Blessedly, dinner was then called. Waved away by Mrs Bennet, Colonel Fitzwilliam stepped forward and offered his arm first to Elizabeth and the other to Miss Bennet, earning him a bright smile from the former. Darcy immediately turned away to hide the stab of jealousy currently piercing his chest.

Dinner was a most miserable affair. Mr Collins seemed intent on remaining at his side and, consequently, Darcy paid little attention to the seat he chose. The parson took the chair immediately to his right, moving it closer to Darcy's than was necessary, and to his left, he found his hostess. Throughout the meal, Mr Collins kept up an endless monologue on the joys of serving Darcy's overbearing and imperious aunt. Mrs Bennet spoke but little to him, which might have been welcome had not the few words she did say border on uncivil as she made remarks about proper gentlemanly comportment and the lack of pleasant company to be had.

Knowing he had not gained the lady's favour when he had spoken so unflatteringly of her daughter all those weeks ago, Darcy turned away from the jabbering Mr Collins and addressed his hostess.

"Mrs Bennet, may I offer my compliments on this fine meal. The watercress soup was particularly delightful. If it is not a great family secret, I would be most grateful for the receipt to send to my cooks in London and at Pemberley."

With her fork stopped midway between her plate and her lips, Mrs Bennet only looked at him for several moments, a most bemused expression on her face as though he had spoken in a language unfamiliar to her.

"I thank you, sir," she said even as she continued to regard him with suspicion. "I will have Cook write it down for you."

Darcy thanked her then turned back to his plate, glancing across the table to where Elizabeth sat only a few seats down. She, too, was watching him with a most peculiar countenance, her eyebrows furled and one side of her lower lip caught deliciously between her teeth. Yes, she was likely very confused by his behaviour; but there was nothing to be done for it. It was imperative that he squash the feelings he harboured for her, be polite to her family for Richard's sake, and find some way to keep breathing despite the loss of his most vital of organs.

Chapter Thirteen

"Good Lord, who is that?" cried Lydia, staring brazenly across the way to where one of her favourite officers, Lieutenant Denny, stood with a decidedly handsome stranger.

"I do not know, but he is terribly good looking," replied Kitty, being no less obvious in her admiration than her younger sister.

"I daresay, he would be much handsomer if he were in regimentals. I think a man hardly worth looking at without regimentals."

"Quit staring so," Elizabeth chided her sisters. "What will they think of you?"

Lydia scoffed, "They will think we are ever so much more fun than you!"

"That is precisely the problem," Elizabeth mumbled under her breath.

After days of listening to Mama's chirping about Elizabeth's suitor and Jane's suitor and pushing Mr Collins to be Mary's suitor, Lydia had had quite enough talk about beaux which had nothing to do with herself. Determined to seek out some male attention of her own, she prevailed upon her sisters to accompany her on a walk into Meryton. It was her expressed intention to learn if Lieutenant Denny had yet returned from his recent assignment to Town, but any officer to cross her path would do just as well.

No less determined than her youngest daughter, Mrs Bennet had pressed Mr Collins into joining his fair cousins. As she pushed them all out the door, she urged Mary to be attentive to the gentleman and warned her eldest daughters to leave Mr Collins to their sister's company; something they were both happy to do. It amazed Elizabeth that Mr Collins possessed the ability to remain silent for more than only a few moments together as he walked beside Mary, uttering not a word.

"Denny!" Lydia hollered across the road, waving her handkerchief and caring not what other attention she may be attracting.

"Lydia!" Jane admonished her, little good it did for the heed the silly girl paid her.

The two gentlemen conferred for a moment before turning to make their way across the main thoroughfare to where the Bennet ladies and Mr Collins stood. Watching their progress, though with more circumspection than either Kitty or Lydia had displayed, Elizabeth was forced to concede that the stranger was, indeed, quite handsome. Tall with dark blonde hair pulled back in a queue, strikingly blue eyes, and a fine figure, it was certainly no hardship to look upon him. Only Mr Darcy could be considered more favourable, in her opinion.

Stop it, Lizzy! she chastised herself. *You have been over this. That gentleman wants nothing to do with you and you are being courted by his cousin, for goodness sakes!*

Shaking away these unwelcome thoughts, Elizabeth turned to greet the two gentlemen. The handsome stranger was introduced as Mr Wickham, a new officer in the regiment having just arrived from London to purchase a commission. The young man expressed himself well with fine manners and an amiable disposition. His smile came easily as did several flattering compliments, delivered in such a manner as to be pleasing without offending or seeming too practised.

Despite Lydia's flagrant attempts to garner both men's notice, Elizabeth could not help but observe how often Mr Wickham's gaze strayed to herself. She felt the compliment of his attentions, but was careful not to display any signs of reciprocation. She offered a slight smile, then turned her gaze away. If she still felt the heat of his gaze on her person, she did not acknowledge it.

The group was still gathered on the walkway, talking agreeably, when their notice was drawn by the sound of approaching hoofbeats. The entire party turned to see Mr Bingley, Mr Darcy, and Colonel Fitzwilliam riding up the street towards them.

Turning to see how Jane bore the sudden appearance of Mr Bingley, Elizabeth's eye caught the countenance of Mr Wickham. Where he had been all ease and friendliness only moments before, he was now pale, tense, and silent. She looked back at the newly arrived gentlemen and saw Mr Darcy and the Colonel in close confederation, though their eyes were narrowed on Mr Wickham.

"Denny," said Mr Wickham, a sense of urgency in his voice Elizabeth had not noticed before. "Should we not return to camp?"

"Oh, but Mr Wickham," Lydia pouted, "should you not like to escort us about our shopping?"

"Wickham!" shouted the Colonel, carefully but hastily climbing down off his mount.

"It was a pleasure to meet you lovely ladies." Offering a perfunctory bow, Mr Wickham turned without pausing to wait for his comrade and hurried down the lane, ducking down and alleyway and out of sight.

"Coward," grumbled Colonel Fitzwilliam as he came to stop at Elizabeth's side. "Typical."

"I beg your pardon, sir," an affronted Mr Denny confronted the Colonel, clearly intent on defending his brother in arms despite standing several inches shorter than his adversary. "Though he is not in uniform, that is a lieutenant in his majesty's militia. You will show him respect."

Pulling himself up to his full, and considerably more impressive height, Colonel Fitzwilliam stepped forward, an imposing figure to behold even with the cane he leant upon. Mr Denny flinched but held his ground. "Though I am not in uniform, I am Colonel Richard Fitzwilliam of his majesty's Fifth Dragoon Guard. I suggest you mind your tone with me, or must I speak with your commanding officer?"

"N-no, sir," Mr Denny stammered, wide eyes full of fear. "My apologies, Colonel, sir."

"No harm done. Pray, tell me, how well do you know Wickham?"

"Not well, sir," Mr Denny answered readily, eager to rectify his mistake. "I met the gentleman in London only last week. He seemed a good sort of chap, friendly and good-humoured despite being in what he said was a desperate situation. Told a good tale about having been mistreated by his benefactor's son and cheated out of his inheritance. It was then I offered to bring him here and help him purchase a commission."

A significant look passed between Colonel Fitzwilliam and Mr Darcy who had joined his cousin. "I would be remiss if I did not warn you to keep an eye on your new comrade. Mr Wickham is not as he presents himself. I would not lend him so much as a farthing, if I was you, and ensure that he is always accompanied when ladies are present. Take every word that falls from his forked tongue with a pound of salt. And I think I will have a word with Colonel Forster, though you will not be mentioned."

"Yes, sir. Thank you, sir."

Mr Darcy stepped forward and spoke in low tones with Mr Denny. Elizabeth could not hear what was said, but an expression of relief softened the features of the latter's face. The young lieutenant thanked Mr Darcy then saluted Colonel Fitzwilliam before bowing to the ladies and taking his leave amidst Lydia's protests.

Dropping the façade of war-hardened soldier, Colonel Fitzwilliam turned to Elizabeth and offered his arm, which she accepted with a smile. When he invited his cousin to join them, Mr Darcy declined, stating his desire to visit the book shop. This vexed Elizabeth as she, too, had intended to inspect Mr Haver's latest shipment, but she held her tongue. She could peruse the shop another time.

"Miss Elizabeth, I apologise for the scene you just witnessed," said the Colonel.

"Think nothing of it, sir. May I presume that you hold an acquaintance with Mr Wickham? We had only just been introduced."

"Aye, I know the scoundrel. Forgive me." Elizabeth felt the muscles of his arms tense as he clenched his fist. "Wickham has been known amongst my family for many years. He has been a plague on Darcy since boyhood. Someday I or Darcy will share the whole of the history with you. For now, it is sufficient to say he is not an honourable man and it would be wise for you and your sisters to avoid his company. He is a practised deceiver."

"I shall warn my sisters, though I doubt it will do any good. Simply by the merit of his being to wear a red coat and possessing a handsome face, Lydia is sure to believe him to be the very best of men, incapable of anything but the most praiseworthy of acts."

"Perhaps I might have a word with your father, in that case. He ought to be made aware of the danger to his daughters. And, I assure you, Wickham is a danger to any young lady."

Elizabeth released a heavy sigh. "You may try, Colonel. My father has never yet exerted himself to check his wife or daughters. He will like as not consider Lydia's silly nature and lack of dowry as deterrent enough to protect her, and any of my sisters."

"Hmm." Colonel Fitzwilliam said nothing further and they walked on in companionable silence for some time until he cleared his throat and changed the topic.

Mr Darcy soon joined them once again, a brown paper-wrapped package under his arm; though he remained quiet and aloof. He answered their inquiries as to his purchases in only brief, vague terms. *So much for our tentative truce,* Elizabeth thought with a sigh. She wondered if he resented the time his cousin spent with her, or if he suspected her of being a fortune hunter and leading the Colonel on. Whatever his concerns, she would not allow them to bother her. The purpose of courtship was to come to know a potential marriage partner better; spending time with one another was essential. One day, Mr Darcy would find himself in the Colonel's position and perhaps then he would understand. Elizabeth would do her best not to tease him too terribly when that day came. As for her being a fortune hunter, she knew her intentions were honourable and cared not for his opinion on the matter.

When they had made an entire circuit of Meryton's main street, their party converged on the small square and began speaking of returning to Longbourn. There were no officers to be seen, so Kitty and Lydia had lost their enthusiasm for the venture. Mr Bingley and Colonel Fitzwilliam offered their services to escort the ladies home; Mr Darcy did not offer, but neither did he object, simply falling into step beside the Colonel, leading his giant grey beast and his cousin's black stallion. This left Elizabeth bewildered and questioning her opinion of the gentleman, yet again. The Colonel had not asked Mr Darcy to lead his horse, nor had Mr Darcy said a word about it. He had merely untied both animals and nodded his cousin towards Elizabeth, which might have been seen in a light of wishing to help further their courtship.

She knew she ought to have been grateful to the gentleman, but she only felt vexed. Could the man not choose one manner of behaving and hold to it? Must he ever be changing from quiet and distant to helpful and kind; from unpleasant and proud to interesting and irresistible? Did he approve of the courtship between herself and his cousin or did he not? Would he help it or hinder it? Oh! He was the most provoking man!

Near the edge of town, the group was met by Elizabeth's dear friend Charlotte and her younger sister, Maria who was likewise intimate with Kitty and Lydia. Greetings were exchanged and Mr Collins introduced to the Misses Lucas and then the entire party set off down the road together.

Upon reaching the lane to Lucas Lodge, Charlotte and Maria bid their friends goodbye and thanked the gentlemen. Before they could depart, however, Mr Collins, who had been much occupied walking and talking with Charlotte to everyone's satisfaction, stepped forward.

"As my fair cousins have ample escort to Longbourn, please permit me to ensure your safe return home, Miss Lucas."

None of the Longbourn ladies could object to a reprieve from Mr Collins' endless rambling, even for a short duration, and so the scheme was agreed upon by all. Mr Collins sent his apologies to Mr and Mrs Bennet for his absence and offered his arm to Charlotte, leaving Maria to follow behind.

Chapter Fourteen

"Colonel Fitzwilliam," Mrs Hill announced as that gentleman shuffled into the drawing-room behind her.

Three days had passed since the encounter with Mr Wickham and there had been little interaction between Longbourn and Netherfield; not that Elizabeth could claim to be surprised. They had dined the following evening at Pulvis Lodge. Several officers had been in attendance and Kitty and Lydia had been in fine form. All evening the foolish girls laughed and flirted and drank too much wine. Even their neighbours, who were well used to their silly antics and wild ways had raised more than a few eyebrows and looked on with barely concealed contempt.

Jane and Elizabeth had made every attempt to curb their sisters' enthusiasm with little success. They might have achieved their aim had their parents roused themselves to check their daughters at all. Alas, Mrs Bennet had been insensible to anything but for crowing over anyone within earshot her good fortune at having three daughters soon to be married—one to the son of an earl! Mr Bennet had found it all rather entertaining.

Had this been the extent of her family's display, it would have been the most mortifying evening of Elizabeth's remembrance. Unfortunately, the Bennets were currently hosting England's most ridiculous man. When Mr Collins was not boasting loudly of the great condescension of his most noble patroness or the costliness of her elegant fireplaces, the absurd parson followed Mr Darcy and the Colonel about like a lost puppy. Colonel Fitzwilliam bore his toadying with composure; Mr Darcy, less so. His face was set in a deep scowl the whole of the evening as his eyes followed Elizabeth's wild sisters about the room and was made to endure the obsequious attentions of her father's cousin.

The only relief had been Mr Bingley's seeming ignorance of the impropriety of her family. That gentleman had eyes and ears only for Jane, despite his sisters' obvious displeasure.

In the days that followed, Elizabeth had existed in a state of expectation, awaiting the letter to her father which would end her courtship with the Colonel and announce the departure of the entire Netherfield party from the neighbourhood.

When her suitor entered the room, she could not bring herself to look upon him. She could, at least, recognise a surge in her respect for the gentleman that he had the good breeding to come to her home and end their understanding in person. Great was her astonishment when he approached, took up her hand, and bowed over it.

"Good morning, Miss Elizabeth," he addressed her with his usual good humour.

Wearily, Elizabeth looked up and was quickly comforted by his warm smile and friendly look. "Good morning, Colonel."

"Oh, but where is Mr Bingley?" Mrs Bennet loudly inquired. "Did he not accompany you, Colonel?"

"My apologies, madam. Mr Bingley and Mr Darcy are much engaged in estate business today. I found myself at my leisure and could not resist paying a visit to the lovely ladies of Longbourn," said the Colonel, flashing his most winsome smile at his hostess.

"Oh, well. I suppose if that must be," replied a flustered Mrs Bennet. "Shall I ring for tea, Colonel?"

"Tea sounds absolutely delightful, Mrs Bennet." With a covert wink at Elizabeth, the Colonel took a seat and turned a bright smile on Kitty. "Miss Catherine, Miss Elizabeth tells me you are fond of art and quite talented."

Elizabeth was forced to cover a rather unladylike snort of laughter with a cough when her mother looked up in alarm at flirtatious tone he adopted. Seeming to decide that there could be no harm in the Colonel getting to know the sisters of the daughter he was courting, Mrs Bennet eyed him warily but said nothing before turning her attention back to her sewing.

A stunned Kitty looked from Elizabeth to her mother and finally to Colonel Fitzwilliam. "Uh, why, yes, Colonel. Well, I mean, I am fond of art. I am sure I could not say as to whether or not I could be considered talented."

"Oh, come now." Richard smiled charmingly and Kitty blushed a marvellous shade of scarlet. "I am sure you are too modest. I am rather fond of art myself. In fact, my father has an original Botticelli in his gallery at Havensworth Hall in Matlock."

"You are joking!" cried Kitty, looking at the Colonel with eyes widened in awe.

"Yes. You must come see it sometime. I am certain we might have a lovely time, walking the gallery and sharing our opinions of the beautiful artwork. I should dearly love to see some of your work sometime."

"Kitty!" Mrs Bennet squealed with a great fluttering of her handkerchief. "Come. Come sit over here with me!"

With one final longing look at the gentleman, Kitty stood and sulked across the room to sit beside her mother who immediately began scolding her in a harsh whisper which was only partially concealed.

"So, Miss Mary," Colonel Fitzwilliam next turned to the middle Miss Bennet, who instantly flushed at his attention. Mrs Bennet started and very nearly fell out of her chair. "I understand you are a brilliant musician. I am inordinately fond of music."

"Colonel Fitzwilliam! You forget yourself!"

"Forgive me, madam. I find myself rather overwhelmed by the charms of your daughters. With so much beauty at hand, how can a gentleman be expected to choose between them?" He gasped as though he had only just come to a realisation. "That must be why ladies of the ton do not often come out into society until their elder sisters are wed. Some ladies may never marry if they are made to compete with their lovely younger sisters." He flashed a dashing smile at Mary with a wink, causing her to blush furiously.

For a moment, Mrs Bennet only looked on the Colonel as if he had spontaneously sprouted antlers. Slowly, however, her eyes began to widen as her eyes darted around the room at all of her daughters seated together like a veritable marriage buffet. Elizabeth watched in amazement as she could all but hear her mother wondering if allowing her younger daughters out before the elder had married had hindered Jane and Elizabeth's chances at matrimony.

The lady of the house leapt from her seat as if it were on fire and pointed out the door. "Kitty! Lydia! Go to your room. I must speak with your father!"

"Oh!" Lydia sulked. "But the Colonel did not yet flirt with me!"

"Go!" Without another word, Mrs Bennet shuffled her youngest daughters from the room, Lydia complaining all the while.

"Thank you," Elizabeth said to her suitor, more than a little embarrassed that his intervention had been necessary to finally make her mother see the dangers in allowing her youngest daughters free rein, but excessively grateful all the same.

"It is my pleasure. They are delightful girls, wanting only a little guidance and maturing." Before Elizabeth could express any more of her gratitude, the Colonel changed the subject. "I do not see Mr Collins this morning."

Elizabeth looked around the room, realising for the first time since the disastrous dinner that her father's cousin had been very little in attendance at Longbourn. Her mind had been much occupied worrying about her courtship and, though she made a great effort not to dwell on it, Mr Darcy's obviously poor opinion of her family. She had given little thought to their inconvenient houseguest's whereabouts.

"No, I suppose not. That is strange. I have not seen Mr Collins much these last few days." She turned a questioning gaze on Mary, who only pressed her lips together and shrugged.

"Mr Collins," supplied Jane, "has been much engaged at Lucas Lodge. I believe he has found a captive audience in Sir William for his effusions over his patroness. Oh, Colonel! Forgive me. I did not—"

"Be at ease, Miss Bennet. I am as relieved as you all must be not to be subjected to the exaggerated excellence of my overbearing and officious aunt."

Again displaying his abundance of tact, Colonel Fitzwilliam glanced out the window and suggested a walk in the fine autumn sunshine. Elizabeth readily agreed while Jane politely demurred by expressing a wish to remain indoors and finish her needlework. Though her words were accompanied by a serene smile, Elizabeth thought she detected a hint of despondency in her sister's tone. She gave Jane's hand a loving squeeze and Mary was persuaded to join them as chaperone.

As they stepped outside, Colonel Fitzwilliam offered an arm to Elizabeth and invited her sister to walk with them, much to Mary's obvious surprise. No doubt, she had expected to trail along behind them, forgotten by the young lovers. But the Colonel seemingly would not have it. He engaged both sisters in lively conversation, addressing as many comments and questions to Mary as to Elizabeth.

Rather than jealously wishing that her suitor had attention only for herself, as one might imagine, Elizabeth was delighted. Considered by many to be the plain Bennet sister, Mary was very often brushed aside or altogether ignored, overlooked at parties and assemblies in favour of her prettier or livelier sisters. Her next younger sister positively came alive under the attentions of the Colonel, brightening especially when he mentioned his horse.

"He is a beautiful animal," said Mary, gazing appreciatively towards the stable where Jonesy was brushing the beast.

"Thank you, Miss Mary. I am rather fond of the great brute. But then, he did once save my life."

"Truly, Colonel?"

"Indeed." The Colonel then went on to relate a tale of such bravery and heroism, complete with danger and intrigue, as to completely enrapture the ladies in wholly undisguised admiration. While entirely impressed and entertained, Elizabeth suspected some of his story to be at least slightly embellished. Mary, however, seemed to hang on his every word. They meandered over to the stables, where Mary verily gushed over the beauty of the animal.

"Do you ride, Miss Elizabeth?" he asked.

"Not at all, Colonel," she answered with a self-deprecating grin. "I took a fall when I was seven and broke my arm. I am afraid I rather lost my enthusiasm for the activity after that."

"That is a shame. And you, Miss Mary?"

"I do ride, Colonel, though not as often as I should like. And I am not as accomplished as I could wish. After Lizzy's fall, Papa did not seem to think it important to give the rest of us instruction."

"Oh, Mary," lamented Elizabeth. "I am so sorry. I had no idea you would wish to learn."

Mary shrugged away her sister's concern. "It is of little matter. I came to the stables so often as a girl, Jonesy took pity on me and gave me lessons when he could spare the time."

A few awkward minutes passed wherein Elizabeth and Colonel Fitzwilliam watched Mary stroking Orion's neck affectionately, having revealed learning to ride by a servant as if she had not been entitled to the attentions of her father. Though it could not be considered in any way her fault, Elizabeth felt a pang of guilt course through her. If she had not allowed her fear to rule her, Mary might have been granted proper riding lessons.

"I have heard," Colonel Fitzwilliam broke the silence, "of some ruins nearby. An old castle. Have I been properly informed?"

The sisters nodded in unison. "Betterston Castle," said Elizabeth. "It is some ten miles to the west. Though I have not been since I was a girl."

"Excellent! What say you we make up a party and go? Make a day of it?"

"That sounds lovely, Colonel."

"And you, Miss Mary? You will join us, will you not?"

Mary, who had turned her attention to the horse when Colonel Fitzwilliam had begun speaking to her sister, started and looked at him in bemusement. "Me? You would wish for me to be one of the party?"

"But, of course. Unless you would rather remain at Longbourn. But I think it would be quite the shame if you should miss it."

"I thank you, Colonel," said Mary timidly. "I should be pleased to be included."

Elizabeth beamed her approval for the Colonel's kind suggestion to her sister. If she was not greatly mistaken, she believed she might have fallen ever so slightly in love with her suitor at that moment.

Chapter Fifteen

*D*inner that evening was a strange affair. Mr Collins had, at last, joined them for the evening meal, having spent the entire day at Lucas Lodge. Though no one had despaired at his absence—save, perhaps, for Mrs Bennet—everyone was disconcerted by the parson's uncharacteristic reticence. Though, to say he was silent would be an untruth.

Upon entering the house, Mr Collins wore an expression reminiscent of the cat who got the cream. He gave his most insincere apologies for having neglected his hosts and thanked them for their most gracious forbearance. As he took a seat amongst them in the parlour, he could be heard mumbling to himself under his breath.

"What was that, Mr Collins?" Mr Bennet inquired, ready as always to be entertained by another's stupidity.

"What? Oh, nothing, nothing. It was nothing at all." A smug grin stretched across his wide face as a most ridiculous giggle bubbled forth from his corpulent lips.

"Are you well, sir?" Mrs Bennet asked, eyeing the parson warily. No doubt she feared the man had lost his mind and might attack them all in their beds as they slept.

"How good of you to ask. I am exceedingly well, madam. Never has a man been so well as I myself am at this very moment." Jumping slightly and raising a portly finger to his lips as if he had let a great secret slip, Mr Collins giggled again. "Ah, but I must say no more! All will be revealed in its proper time."

Dinner was then thankfully called and the family made their way to the dining room. Mr Collins stood back and allowed his relations to precede him, positively shivering with barely concealed glee. Throughout the meal, he mumbled to himself as he peered at each of his companions over his fork or his wine glass. When asked to repeat himself, he would only respond with a stupid smirk and mutter "Oh, nothing, nothing." Tired of the foolish man's antics and choosing to take him at his word, the family quickly ceased to inquire after his meaning and simply ignored him. This only increased the frequency and volume of his absurd giggles.

When the meal came to its merciful conclusion, Kitty and Lydia made not the slightest objection at being made to retire early, no longer being considered as out until at least one of their elder sisters married. Though they—most especially Lydia—had objected most strenuously when the verdict had been handed down, neither gave the least bit of trouble upon being excused from joining the family for tea.

The rest of the family retired to the parlour—Mr Bennet, having had more than enough entertainment at his ridiculous cousin's expense, would not subject himself to a half an hour alone with the buffoon. There, Mr Collins offered to read aloud and chose from *Fordyce's Sermons for Young Ladies* a lengthy diatribe on the importance of female meekness. Very often he would interrupt his reading to insert his own dubious words of wisdom on how a young lady had best go about attracting a husband, much of which consisted of keeping her thoughts and opinions to herself and always submitting to a man's dictates.

At an unprecedented early hour, Jane, Elizabeth, and Mary stood as one the moment Mr Collins finished the first sermon, bade hasty goodnights, and fled the room.

Waking at her accustomed time the next morning, Elizabeth sent forth a fervent prayer that her cousin's strange behaviour from the evening prior did not extend to a sudden penchant for early mornings. Her worries were needless as the only soul she encountered as she slipped from the house for her daily constitutional was Cook who pretended to scold the young miss as she nicked a muffin from the kitchens on her way out of doors.

Her ramble was a lengthy one; each time she considered returning to the house, memories from the previous evening begged her to go a little further. Alas, she could not very well stay away for the entirety of the day and, at last, turned her feet towards home.

"Had you a pleasant walk," Charlotte Lucas greeted her as she stepped off the path into the back garden.

"Charlotte!"

"I have been waiting on you this past half hour. I suppose you have been lost in your thoughts, dreamily imagining yourself as Mrs Elizabeth Fitzwilliam! How well that sounds!"

Elizabeth laughed at her friend's teasing when in truth she was quite alarmed at herself. Her suitor had not crossed her mind the entirety of her walk. The majority of her outing had been occupied with the simple admiration of the beautiful autumn morning. There had been a funny little squirrel who was most happy to accept crumbs from her muffin and followed her a great distance. The vivid golds, oranges, and reds of the changing leaves begged to be admired and enjoyed. If the good Colonel had entered her thoughts, it had been only fleetingly and in regards as to his relationship with Mr Darcy.

"What do you do here, Charlotte? You know I am always happy to see you, but it is rather early, is it not?"

Charlotte looked away then, avoiding Elizabeth's eyes. It was then that Elizabeth noticed the handkerchief being twisted in her friend's hands.

"Charlotte, whatever is the matter?" Elizabeth asked, stepping forward to take Charlotte's hands in her own.

Pulling away gently, Charlotte began pacing, gesturing impatiently. Her next words came out in a rushed jumble. "I have something to tell you, Eliza, and I wished you to hear it from me. I am just going to come right out and say it. Mr Collins has offered me his hand in marriage and I have accepted him. Despise me if you must, but what is done is done and I will not apologise for it. I know what you must think and how you must feel but we are not the same. I am not romantic, Lizzy. I never have been. I ask only for a comfortable home and respectability. I am convinced my chances at happiness with Mr Collins are as fair as any two people can boast upon entering the marriage state. You will not change my mind so do not even attempt to do so."

This monologue had the effect of rendering Elizabeth speechless for several moments. There was no denying she felt her friend's choice a foolish one. Mr Collins was the most ridiculous man she had ever had the misfortune to meet. The way he spoke of his patroness bordered on obsession. He made no disguise of relying upon her supposedly superior opinions in all matters, great or small. Elizabeth had felt from the beginning of their acquaintance that whomever the silly man duped into accepting his hand would always be second in her husband's esteem, always subject to the whims of Lady Catherine de Bourgh. Even had she not been engaged in a courtship with Colonel Fitzwilliam, Elizabeth could never have been prevailed upon to accept such a man.

But Charlotte was correct. Though as dear to one another as two friends could possibly be, there could be no denying Elizabeth and Charlotte were very different creatures. Somewhat impetuous and unapologetically romantic, Elizabeth was, first and foremost, guided by her heart. She longed for a marriage founded upon mutual respect, admiration, and love. Only a man who stirred both her heart and her mind would do. Marriage to a man such as her cousin would be nothing short of the worst sort of torture.

Her friend, however, placed her hopes in more practical considerations. At seven and twenty, Charlotte was considered by many to be firmly on the shelf. She had neither beauty nor fortune to attract a husband and few men could be relied upon to appreciate her sensible mind. If she did not accept Mr Collins, it was likely she would never receive another offer of marriage and would end her days a poor spinster, dependent upon others for support.

Choosing her words and her tone carefully, Elizabeth stepped forward and took up her friend's hands again. "Charlotte, are you happy with your choice?"

"I am," answered Charlotte, almost defiantly.

"Then I am happy for you. It is true that I could never be happy with a man such as my cousin, but I have not your good sense and patience. I am sure you shall be the making of him. And you shall make a wonderful mistress of Longbourn."

"I...thank you, Eliza." Charlotte eyed her friend warily, as if trying to determine if her words might be trusted. Elizabeth smiled sweetly, knowing they would never see eye to eye on the subject and feeling it was not worth losing her dearest friend over. After a moment, Charlotte released a heavy breath. "I know you are disappointed in me, that you do not understand my reasons. But your support and friendship mean a great deal to me."

Elizabeth thread her arm through Charlotte's and they began walking down the garden path. "And you shall always have it. As I said, I desire only your happiness."

"Your mother will be very angry. I am afraid...that is, will Mary be terribly upset, do you think?"

As they walked, Elizabeth considered her sister. Though seemingly suited to the life of a parson's wife, Mary had made no indication she would have welcomed Mr Collins' suit had he taken Mrs Bennet's hints. Last evening, she had been as eager to vacate the parlour as any of her sisters.

"No. I do not think even Mary could have been induced to accept such a man. Oh!" Pursing her lips together, she sent her friend a sheepish glance. "Forgive me."

"Oh, Lizzy!" Charlotte laughed.

"Will you come in for breakfast?"

"No. I will call with my parents later. Mama is eager to boast our good fortune all over the neighbourhood. She considers it quite the triumph to have a daughter wed before any of the beautiful Bennet girls. Even if you are being courted by the son of an earl."

When the Lucases came to call later with their announcement, Elizabeth continued to show her support by congratulating her friend heartily. Whilst Mrs Bennet sat stunned and speechless at the news, her two eldest daughters expressed their relief at knowing their beloved home would be in good hands when the sad day came that their father must pass on to his eternal reward.

To their great relief, Mrs Hill entered, announcing the Colonel—looking rather dashing in his red officer's coat—Mr Darcy, and the Bingleys just as Mrs Bennet was regaining the use of her tongue. Though no less put out at having lost Mr Collins to none other than the plain spinster Charlotte Lucas, she was suitably comforted by the presence of two of her own daughters' suitors—both of whom were far superior to Mr Collins. Amidst all the activity, no one noticed Mary slip quietly from the room.

The newcomers were quickly called upon by Lady Lucas to extend their congratulations to her daughter. Mr Darcy, being nearest offered his sincere felicitations before stepping back to allow the others to pay their respects. While the Colonel and Mr Bingley were warm in their well wishes, Miss Bingley gave the briefest of nods before taking a seat as far removed from any of the others as possible. To Elizabeth's great surprise, Mr Darcy crossed the room and came to a stop before her.

Slipping a hand inside his coat, he pulled out a worn leather book and awkwardly held it out to her. He coughed slightly before saying quietly, "I thought you might enjoy this."

With a curious glance up into his face, she gingerly took the book from his hands. Turning it over, she saw it was a journal of some kind. A brief perusal revealed page after page filled with a neat, masculine script, simple drawings of symbols, figures, and strange animals.

"What is this?" she asked, carefully flipping through the pages with interest.

Mr Darcy shuffled his feet and reached up to rub the back of his neck. "It is the notes I kept from my studies of the Scandinavian cultures at university."

"Oh, Mr Darcy!" she uttered breathlessly. "This is wonderful! I mean,"—she turned the page to discover a full-page, detailed sketch of a Viking ship and gasped—"absolutely marvellous!"

"I am glad you approve. This is but one of six journals I kept on the subject. If you enjoy it, I would be happy to lend you the others, as well."

Closing the book and hugging it tenderly to her chest, she smiled shyly up at him. "Thank you, Mr Darcy. I shall take very good care of it."

"I have no doubts you will, madam."

Colonel Fitzwilliam approached and bowed over Elizabeth's hand. "We have come on purpose of issuing an invitation. Well, two invitations, really. Having consulted with my companions, we have decided on Tuesday next for our excursion to the ruins. Will that do?"

"That sounds lovely, Colonel."

"And," piped in Mr Bingley, pulling an elegant invitation from his coat and motioning for his sister to join him only to be ignored, "the Thursday following shall be a grand ball at Netherfield!" He produced an elegant invitation from his inner coat pocket.

"Oh, a ball! Oh, Lydia!" cried Mrs Bennet. The lady looked about her for her youngest daughter, no doubt to indulge in her rapturous delight, before recalling that both Kitty and Lydia had been remanded to the schoolroom. In a clear sign of increasingly agitated spirits, her handkerchief began to flutter as her lips trembled. As her eyes swept from one side of the room to the other, she caught sight of Colonel Fitzwilliam, sitting beside her most troublesome daughter, smiling adoringly at her. As if by some miracle cure, her hands stilled and a look of calm washed over her features. She turned her sights upon Jane who was on the receiving end of Mr Bingley's attention, his invitation having been extended. "You do us great honour, sir."

With their own invitation in hand, the Lucases soon took their leave, anxious as Lady Lucas was to spread the word of her daughter's engagement; perhaps the desire to be removed from her friend's prettier daughters and their far more impressive suitors added haste to their departure. They had no sooner quit the room than Miss Bingley leapt to her feet and announced that they, too, had best be on their way, having more invitations to deliver for their ball. A reluctant Mr Bingley peeled himself away from Jane as Mr Darcy and his cousin also rose to leave.

"We have an appointment to speak with Colonel Forster about our old playmate," the Colonel explained.

Elizabeth walked the cousins out, Mr Darcy's journal still held possessively to her chest. As she watched them ride away down Longbourn's drive, she purposefully did not give thought to why her eye followed the tall and stately gentleman who most assuredly was not her suitor.

The remainder of the day was spent in quiet, fascinated study of his meticulously written journal. His strong, tidy hand was nearly as interesting to her as the words which they formed. When she lay her head down on her pillow that night, the journal carefully placed on her bedside table, her thoughts were for the most confusing gentleman she had ever met. More than once she caught herself and firmly turned her thoughts to the Colonel. He was a very fine man, amiable and gregarious. Not at all like his cousin, who was more often than not silent and grave. Yet, she had known him at times to be perfectly friendly and engaging, such as when they had debated Shakespeare at Netherfield or sat together atop Oakham Mount and discussed lore and mythology.

Oh, dear! Elizabeth fretted into the darkness. *Why am I still considering Mr Darcy?!*

She turned over, punching her pillow into a more comfortable shape. Surely her inability to turn her thoughts away from that man was nothing more than her delight in his university journal. She was a woman who loved to obtain new knowledge and he had provided an opportunity to learn, that was all. It was little wonder he had piqued her curiosity. Mr Collins might have done the same had he approached her with a new and obscure branch of study to explore. Mr Darcy's handsome face, fine figure, and mysterious nature had nothing at all to do with it.

Chapter Sixteen

Riding away from Longbourn, neither cousin spoke, each lost in their thoughts as they were. Sending away to Darcy House for the journals had been done with very little forethought. When he had done so, Darcy rationalised that he desired them for himself. Speaking to Elizabeth on the subject had merely renewed his interest and he wished only to review what he had learnt all those years ago. Upon their arrival, however, he knew he had been lying to himself. The moment the books were laid in his hands, he could not help but imagine the bright smile that would grace her lovely lips when he presented them to her. He had foreseen with great clarity the very same spark of interest in her magnificent eyes which had become reality not half an hour ago.

Knowing the pleasure he would be bestowing and the effect it would have on himself, he had hesitated. What might be the consequence to his heart to give such joy to this woman knowing it would not be his privilege to do so for the rest of his life? If he did wish her to have it, he ought to have given it to

Richard to present to Elizabeth; such would have been proper. In the end, a strong desire for her happiness had won out—along with the selfish wish to be the one to bring it about, if just this once.

"The book you gave Miss Elizabeth," Richard's voice cut into his thoughts, almost as if he had read them. "You have made her very happy."

Darcy shifted uncomfortably atop his mount. "'Tis a loan. And it was only a book."

"Ah, but it was much more than that. It shows that you value her mind. That is very important to Miss Elizabeth."

"I do not value her at all, except as your future wife and my future cousin."

At this, Richard chuckled and Darcy turned his face away so as not to betray the blatant falsehood he has just uttered.

"Well, I am glad you like her. And I am excessively glad you can keep up with her. She has such an exquisite mind, keener than any woman I have ever met. I am no simpleton, yet I often find myself at a loss in our conversations. You shall have to be with us often so that she has someone with whom to debate!"

"When will you propose," Darcy asked mostly to avoid making any commitments he would not be able to keep. Already he was beginning to fear he might have to give up his cousin's company altogether. How was he ever to bear meeting with Elizabeth once she became Mrs Fitzwilliam? It was near enough devastating meeting with her now knowing that had it not been for his damnable pride, it might be him granted the pleasure of courting her.

"As to that, I could not say. Miss Elizabeth will not marry where she does not love, and I do not think she is there."

To this Darcy made no reply. His insides were burning with the shameful hope that Elizabeth might never come to love his cousin and he would never have to witness their marriage, her growing large with Richard's children, bestowing her love and adoration on an eminently worthy man so wholly connected with himself.

Silently, he berated himself. Whether Elizabeth married Richard or not, she would never be his. Even if their courtship did not lead them to the altar, Darcy could never betray his most beloved cousin by entertaining hopes towards the woman Richard had once meant to call his wife. Either way, Elizabeth was lost to him. He would get the better of these terrible, envious thoughts. Richard was as a brother to him, and he wished for nothing more than that dear man's happiness even if it meant Darcy's being miserable forever.

They pulled the horses to a stop outside Colonel Forster's lodgings, dismounted and tossed the reins and a few coins to the boy who rushed out to meet them. They entered the house and were greeted by a very young ensign seated behind a desk who leapt to his feet and saluted when he saw Richard's bright red coat and colonel's insignia.

"At ease, soldier. I am Colonel Richard Fitzwilliam of his majesty's Fifth Dragoon Guard. This is my cousin, Mr Fitzwilliam Darcy. I believe Colonel Forster is expecting us."

"Aye, sir. Of course, sir. If you'd just follow me, please."

The young soldier led the two gentlemen to a small parlour situated at the back of the house which had been converted to a study of sorts. In the middle of the room sat a large oak desk, which took up a majority of the space. Behind it was a fine leather chair and two smaller chairs were placed before it. Behind the desk stood a large cabinet and a sideboard holding several bottles of spirits. Against the wall opposite was pushed a worn sofa. The whole of the room might have fit in one half of the master's study at Pemberley.

"Colonel Fitzwilliam!" Colonel Forster greeted his comrade cheerfully, gesturing them into the chairs before the desk. "Mr Darcy! Can I offer you gentlemen a drink?"

"No, thank you, Colonel," answered Richard. "How is your brother?"

"Quite well, much thanks to you. My family owes you quite the debt of gratitude. My mother gives thanks every day that you were on that battlefield that terrible day. James might not be with us today had you not been."

"'Twas nothing, I assure you. I was only doing my duty, as any soldier might have done."

"Stuff and nonsense!" Colonel Forster turned to Darcy. "Did you know what a hero your cousin is, Mr Darcy? This man saved my brother's life. Have you heard the tale?"

"Indeed, I have heard the, no doubt embellished, story."

"Ha! Indeed! Well, Fitzwilliam, do I hear correctly? You are courting the lively Miss Elizabeth Bennet?"

"The rumours are true, my friend."

"My congratulations. She is a pretty young thing. A little wild for my tastes, but no doubt you will enjoy taming her, eh!" Colonel Forster laughed at his own bawdiness, oblivious to Richard's weak smile and Darcy's scowl and clenching fists. "And what of you, Mr Darcy. Have you set your sights on your own Bennet sister? Your friend seems well pleased with the eldest. What of the middle one? What's her name? Martha? Margaret? Mary! There it is. Oh, she is nothing to her sisters, but still quite lovely in her own right."

"You are wide of the mark, Colonel. My cousin is determined to make a splendid match. A simple country lass, no matter how lovely, will never do for a Darcy."

"Well, I wish you both all the best. Now, I cannot imagine you took time away from your lady to come see me for nought but idle chitchat. What can I do for you gentlemen?"

"Colonel, we have come to speak to you about one of your men, a recent recruit."

"Oh? Who might that be? A Lieutenant George Wickham, perchance?"

The cousins exchange an exasperated look. Richard turned back to the Colonel. "I see he has gotten a jump on us. Seeking to discredit whatever we might have to say against his character, I have no doubts."

"He may have made mention that you two might come telling tales on him. He seems to think himself greatly wronged by you, Mr Darcy."

"I wish I could say I was surprised. Something about a stolen inheritance, if I am not mistaken?"

"Spot on."

Reaching into his coat, Darcy pulled out a folded document. Opening and smoothing it out, he laid it on top of the desk in front of Colonel Forster. As the military man picked it up and perused the paper, Darcy explained.

"I assure you, Colonel, we have ample evidence to support our *tales*, as Wickham puts it. The living he claims I denied him was, in fact, refused. When my father died, Wickham declined any interest in the church and requested compensation in lieu of it. As you can see, he asked for, and was granted, three thousand pounds in addition to the one thousand already bequeathed in my father's will."

The amused smile dropped from the stunned Colonel's face as he looked over the top of the page. "Four thousand pounds?"

"Just so. He expressed an interest in studying the law, though I did not think him serious. Some years later, when the incumbent died and the living fell vacant, Wickham wrote to me declaring his situation to be desperate and requested I now grant him the living he had previous spurned. I felt justified in refusing, feeling my duty towards my father's godson already fulfilled."

"I have no doubt," chimed in Richard, "that we could call forth no less than a dozen credible witnesses to his black character with very little effort."

"No. No, that will not be necessary." Colonel Forster laid the contract down and dragged a hand across his suddenly weary face. "I confess, gentlemen, I am shocked, indeed. Wickham has such a charming, friendly manner. If I had not seen this,"—he gestured towards the document—"for myself and did not know you to be honourable men, I would find this very difficult to comprehend. He is well liked by his fellow soldiers and the neighbourhood."

Darcy leant forward in his seat. "Mr Wickham is talented in making friends wherever he goes. His talents in retaining those friendships, however, are far less honed. He leaves debt, debauchery, and regret in his wake. He ought not to be extended credit in the local shops, loaned any sum of money, or left alone in the company of young ladies, most particularly maids or merchant's daughters."

"Bloody hell," cursed Colonel Forster. Abruptly, the man stood and stomped to the door, throwing it open and shouting for someone named Fernsby. This accomplished, he crossed back across the room to the sideboard and poured himself a healthy measure of brandy, throwing it back in one swallow.

A few moments later, the young ensign who had shown Darcy and Richard in appeared at the door with a warbly "Sir?"

"Bring me Wickham at once."

"Aye, sir." He was gone as quickly as he had come.

"I thank you gentlemen for bringing this to my attention. A regiment of soldiers does not receive a ready welcome everywhere, and it is because of villains like this hiding amongst honourable men. Have you any thoughts for the reprobate's fate?"

A silent conference occurred between the two cousins, wherein they came to a swift agreement. At Darcy's nod, Richard smiled and answered the question.

"Mr Wickham is currently under the jurisdiction of his majesty's army. His discipline is, by rights, your responsibility."

"Very good." Colonel Forster motioned towards the sofa on the back wall and the two gentlemen stood and relocated to where they would not be readily perceived by anyone entering the room. Nearly a quarter of an hour passed with the colonels making small talk as Darcy gazed absently out the window, a thrum of excitement building within as the final moments of being plagued by Wickham closed in.

Voices were heard beyond the door and the three men snapped to attention. The door opened and Wickham came swaggering in, tossing a lazy salute to his commanding officer.

"My good Colonel, how may I be of service?"

"Wickham, close the door." Seeming to sense danger, Wickham's shoulders tensed and his fist clenched before he did as he was told. Darcy took a great deal of satisfaction out of watching the colour drain from his nemesis' face when he caught sight of his former friends seated in his commanding officer's study. Colonel Forster nodded to where the other two men sat. "I believe you are familiar with my guests."

Wickham whirled around to face his colonel and immediately went on the defence. "Did I not tell you? I said they would come and spread their poison about me. No doubt they have told you all manner of vile slander against me."

"I have certainly heard some rather unflattering points regarding your character, Lieutenant," Colonel Forster confirmed calmly.

"You see! They have only proved my words!"

"Interesting choice of words, Wickham. What proof have you to offer to refute their accusations?"

"Proof? What proof can I offer of their hatred for me? They have hated me since we were boys for the great crime of having been born the son of a steward. Darcy, in particular, could never stomach that his father loved me better."

"So, you have no proof? Because these gentlemen claim to have ample. Something about a contract signed by you, refusing all claims to the living you claimed had been stolen."

What colour he had regained from his impassioned speech quickly drained from Wickham's face again. He licked his lips as he sent a venomous glare towards his foes. "Lies. Only further lies."

With a heavy sigh, Colonel Forster picked up the contract and held it out to Wickham. "Then explain this."

When he had taken no more than a cursory glance at the paper, Wickham swallowed hard, recognition plain on his face.

"Shall I also send for the receipts of the debts I own against you, Wickham?" Darcy offered nonchalantly. "It shall only take a day or two. Do you even know how much you have squandered over the years? Would you like to?"

"Or," input Richard, "we might summon the fathers of the countless daughters you have ruined. How many children have you sired, Wickham?"

"Think very carefully, Wickham, before you speak," Colonel Forster warned, his voice as hard as flint. "I do not appreciate being lied to. Now, was there any truth to the narratives you shared with me, and several of your fellow officers, regarding Mr Darcy?"

A muscle twitched in Wickham's cheek and Darcy could see the battle raging within. Admitting his faults would taste bitter, indeed—especially in the presence of his enemies. Through clenched teeth, he confessed, "I may have...misspoke...in some regards."

"I see. Very well. In case you should be tempted to *misspeak* again, you ought to know that Mr Darcy is well within his rights to call in the debts owed to him. Should he do so, you would be required to pay the whole of the amount, or face debtor's prison or deportation." Wickham's eyes widened in panic and Darcy smothered a smile while Richard made no effort to disguise his snicker. "However, seeing as you are under my command, both gentlemen have agreed that the consequences of your deceitful actions will fall into my hands. Make no mistake," Colonel Forster admonished when Wickham's shoulders relaxed a fraction, "should you step one toe out of line, I will not hesitate to recommend Mr Darcy call in every farthing against you.

"Now, from this moment forth, you will be accompanied by at least one other officer at all times. Each quarter, an inquiry will be made at the local shops and your wages will go to satisfy any debts with the merchants of Meryton. Anything which remains will then be granted to you. Debts of honour with any of your fellow militiamen will be your responsibility.

"And, finally, I will remind you that desertion at a time of war is punishable by hanging should you have any thoughts of attempting to sneak away. Even in the militia." He looked to the two gentlemen seated across the room. "Are you gentlemen agreed to these terms?"

"Agreed," the cousins said in unison.

"Wickham, do you understand these terms."

"Yes," the blackguard murmured.

"I beg your pardon? I am your colonel, son."

Straightening his back and snapping his shoulders square, Wickham lifted his chin. "Yes, sir."

"That is better. You may be dismissed to your barracks. You are to remain there until instructed otherwise."

"Yes, sir." With a final, hate-filled look to the two men who had once considered him as a brother, Wickham turned on his heel and left the room, taking with him years of grief, animosity, and hard feelings from the shoulders of his former friends.

Chapter Seventeen

orning dawned upon an excessively frustrated and annoyed Elizabeth. Sleep had proved stubbornly elusive as she wrestled with her thoughts and inconvenient feelings all through the night. No matter how she tried to centre her thoughts on one gentleman, images and musings of another would intrude. Unfortunately, the man upon whom her mind insisted upon dwelling was most assuredly not the man who was currently paying her court.

When she could stand to remain abed not a second longer, she threw the bedclothes aside and hurriedly dressed in a plain walking gown. Deftly twisting her long, dark curls into a simple knot at the back of her head, she glared at her reflection as she secured her hair in place with pins.

"That is quite enough out of you, Miss Lizzy," she chastised herself in the mirror before turning and fleeing the house and her thoughts.

Setting out at nearly a run, she made Oakham Mount her destination. If the exertion of the climb did not free her thoughts, the views from the summit had never yet failed to calm her troubled mind and deliver much needed clarity.

Except, once she reached the base of the mount, she was reminded of the last time she had come to this place. Almost as if he stood before her, she could picture Mr Darcy in his dark riding jacket, tan trousers, tall Hessian boots, and his fine beaver hat. A hint of a smile had played at his lips and the corners of his eyes. Lord, but he was a handsome man!

"Oh, stop it!" she shouted at the vision. With a swish of her skirts, she turned and marched up the slope of Oakham Mount. A mere memory of a man would not defeat her. It was madness to even entertain such thoughts. What was she doing borrowing such trouble? Her mother was not entirely unjustified in her worries regarding her second daughter. Despite being considered a famous local beauty, no gentleman had ever taken a serious interest in her. Besides having no dowry, her impertinent manners, fierce independence, and unabashed intelligence did not appeal to the male sex. She was fortunate the Colonel had taken an interest in her; why could she not be content with that? Was she so vain she would covet the notice of his taller, much more attractive cousin, as well?

Such notions were not only foolish, they were dangerous. Mr Darcy was a wealthy, high-born member of the ton. Men such as he did not choose wild, dowerless daughters of insignificant squires to wed. The future Mrs Darcy would no doubt be an elegant, accomplished heiress who brought fortune, connexions, and, likely, a title into the union. She would never be an outspoken country miss with a propensity for dirtying her hems on long solitary rambles and could only claim adequate skills on the pianoforte. Allowing this absurd attraction to run amok could only end in heartache and upend her world.

Not a moment after she thought it, did the world truly tilt on its axis as the toe of her walking boot caught the very same troublesome root as had given her such delicious memories on her last climb. Only this time, there was no strong, gallant gentleman to take her into his arms and prevent her from spilling on the path. Her hands took the brunt of the impact as she crashed rather inelegantly to the ground with a very undignified "Oof!" Her knee met with a rock to painful results and she ended flat on her stomach.

With a deep groan, Elizabeth rolled over onto her back and stared up at the thinning golden canopy above. A moment's evaluation assured her that she was not seriously injured. Her palms stung slightly, but her gloves had thankfully provided some protection against the rocky ground, and her knee smarted something fierce. Otherwise, she was unharmed. Mostly, she was just grateful there had been no witnesses to her inexplicable clumsiness.

A laugh bubbled up from she knew not where and soon grew until she was gasping for breath. She had taken this path hundreds of times; knew it as well as the hallways within Longbourn. Never had it given her such trouble! Then comes along one handsome gentleman and twice she trips over a root she had ever known to avoid.

"Oh, Lizzy Bennet," she chided herself as she wiped away tears of mirth, "you are a hopeless creature."

Climbing to her feet, Elizabeth brushed out her skirts and resumed her trek, though with a better attitude than before. She was focusing, she concluded to herself, on the wrong problem. Mr Darcy was an incredibly good looking, intelligent, intriguing gentleman; it was hardly surprising she would be captivated by him. Fighting her attraction for him was a futile endeavour. Even should she marry the Colonel—or any other man for that matter—she would likely always consider his cousin the most interesting and handsomest man of her acquaintance.

Perceiving a man as well favoured, however, by no means equated to love. Such feelings did not mean that she could not grow to love Colonel Fitzwilliam with a deep and abiding fervour despite her opinions on his cousin's fine countenance. Rather than endeavouring to rid herself of her inconvenient fascination with Mr Darcy, she would seek instead to find common ground with his cousin, focusing upon his finer virtues and that which she already admired in him. As she sat atop Oakham Mount, gazing unseeingly over the scene laid out beneath her, she came upon the perfect solution—if only she could muster the courage to see it through!

🌿

*E*lizabeth stopped outside the stable doors and took a deep breath. *You are being silly, Lizzy. They are just animals. Very large, very strong animals.* Before she could talk herself out of it, she pulled the door open and stepped into the dimly lit stable. For a moment, she only stood there, allowing her eyes to adjust to the low light and breathing in the scent of the hay and the horses. When her heart had slowed a fraction, she took a few tentative steps nearer the first stall where Nelly was kept. That was probably the best place to start; Nelly was so old and docile, Papa often complained she was not even worth selling.

Reaching out a trembling hand to Nelly's nose, Elizabeth had just grazed the soft velvet when a muffled sniffling caught her attention from deeper in the stables. So tense was she, the unexpected sound startled her and she quickly pulled back her hand, pressing it to her chest where her heart had very nearly escaped its confines. Squinting into the shadows, she could just make out a dark object nestled in the hay piled in the corner. Taking several slow steps towards the object, she determined the object was a person in a dark gown.

"Mary?"

At Elizabeth's voice, Mary scrambled to extricate herself from the hay as she tried to inconspicuously wipe her eyes on her handkerchief.

"Oh, Lizzy. I-I did not know you came here." Her voice was thick and strangely high-pitched and she would not raise her eyes to meet her sister's.

"I do not often. Or at all, really," Elizabeth answered. "Dearest, what is the matter?"

"No-nothing. Nothing is the matter. I am well."

"Mary," said Elizabeth gently, "I can see that you are not. Will you not tell me what troubles you?"

Mary clasped her hands in front of her and pressed her lips together. She was quiet for several moments as she looked anywhere but at her sister. Elizabeth was sure Mary would refuse to answer when suddenly she spoke, the words erupting from her lips in a rushed, anguished cry.

"Why...why am I...so-so unlovable?" She burst into tears as her face fell into her hands and her shoulders shook with her sobs. Elizabeth had never seen her middle sister display so much emotion and was momentarily at a complete loss as to what she ought to do. Suddenly realising herself, she wrapped Mary in a tight embrace and held her close.

"Oh, darling, you are *not* unlovable!"

"Of course, I am!" Mary mumbled through her fingers against Elizabeth's shoulder. "Even *Mr Collins* did not want me!"

"I should think that cause to rejoice rather than weep." The jest came out before Elizabeth could think better of it and she cursed her flippant tongue as Mary only sobbed harder. "Oh, Mary. Forgive me. That was thoughtless of me."

They stood there for several minutes, Elizabeth feeling acutely awkward. She had never had very much to do with Mary and only now did she realise what a failing that had been. More often than not, she actively avoided her next younger sister and Mary's pedantic moralising. They had little in common and Elizabeth had always supposed that Mary was as content with their relationship as she was. Besides, she had always been closest with Jane. Surely, her sister understood that and would not begrudge their bond. After all, Mary had...well, she always...there was Kitty and Lydia and...oh, dear. All at once did Elizabeth see the unfairness of five sisters pairing off. She had never meant to neglect Mary, or give her the impression she was unloved. A rush of affectionate gratitude flooded her heart for the Colonel's kindness towards her middle sister the other day.

When the tremor in Mary's shoulders calmed, Elizabeth gently nudged her to lift her head and gave her as sweet a smile as she could muster. "Did you...did you wish to marry Mr Collins?" She tried so very hard to keep the revulsion at such a thought off her face and out of her voice. How well she succeeded, she could not be sure.

"Yes! No. Oh, I do not know." Mary threw up her hands, narrowly missing Elizabeth's cheek, and turned to sit heavily on a nearby stool. "Our cousin is not handsome, nor clever or lively. He is vain and vacuous and conceited and has no respect whatsoever for the female sex." Mary took a deep breath. "No. I do not wish to marry him. But if even a man such as that believes I am not worthy, what hope have I that any man will ever want to make me his wife?"

"You have it entirely wrong, Mary. If Mr Collins could not recognise what a wonderful woman you are, that is proof only of his stupidity, not your unsuitability. You would make an excellent parson's wife." Mary bristled and Elizabeth wondered at it. "Would that not please you, dear?"

"I think the church a fine occupation for any gentleman but I do not think I should like to be a clergyman's wife."

"Would you not?" Elizabeth asked with no little amount of surprise. When Mary merely shook her head, she pressed further. "But you are always quoting scripture and reading all those religious texts."

Mary heaved a great sigh as she stood and wandered over to one of the stalls. A long, dark face poked over the wall and Mary absently stroked the white stripe along the horse's nose. "I am not beautiful like all my sisters. I thought...I thought that if I could distinguish myself in some other manner, perhaps I might be better noticed. I do not wish to be as silly as Kitty and Lydia and could not hope to match Jane's sweetness nor your cleverness. You are the only one Papa does not consider to be excessively silly. I had thought that if I read some of his books, he would notice me as he does you." Mary's countenance fell and her shoulders slumped. "Only, I did not understand them."

"Oh, Mary. I did not understand them, either."

"You did not?" Mary asked.

"Not at first." Elizabeth smiled at the look of wonder on Mary's face. "I would read a passage and then discuss it with Papa and he would help me to understand what I had read. I should be happy to discuss Papa's books with you if you were inclined to try again. And I am sure Papa would love to share his knowledge with you as he did me. Papa and I have canvassed nearly everything in his library. I believe it would be a delight for both of us to have some fresh discussion." As she considered all she had just learnt of her sister, a new thought struck Elizabeth. "Is that why you have always practised the pianoforte so diligently? To be noticed?"

"Yes, little good though it did me. Everyone still enjoys your playing to mine though you hardly ever practise."

Elizabeth hesitated a moment. It had been many years since she had held such an intimate conversation with her middle sister and greatly wished to say only the right things. "Mary, do you...do you enjoy music?"

Mary shrugged. "It is a worthy diversion and I am pleased whenever I master a new piece."

"That is a good start, but, Mary, music ought to come from the soul! If you are not moved by the music, how can you expect to move others?"

"I...I had not thought of it in such a way."

"Shall we make a bargain?" Mary nodded and Elizabeth smiled. "If I teach you to find enjoyment in literature and music, will you teach me to ride? I know it is an activity the Colonel greatly enjoys and I am determined to learn."

"Very well, I agree," said Mary. She gave a soft sigh before adding, "The Colonel is a fine man. I am very happy for you, Lizzy."

"He *is* a good man, Mary," answered Elizabeth, perhaps a little too vehemently. In a gentler tone, she said, "And I know there is just a such a man out there for you."

"I hope so," was Mary's wistful reply.

Chapter Eighteen

"Kitty, may I borrow this?" Elizabeth asked as she pulled a lovely rose-coloured gown from her sister's closet.

"But my gowns will not fit you? I am taller and you have more bosom than I," Kitty replied with a pout.

"I would happily trade you some of my bosom," Elizabeth laughed, "for a touch of your height! You cannot know how maddening it is to be forced to look up at all my younger sisters! Besides, 'tis not for me, but Mary."

"Mary?" Lydia cried, sitting up from where she had been lounging lazily on her bed. "Lord, what on earth would Mary do with such a gown? 'Tis far too pretty for the likes of her."

"She will wear it to Aunt Phillips' card party tonight," Elizabeth answered simply, though she knew very well the effect such information would have on her youngest sister.

"What?! Aunt Phillips' card party? No one told me of this! I must prepare!"

Leaping up from the bed, Lydia ran to the closet and began pulling gowns out haphazardly, dismissing each one as insufficient. Carefully, Elizabeth laid the borrowed gown upon the bed to avoid wrinkling it, then walked over to the closet, grasping Lydia by the arm and pulling her away.

"Nobody told you, Lydia, because you are not to go."

"What?!" the young girl screeched. "Of course, I am to go! The officers will miss me most dreadfully!"

"And we will inform them that you are but a fifteen-year-old girl no longer out in society."

"Oh, Lizzy! You would not!"

"I would. It is nothing more or less than the truth."

With a petulant pout on her lips, Lydia eyed her sister as if gauging the seriousness of her threat. Flipping her hair, she spun back to the closet. "Mama will let me go, so it is of little matter."

"You may think that, Lydia," Elizabeth quipped, picking up the rose gown, "if it gives you pleasure. But it is not only Mama you must convince, but Papa, also. If you wish to have any hope of seeing an assembly before you reach your majority, you had best learn how to behave in a rational manner and cease all this disgraceful flirting and chasing after anything in a red coat. Not one of them can afford to take a silly country miss with no dowry to wife. But as I can plainly see you are not listening to a word I say, I shall keep my breath to cool my porridge."

With that, she picked up the gown and swept from the room, pleased to see Kitty, at least, appeared a little troubled and more thoughtful than was her custom. Whether her words would have a lasting effect on the impressionable young girl, one could only guess. But Elizabeth had other matters to attend to for the moment.

Slipping down the hall, she entered Mary's room with a flourish, the borrowed gown held out before her like a priceless treasure.

"This," she said, "is what you shall wear tonight."

Mary's eyes widened at the sight as Jane exclaimed her approval. "Oh, Mary! 'Tis perfect for you! This colour will look absolutely marvellous against your skin."

"But, but, but I have never worn anything like this," Mary protested. "I am uncertain that I can."

Elizabeth gave her sister a reassuring smile. "Of course, you can. I chose this gown not only for the lovely colour, but for the higher neckline. And with a lace fichu, it will be perfectly modest. I have no wish to make you uncomfortable, dear Mary. Only to make you feel as beautiful as you are."

"They are correct," a timid voice said behind them. The three eldest sisters turned around to find Kitty hovering in the doorway. "It is an excellent colour for you."

Jane sweetly invited Kitty to join them, which she did after ensuring she would not be in the way. For the next hour, the four sisters laughed and talked as they worked together to prepare Jane, Elizabeth, and Mary for the party. Though Kitty looked on wistfully, she did not utter one complaint as she helped Mary pin her hair in a much more flattering style than her customary severe bun. Soft curls framed her round face as a simple ribbon wrapped around the crown of her head. When all their preparations were complete, Mary stared at her reflection in awe.

"Oh, I do not know. Is it not a sin to indulge in vanity?" she asked in a strangled voice.

Elizabeth wrapped an arm around her shoulder, laughing. "It is not vanity simply to be beautiful, Mary. 'Tis only vanity to place too great an importance upon one's beauty. Look at our dear Jane." She shifted Mary to look upon their radiantly beautiful sister. "There are few who can boast such pulchritude, yet you would not consider Jane vain or sinful, would you?"

"No. Of course, not."

"You see? Beauty in and of itself is not a sin. We must simply take care as to not fall into the trap of believing it to be our only, or even most valuable, virtue. Beauty fades, my dear. We must ensure that when it does, we have other, more worthy, accomplishments to sustain us."

The three sisters were seen graciously off by Kitty, as Lydia had stomped resentfully to her room having failed to talk her parents round to her own way. As it was a novel experience, she did not take kindly to being denied. Though Mrs Bennet twisted her handkerchief violently as her favourite child's screams carried down the stairs, she nevertheless held firm. Elizabeth took further comfort from Kitty's thoughtful expression. When Papa invited her to sit with him in his study and learn to play chess after bidding his elder daughters goodnight, Elizabeth could have kissed him.

Upon entering the Phillips' home, she was forced to temper her smile at Mary's reception. Aunt Phillips at first mistook her for Kitty, then exclaimed her disbelief aloud when she looked again. As they made their way further into the room, their neighbour's eyes followed the ladies' every move, though Elizabeth was certain their scrutiny was for one sister. Sam Goulding brazenly stepped forward, greeting them enthusiastically and bowing especially deep over Mary's hand. Several officers approached; rather than asking after the absent Kitty and Lydia, each requested an introduction to this mysterious beauty. Unused to such notice having ever been the invisible daughter, she kept close to Jane and Elizabeth.

Elizabeth knew a slight twinge of remorse when Mr Collins—who had departed Longbourn early for Lucas Lodge to escort his betrothed to the party—stepped away from Charlotte to stare slack jaw and wide-eyed at the *plainest* Bennet sister. For once, words failed him; yet his roaming gaze spoke of a touch of regret for having passed over his cousin for consideration for the role of Mrs Collins.

Occupied in observing the attentions Mary so deservedly received, Elizabeth had not noticed that it was she who was the primary object of interest to one particular gentleman in the room. But when her sister had retired to the relative safety of the pianoforte with Maria Lucas, Elizabeth was at leisure to seek out other company. Looking about the room, she was startled to see Mr Wickham standing amongst a group of officers, his gaze fixed unwaveringly upon her person. A strange sort of smile played at his lips that sent a shiver of unease down her spine.

Though she endeavoured to put the man from her mind and enjoy the company of her friends and neighbours, she could not escape the awareness of his scrutiny. Indeed, he seemed almost to position himself in such a way as to be always within her line of sight; and each time her eyes landed upon him, he was staring unabashedly back at her. She was comforted somewhat when nearly an hour passed and he made no attempt to approach her.

Just when she was beginning to relax and had convinced herself that he meant to avoid her the whole of the night, she stood from the whist table and turned around to find him standing directly behind her. Hoping it to be nothing more than a coincidence, she gave him a curt nod and made to move on but he stood firmly in her path.

Mr Wickham bowed and flashed what she was sure he believed to be a most winsome smile. Perhaps if she had not been forewarned by Colonel Fitzwilliam, she might have agreed. He was certainly handsome and carried himself with an air of unaffected confidence, but she looked upon it all with distrustful eyes.

"Miss Elizabeth, what a joy to see you here tonight."

"Mr Wickham." As she could not honestly claim any pleasure in meeting him, she said nothing further.

For several minutes, he spoke of nothing more exciting than the weather or the state of the roads. Reluctantly, Elizabeth was forced to acknowledge to herself that he was a skilled conversationalist, making even such mundane topics as these seem interesting. Still, she wished to be away from him and sought an opportunity to do so politely when he turned the subject.

"I do not see Colonel Fitzwilliam and his cousin here tonight."

"No. I understand they had a previous engagement," was all she would say.

"Ah, yes. I am sure that is the reason."

He looked away then with an expression that spoke to his having more he wished to say but struggled with whether he ought. Elizabeth was on the cusp of excusing herself, having no wish to hear anything more from this man when he spoke again in a most urgent manner, looking around to ensure he was not overheard.

"Miss Elizabeth, I would be remiss—I could not forgive myself if I did not speak. I must warn you as to the true character of the two gentlemen of whom we have just spoken. They are, neither of them, what they seem. Having the benefit of the best tutors and instruction, they may present themselves as honourable gentlemen but are, in truth, the furthest thing from.

"I have been much in the company of high-born gentlemen with little enough to occupy themselves but the spending of their fortunes and looking down upon those who have not been born to the same privileges as they. Often enough, the diversions they indulge in are innocent enough, gambling, boxing, the taking up of mistresses. But there are those who seek other means to satisfy the tedium of high living."

He looked away as if it pained him to continue. But when he turned back, his face was set with determination. "I am given to understand you have been an object of interest to Colonel Fitzwilliam. That you are engaged in a courtship with him."

"I am."

"It pains me to inform you, madam, that the Colonel has no honourable intentions towards you. It is a game he and his cousin play. Singling out a young woman from a lower stratum with little enough protection and engage her affections. Just when the young lady anticipates a proposal, she is left abandoned and heartbroken, on occasion even ruined, whilst they laugh about their conquests at their club over brandy and cigars. You are hardly the first to fall victim to their cruel schemes, and will surely not be the last."

Elizabeth regarded the lieutenant with suspicion, Colonel Fitzwilliam's warnings ringing in her head. "You are very kind to wish to put me on my guard, sir."

"I can see you doubt my claims. Perhaps you have been warned against me." Though she fought to keep her expression impassive, he must have read the truth in her eyes. A rueful smile crossed his lips. "Ah, yes. I should have known they would seek to discredit me before I could expose them. They have been to speak to my colonel, as well. Though I have sought to make something of myself, and can boast of my success, I am to be punished all my life for the reckless misdeeds of my youth. Those who have had all the advantages of education and wealth will hold my humbler beginnings against me all my days. Am I never to escape their hatred and prejudice? Can they not accept that a man can change?"

His performance was convincing, from the tremble in his voice to the clenching of his fists and teeth to the agitated way he averted his eyes. Still, she was not swayed. *He is a practised deceiver* Colonel Fitzwilliam had warned her.

"Mr Wickham," Elizabeth sighed, but he did not let her finish. His next words settled uneasily in her chest, speaking to the concerns she herself had felt.

"Tell me you have not questioned the Colonel's interest yourself. Despite your manifold attractions, the dowerless daughter of an insignificant country squire could hardly be considered a suitable match for the son of an earl, even a second son. But I can see you are not to be persuaded. I am sorry for it. But I had to try. Forgive me for intruding on your time."

With a swift bow, he turned away and was gone. Elizabeth watched him go with relief and sought out better company. Though she was determined not to give any credence to his words, they nevertheless needled at the back of her mind like a misplaced hairpin.

By the time she readied for bed later that night, the poison with which he had laced her thoughts had begun to take effect. If she had considered it so incredible that a mere gentleman such as Mr Darcy could look favourably upon her, how much more improbable ought it be to capture the attention of a son of nobility? Colonel Fitzwilliam had painted Mr Wickham as a despicable liar—yet Mr Wickham had said the very same of his accuser. Who was to be believed?

The Colonel and his cousin had given her no cause to question their integrity. Colonel Fitzwilliam had never been aught but amiable and agreeable. Though Mr Darcy had not given off the best first impression, she had come to respect and even like him. Indeed, perhaps a little too much. Was it all an act?

She recalled the first meeting with Mr Wickham on the streets of Meryton. He had presented himself as everything respectable and charming. But for the Colonel's caution, she might still consider him so. Yet when they had come face to face, it had been Mr Wickham who had fled the presence of the other gentlemen. Did that not speak volumes as to his guilt? Or had he simply been avoiding the company of two powerful men who held umbrage against him?

Whilst she ruminated on the troubling puzzle of who was lying to her and who she ought to trust, Jane entered her bedchamber to bid her goodnight. Seeing the agitation on her face, she instantly inquired as to her wellbeing. When Elizabeth had related all that Mr Wickham had told her, her sister was amazed. Gentle-hearted Jane was sure there must be some kind of misunderstanding wherein all parties might, in time, be found blameless.

"I cannot believe the Colonel could be capable of such wilful deceit. He has been everything charming and amiable, and he looks upon you with such fondness. I am sure he must be sincere in his attachment. Though, I cannot believe Mr Wickham could be so dishonest. Perhaps he has been deceived by another?"

"And who has deceived that party, dear Jane? Or shall we be obliged to think ill of somebody down the line?"

"Laugh all you wish, but you will not laugh me out of my opinion. Only think of what a disgraceful light it places Colonel Fitzwilliam and Mr Darcy. It paints them as the very worst of scoundrels, ruining young ladies' reputations for sport."

"I confess, that is difficult to imagine."

"And, just think, how could Mr Bingley not know of such despicable behaviour? Surely, he would not maintain the acquaintances if they were so very bad?"

To this, Elizabeth had no response. Was it more likely that Mr Wickham had blatantly lied to her or that Mr Bingley was being grievously imposed upon by those whom he called friend? Or, though she would not burden her dear sister with such thoughts, was Mr Bingley as much a black-hearted villain as his friends, if they were so very bad?

Blowing out her candle after Jane had bid her goodnight and left her alone, Elizabeth lay in the darkness, desperately trying to be reasonable. She had known the Colonel above a month and had been given no reason to doubt his integrity. But for her own insecurities, their courtship appeared legitimate. Of his cousin, she had less reason to be suspicious. Still, Mr Wickham's words would not leave her in peace.

Just before sleep finally claimed her, she determined there was nothing else to be done but to be on her guard until she could be assured of all three gentlemen's characters. When next she saw the Colonel, she would confront him with her concerns. If he could not satisfy her, she would put a hasty end to their courtship.

Strangely, the thought that Mr Darcy could hold any portion of blame gave her more discomfort than believing the Colonel might only be sporting with her. She forcibly pushed those thoughts to the side, certain no good could come from exploring their meaning.

Chapter Nineteen

uesday arrived much sooner than Darcy was prepared for. Riding alongside the carriage from Netherfield to Longbourn, where the party would gather for their excursion to Betterston Castle, he wondered if it was too late to make his excuses and refuse to go.

When he had agreed to this scheme of Richard's, there was nearly a week's time to inure himself to the idea of spending an entire day in Elizabeth's presence, witnessing her bright smiles, hearing her musical laugh, watching Richard woo and make love to her. He had felt himself equal to the task then, certain he would be master enough of himself well before the day arrived.

How naïve he had been. The bewitching woman filled his every idle thought by day and tormented his dreams by night. He was torn between sweet visions of holding her in his arms, imagining what pure bliss it would be if she were his, and horrifying images of watching her marry his cousin. He had grown half-mad with both craving her presence and wishing he had never met her.

But he could not bow out now. Even if he could manufacture an excuse the company would accept as valid—and Richard would not see through in an instant—if he returned to Netherfield, Miss Bingley would certainly insist on joining him. Already tortured by his own mind's preoccupation, the last thing he needed was to spend an entire day subject to that lady's fawning ministrations with no escape.

So, he would go. He would put on his usual mask and avoid Elizabeth as much as he was able. Perhaps he might seek out a path to explore on his own, away from the others. Perhaps he would find a shady spot beneath a secluded tree and nap the day away. Lord knew it had been years since he had indulged in such indolence and he wondered if it was not just what he needed.

They turned into Longbourn's sweeping drive and Darcy felt his anxiety heighten. Down the lane, standing before the house, stood four ladies and a gentleman, awaiting their party. Only one garnered his attention. Standing between her two sisters, Elizabeth stood out as brightly as a beacon. At least to him, she did. To his right, he could hear Richard babbling away about something which had caught his notice in the distance. How his cousin could have a mind for anything but the glorious woman who awaited him at the end of the lane, Darcy could not fathom. He had half a mind to knock the idiot off his horse.

When they came to a stop where the Bennet ladies, Miss Lucas, and Mr Collins waited, Darcy was instantly aware of something amiss. Elizabeth greeted them civilly with her sisters, but her smile was polite at best and did not reach her magnificent eyes. It did not escape his notice that she met no one's gaze and held herself slightly apart from the others. Until Richard approached, she made no attempt to engage with anyone.

"May I have a word with you, sir?" she requested of her suitor, though her tone and arms folded tightly across her chest provided little room for refusal.

"Of course. I am at my lady's command." Richard gave a gallant and exaggerated bow, but Elizabeth was not amused. She only raised one of those exquisite brows and turned to lead him a few yards away where they might speak in private. Pausing only a fraction of a second to send Darcy a look of confusion, Richard followed.

Darcy watched the couple through the corner of his eye. It was poor manners to invade their privacy in such a way, but he could not help himself. It was absolutely absurd, but he could not stop himself envying Richard's position. What he would not give to be the one on the receiving end of her displeasure that he would have the privilege of being the one to make right her concerns; that it might be he who was granted the blessing of her adoration when all that troubled her was resolved by his hand.

Their conversation was not an animated one. Elizabeth held her head high with her hands placed defiantly upon her hips as she briefly spoke her piece. He could glean nothing from Richard's expression as his cousin listened patiently. When it seemed she had finished, Richard visibly sighed, shaking his head. They exchanged conversation back and forth but their vague gestures gave nothing away. Once, they both looked to where he stood, and Richard seemed almost amused. After only a few minutes, Elizabeth's face lit up with her beautiful, bright smile and Darcy could look on no longer.

"Not yet even engaged," Miss Bingley snickered over his shoulder, "and already she berates him like a common fishwife. The poor Colonel. But then, what else was to be expected from courting such a girl from such a family."

Both irritated and grateful for the distraction, Darcy turned to face her. "Whatever their quarrel, it can be nothing to either of us." Glancing back towards the couple, he saw they had finished their conversation and were walking back to the group, Elizabeth's hand wrapped around Richard's arm. Swallowing down his jealousy, he said, "And it appears as if all is well, in any case."

"Tell me you are not concerned for the fate of your cousin? Attaching himself to such a family? Such a mother-in-law! You would do him a great kindness by giving him a hint of your disapproval."

"But I do not disapprove. Not in the least. Miss Elizabeth is a lovely, lively young woman who will make a delightful addition to the Fitzwilliam family." He did not add that he wished with all his heart that it might be through himself that she would become connected to his relations. "Mrs Bennet is a mother with a concern for her daughters' futures. I have seen just such behaviour, and worse, amongst members of the ton with much less provocation. Only it is excused by virtue of their position and fortune. Furthermore, I wish for nothing more than the happiness of my cousin. Should he find that happiness with Miss Elizabeth, a governess or a milk maid, I would not interfere." Though this was a gross exaggeration, Darcy was tired of the conversation. He gave a slight bow and stepped away just as Richard and Elizabeth joined the party.

"Shall we be off then?" Richard inquired enthusiastically. "I am keen to begin exploring."

General assent was given and the ladies were assisted into the carriage, as Mr Collins climbed atop to sit in the driver's box explaining, in as many words as possible, that he did not ride. Darcy did not envy the occupants within. Miss Bingley was already in a sour mood, having only agreed to attend at Bingley's insistence. The evening previous, she had treated them all to exactly what she thought of *tramping about an old pile of rocks with such tedious company.* He doubted she would make a pleasant travelling companion, especially as she had not understood why the Hursts had been allowed to cry off simply because her sister had been feeling unwell of late.

Mr Collins would certainly be no better. The buffoon had not ceased speaking since the carriage came to a stop at Longbourn—and had probably been speaking long before they arrived—completely oblivious that no one paid him any attention. Elizabeth had described her friend Miss Lucas as a sensible, intelligent woman. Darcy wondered if those words had different meanings in Hertfordshire if the lady was willing to shackle herself to such a man for life. He would wager a handsome sum the carriage was currently filled with Miss Bingley's snide remarks and Mr Collins nasally droning.

"Are you not curious?" Richard's voice broke into Darcy's musings. He had hardly noticed they had been riding silently side by side for several minutes.

"About?"

"My conversation with Miss Elizabeth, of course."

"I assumed it was a matter between a courting couple and none of my business." He turned his face away, hoping to put off his cousin. Now that it was before him, he found that, no, he had no wish to know what affairs Elizabeth would discuss with her suitor.

"Normally, you would be absolutely correct. Only this time it does concern you."

Wild thoughts began circulating in his head. Guilt-filled hope and shameless imaginings stuttered around in his chest. Had she been as affected by him as he was of her? Did she intend to throw Richard over? Might he have a chance to gain the affections of the only woman who had ever piqued his interest so thoroughly?

A moment later, he cast off these thoughts. Of course, he had no chance. Even if Elizabeth declared she would never have his cousin and professed her most ardent love for himself, he could never betray Richard in such a manner.

"It seems we did not manage to scare Wickham straight, after all."

"What?" It took a moment for Darcy to pull his thoughts away from Elizabeth and process Richard's words. "What do you mean?"

"The ne'er-do-well approached Miss Elizabeth at a party the same day we paid him a visit. Spun a wild tale of debauchery and deceit."

"What?! He confessed—"

"Against us." Darcy could not find the words to express his incredulity and affront so Richard continued. "Apparently, you and I get our jollies from courting innocent young ladies, engaging their affections then breaking it off, leaving fair maidens heartbroken and ruined. Breaks up the monotony of being so rich and spoilt, you see."

"Rich and spoilt," Darcy muttered under his breath. "I had no idea I had it in me."

"Ha! Neither did I!" Richard laughed. "Miss Elizabeth wished to know what my intentions were."

Darcy twisted quickly in his saddle, causing Sleipnir to protest against the reins. "She did not believe the scoundrel?"

"Believe is a strong word. There was some concern, and I cannot say I blame her. We have been acquainted only a short time and she will not be the only one to question why the son of an earl would take a fancy to a young lady with no fortune or family."

"Perhaps at first," said Darcy, gazing through the carriage window to where Elizabeth sat, her musical laughter drifting out the open window. "One need only spend a few moments with Elizabeth to understand why any man would be drawn to her."

Distracted as he was, Darcy did not notice Richard's raised brow at this statement. "You were not."

Tearing his eyes away from the lovely vision before him, Darcy cleared his throat. "No, I was not. Am not."

"Oh, but I thought it was no secret why any man might be drawn to her."

"Any man who is not bound by duty to his estate and family."

"Balderdash. Miss Elizabeth will make an excellent mistress to any estate. Already she is better acquainted with the business than I."

"Well?" asked Darcy, steering the conversation away from anything which could cause him to say aught else that would betray his admiration for a lady for whom he had no right to possess such feelings.

"Well, what?"

"What did you tell her about your intentions?"

"Oh. I assured her that I had nothing but honourable intentions, of course. That, but for you and Georgie, there is no one whose happiness I desire more than hers."

Therein lie the rub, did it not? Elizabeth's happiness was rapidly becoming paramount to Darcy, equal to his concern for Richard's. Yet, the happiness of those two souls would likely mean misery for Darcy for the rest of his days. If Darcy were to achieve his greatest happiness, it could only come at the expense of his most beloved cousin.

"I encouraged her to write to her aunt in London," Richard continued, thankfully oblivious to Darcy's turmoil. "Such a reputation would be easy enough for the lady to uncover. And, of course, I offered to provide whatever evidence she required of Wickham's depraved nature. Then, perhaps most of all, there is the fact that my mother would box my ears and skin me alive if ever I were to behave in such a despicable manner! In the end, I believe I was able to convince Miss Elizabeth that we are both fine, upstanding gentlemen. You more than I, certainly."

Darcy said nothing for a moment, grateful to be exonerated yet it felt a hollow victory. At last, he decided to address something which had been bothering him.

"Why do you call her that?"

"What? Miss Elizabeth?"

"Aye."

"'Tis her name," Richard answered with a shrug. Did he purposefully avert his gaze or was he simply watching the road?

"But you are courting her. It would not be inappropriate to use her Christian name. Not amongst family."

"Well, as you say, I am merely courting her. It is not as if we are engaged. We are still coming to know one another."

"But cannot familiarity breed affection?"

Richard threw a hand into the air. "For God's sake! I do not know what you want, Darcy! We have not spoken of it."

"Forgive me, Richard. 'Tis hardly my business."

Companionable silence fell between them for the remainder of the journey. Yet Darcy could not help but feel that if he were granted the privilege of courting a woman as special as Elizabeth, he would cherish the right to caress her name on his lips as often as he was able.

Chapter Twenty

B etterston Castle was just as Elizabeth remembered it, except perhaps a little smaller. She had not been here since she was a girl. Then it had seemed an enormous, enchanted fortress filled with untold stories of dragons, knights, imprisoned princesses, and evil stepmothers. She, of course, had never played the part of the helpless maiden; Elizabeth much preferred the role of brave rescuer or vanquisher of the fiery guardian. On occasion, the great beast was her friend, and she, its keeper.

It was much less impressive from this side of childhood and, for but a moment, Elizabeth mourned that carefree dreamer she had once been. Everything had seemed much simpler then. She had ever imagined one day she would meet a handsome man; they would fall immediately in love and, of course, live happily ever after. She glanced out the carriage window to where Colonel Fitzwilliam was sitting atop his great black mount, looking down upon Mr Darcy who had already dismounted. If only someone had told her that real-life romance did not play out as neatly as the fairy tales her father read to her in his library. Still, she was no less averse to adventure today than she had been all those years ago.

The carriage door was opened and Mr Collins bounded out, immediately expressing his admiration for the scene before him, but forgetting entirely the ladies who remained within the vehicle. Mr Bingley took up the gentlemanly task of handing out the ladies, helping Charlotte and then his sister to debark. But when Jane gave him her hand, all else seemed to vanish before him as he walked away, tucking Jane's gloved fingers around his arm. Elizabeth and Mary exchanged amused looks before Mary alighted from the carriage.

A large gloved hand appeared before her when Elizabeth moved to the door. Laying her own in it, she looked up into Mr Darcy's handsome face. His hand wrapped securely around hers and she felt a tingling warmth spread through her fingers and up her arm. Despite the unseasonable warmth of the bright autumn day, a shiver coursed down her spine all the way to her toes.

"Are you warm enough, Miss Elizabeth?" Darcy asked her in a gentle, almost intimate tone.

Though she knew she ought to look away, she was held captive by the piercing, unfathomable depths of his dark eyes. "I...yes. Yes, thank you. I..."

"There we are!" Richard beamed down at her and she pulled her hand away from his cousin's so quickly, her glove nearly slipped off. "Forgive me for not handing you down, Miss Elizabeth. I am afraid I have not yet mastered a faster means of dismounting from my horse."

"Oh," Elizabeth breathed, still reeling from the effects of Mr Darcy's touch. "Think nothing of it, sir."

"I am grateful to you, Cousin, for being on hand in my stead yet again! Perhaps you ought to be the one conducting this courtship!" Colonel Fitzwilliam joked and Elizabeth attempted to join him in his merriment, though her laugh came out as a rather feeble huff.

Mr Darcy merely turned away, clearing his throat. He mumbled a gruff, "Well, shall we?"

The party set out as one large group, meandering about the ruins. Soon enough, however, separations began to occur. Mr Collins expressed a wish to see the ruined rectory and led his betrothed in that direction. Colonel Fitzwilliam suggested taking the path which led up a small hill behind the castle. Jane, who was not so great a walker as her sisters, demurred and was joined with alacrity by Mr Bingley. Miss Bingley, who had thus far clung to Mr Darcy's arm and showed little desire to relinquish him, was at last persuaded to stay behind, owing to the fine satin gown and dainty slippers she had insisted on wearing that day. The remaining four carried on, Elizabeth on Colonel Fitzwilliam's arm and Mary on Mr Darcy's.

They were a merry party, many thanks to the efforts of the Colonel; though Elizabeth chafed slightly at the slowness of their pace and Mary and Mr Darcy appeared uncomfortable with one another. But her companion managed to keep the conversation light and even Mr Darcy was induced to flash a smile from time to time.

"Did you come here often as girls?" Colonel Fitzwilliam asked the sisters.

"Not often, no," said Elizabeth. "No more than two or three times, perhaps."

"Oh, but the last time," Mary smiled, "we came with the Lucases. I was but nine and Lizzy ten. After, John and Robert insisted on playing knights when we returned to Meryton. They made Jane and I sit atop the woodpile behind Lucas Lodge and pretend to be princesses locked away in a tower."

"What of you, Miss Elizabeth?" the Colonel asked. "Were you made to play the damsel in distress, as well?"

The sisters shared a look then broke into merry laughter.

"Oh, Elizabeth refused to be rescued!" Mary answered in her stead. "She had climbed up a tree insisting she was the dragon, which the boys would have none of. When John came to liberate her, she climbed higher and higher until even he would go no further. But then, Lizzy could not get down either, though she would not admit it!"

"Oh, my! What happened? Were you able to rescue yourself?"

"After a manner," Elizabeth evaded a true answer.

"We had to go for Papa—" Mary began.

"Which vexed me greatly. I was quite determined to be my own hero."

"By the time we returned with Papa, Lizzy had managed to get down to the lowest branches, but..." Mary looked to her sister.

"On the verge of victory, I stepped on my skirts and fell from the tree, landing right at my father's feet and dislocating my shoulder."

"Oh, no!" Colonel Fitzwilliam cried through his laughter.

"Even before it was healed," Mary gasped through her own merriment, "she was trying to convince Papa to allow her to wear breeches whenever she climbed trees!"

The entire party burst into laughter and Elizabeth felt a thrill of delight seeing her sister at such ease and in good spirits. When she looked upon the Colonel, she felt a wave of affection for the dear man. He was kind and jovial and she regretted ever giving even the slightest heed to the despicable Mr Wickham's lies. Whether the emotions she experienced were what she ought to feel towards a man she would marry, she could not be sure. How could she be? Their acquaintance was still young and she had, after all, never been in love. Perhaps this was what love felt like?

Then she turned her gaze on Mr Darcy and knew instantly she was wrong. He looked upon her with a devastating smile and a look which she could not interpret yet sent her heart skipping and caused her insides to warm. Her cheeks flushed and her breath caught in her chest. No look from the Colonel had ever affected her in so powerful a manner, his touch did nothing for her. What it might mean, she did not wish to think on.

"What say you to a change of partners?" Colonel Fitzwilliam suggested and Darcy's smile faltered. She watched his cravat shift as he swallowed and he looked away. "I have held you back long enough, Miss Elizabeth, and I should like to come to know your sister better."

"Would we not be better served to turn back?" asked Mr Darcy sounding somewhat desperate. He even took a few steps in the direction they had come.

"Not at all! I know you are as keen as I to press on, you have only the greater ability. Do not pity me, Cousin! I will not allow it."

"Oh, but I would not wish to abandon you," said Elizabeth in a tremulous voice. "Certainly, we might find a path we can all take."

"Nonsense! You have been very kind to indulge an old invalid, but now I beg of you to go, explore to your heart's content and take my surly cousin with you. I assure you, he is an excellent walking companion. Much quicker than I, that is for certain."

She did not know how to refuse further without giving away her own troublesome feelings or offending Mr Darcy, and he made no more objections; though he did not look comfortable. So, the two bid their companions adieu and set off together further up the hill.

They walked along in silence along a tall stone wall. He did not offer his arm for which Elizabeth was grateful; she was not sure what would happen if she took it or if she could countenance any more disturbances to her sensibilities! She chanced a glance up at him a time or two, only to catch him pulling at his cravat or rubbing the back of his neck. Whether his discomfort stemmed from a distaste for her company or if he was as affected by their closeness as she, she could not say.

She was certain, however, that if they did not break the silence, the awkwardness would soon become unbearable.

"And how do you find Hertfordshire, sir?" she asked her companion. "Is it much different from Derbyshire? I have never been."

He seemed startled by her voice but quickly recovered himself. "It is very different. Your county is much flatter and feels...tamer, somehow. Derbyshire is full of mountains and moors. Pemberley sits in a low valley surrounded by rugged peaks and wild forests."

"It sounds beautiful. You must never wish to leave it."

"I love my home dearly. To me, it is the most beautiful place in the world." He hesitated a moment then said, "Though Hertfordshire is not without its own beauties."

He did not look at her as he said this, but the tips of his ears pinked; she felt a flush creep across her cheeks in response. Was Mr Darcy flirting with her? He ought not to be, yet she harboured a secret hope that he was. Unlike his cousin, Mr Darcy was not naturally flirtatious; if he flirted at all, it was likely quite by accident! But, as such, it was also more genuine than the pretty practised words tossed about by men such as Colonel Fitzwilliam or Mr Bingley and, therefore, more worth the earning. His quiet, hesitant flirting filled her with a greater thrill than any of the Colonel's blatant flattery ever had.

Unsure of how she ought to respond—unsure even of her own feelings—she took a slow, shaky breath.

"Oh? Any beauties, in particular, you have grown fond of?" The words tumbled out of her mouth before she had the chance to think better of it; she certainly had not intended to sound so coy!

"Oakham Mount," he answered instantly, fixing her with that piercing gaze of his. "I think I shall always think on that place with fond remembrance."

"Yes, it has ever been a favourite of mine, as well. Though, lately, I find it has grown even dearer to me."

Mr Darcy looked at her then with an expression that very nearly broke her heart. It spoke of longing and desire, of love and promise. But there was also anguish, guilt, and regret for he had no right to make any declarations, nor had she any right to accept such.

Though they were near-strangers, having shared only a handful of conversations, there could be no denying the electric force which pulled them together. Whenever they were in company together, she was inexplicably, powerfully aware of his presence and every move. Even before they had been introduced, the moment he entered the assembly rooms that first night, her eyes had been drawn to him and something within her had shifted.

She had attempted to deny it; to bury her fascination under her indignation to his slight at the ball. Still, he took up far too much space in her thoughts to be able to claim herself indifferent—even before his fine apology at Netherfield. For sure, much of her contemplation of the gentleman had been frustrating and confused, but it had been near constant.

How long they stood there, gazing into one another's eyes, she could not say with any degree of accuracy.

"Miss Elizabeth, you ought not to provoke me to say things I should not."

"Then you really ought not to provoke me into wishing to hear what you would say."

"Elizabeth...I cannot..." He swallowed and took a step nearer, pulling off his glove as she held her breath. He raised his bare hand to hover over her cheek and she felt her skin tingle in anticipation of his touch. She knew not what was happening or what the consequence might be, neither could she bring herself to care overmuch at that moment. All she knew was that if he did not touch her, she would burst.

"Mr Darcy, Lizzy! Hurry! Colonel Fitzwilliam has taken a fall!"

Chapter Twenty-One

*urried footsteps were heard just before Mary burst into view around a bend in the path. Elizabeth spun around as Mr Darcy took a step back, shoving his hand back into his glove. Though nothing had actually happened—he had not even touched her—sharp guilt pierced her gut. She was being courted by a very worthy man, and here she was, *flirting with his cousin!*

"Come quickly! I think he has injured his leg," Mary cried.

Mr Darcy's eyes met Elizabeth's for but a moment before he grabbed her hand and pulled her along back down the path. They raced around the corner of the castle and saw the Colonel on the ground just off the path, clutching at his leg and groaning.

"Richard!" Mr Darcy called, dropping to his knees at his cousin's side and pulling Elizabeth with him. Only then did he release her hand. Thankfully, she had greater matters of import to concern herself with than to mourn the sudden loss of his hand wrapped around hers. "What happened?"

"I should think that would be obvious," Richard answered through gritted teeth. Clearly accustomed to his cousin's irreverent manner, Mr Darcy ignored the sarcasm and looked to Mary.

"I am uncertain, sir. He dropped his walking stick and it rolled into that ditch." Mary pointed to a low point some ten feet away. "I went to fetch it for him when he cried out. When I turned back, he was on the ground." She covered her pale cheeks with her hands and shuddered. "I ought to have been more attentive!"

Mr Darcy reached up and gently squeezed her arm in a comforting, brotherly fashion. "No, Miss Mary. There is nothing which you might have done to prevent this. I thank God you were here to fetch help." He turned back to his cousin. "We need to get you back to the carriage. Can you walk?"

"I can certainly try. Where is my stick?" Mary cried out, having forgotten the wayward cane in the excitement. "Never mind that. Give me your hand, Darcy."

Mary went to fetch the recalcitrant walking stick while Mr Darcy helped the Colonel to stand; though he cried out in agony when he attempted to carry any weight on the injured leg. Mr Darcy pulled his cousin's arm around his shoulder, supporting the weaker side. With nary a hesitation, Elizabeth slipped under the Colonel's other arm and wrapped it around her neck.

Colonel Fitzwilliam immediately protested, "Miss Elizabeth, I am too heavy for you!"

"Nonsense. I am stronger than I look."

"This is unnecessary," added Mr Darcy. "I can manage him."

"No one is questioning your strength, sir. But we must get the Colonel back to Netherfield as quickly as possible so that he may be seen by a doctor. Surely, the task can be carried out much more speedily if I assist. Now, both of you cease arguing and allow me to help."

"Says the lady," the Colonel grumbled, "who would not be helped down from a tree."

Elizabeth threw him a saucy glare from under his arm. "When I was but ten years old, sir. Tell me, have you no greater wisdom than a young girl? If that be the case, then I weep for the state of our army."

"Let us just get on with it. This is humiliating enough as it is."

Slowly, carefully, the party made their way back down the path to the front of the ruins where Jane and the Bingleys waited. When they came into view, Jane cried out in dismay and Mr Bingley hastened to relieve Elizabeth of her burden. Miss Bingley seemed oblivious as to the true concern and inquired only after Mr Darcy's well-being, trying in vain to convince him to relinquish his place to a footman. A coachman was dispatched to fetch Mr Collins and Charlotte whilst they determined the most efficient manner of conveying the Colonel back to Netherfield.

It was quickly decided that he could not ride and would require a bench to himself in the carriage to best keep his leg stable. This, however, meant at least one lady would have to give up their place for the journey back as the four remaining ladies squashed together on one bench. While the three sisters each offered to sacrifice her seat, Miss Bingley made no pretence whatsoever of being so magnanimous.

"Miss Eliza is, as we all know, a very great walker. I think the choice is obvious," said she imperiously.

"Oh, but would you not wish to remain with the Colonel, Lizzy?" Jane asked.

Though it galled her to agree with Caroline Bingley, Elizabeth had to admit the lady was right. "Of course, I would. But Miss Bingley is right. I am far more suited to walking the eight miles back to Longbourn than any of you. It shall not take me long, two hours at the very most."

Still, Jane was uneasy. "But already it is growing late."

"All the more reason that we ought to get the Colonel loaded in the carriage and all of you on your way that I may begin. The longer we stand around here discussing the matter, the later shall I arrive."

"I shall ride on ahead now," declared Mr Bingley, already climbing atop his horse, "and send for the doctor." This excellent thought earned him a look of pure adoration from Jane, who watched him ride away with a beatific smile on her face, concern for her sister seemingly temporarily forgotten.

Taking advantage of her compliance, Elizabeth ushered her sisters into the carriage after Miss Bingley. With great care, Mr Darcy helped his cousin to climb in and situate himself across the rear-facing bench.

"Darcy, you will accompany Miss Elizabeth, will you not?" Colonel Fitzwilliam asked after Mr Darcy had climbed back down. To Elizabeth he added, "It would ease my conscience a great deal knowing you are accompanied and protected."

"Of course, I will see Miss Elizabeth safely returned," said Darcy, though he barely glanced in her direction.

"That is very kind of you, sir, but surely unnecessary. The Colonel ought to be your priority."

"Miss Elizabeth, I could not call myself a gentleman if I allowed you to walk eight miles alone when it is no imposition to me to go with you. Bingley and Mrs Nicholls will see to my cousin in my absence. I should be more in the way than of assistance."

He sent her a look full of meaning. No doubt he felt the same as she; they ought to spend as little time alone in one another's company as was possible. There was little to be done about it now, however. It was too great a distance for a young lady to walk alone, Elizabeth could begrudgingly admit, and there were no other gentlemen to offer their assistance. Mr Bingley had already gone ahead and Mr Collins...she would be better off walking alone.

"Very well," Elizabeth conceded. "I thank you, Mr Darcy."

Mr Collins and Charlotte soon arrived and, after a good deal of the former's fussing over his noble patroness's august nephews—he would not be easy until he was assured of the wellbeing of *both* gentlemen—the carriage was loaded and prepared to be off. Elizabeth's sisters, friend, and suitor each offered their assurances that the carriage would be sent back as soon as they had been delivered to Netherfield; Miss Bingley directed her own pointed promises for a swift rescue directly to Darcy.

"Perhaps you might like to sit atop Sleipnir—" Darcy began to offer but Elizabeth quickly cut him off.

"No! Thank you," she hastened to add. "Forgive me, sir. I do not ride and certainly not on so large a beast as that!"

"I assure you, Sleipnir is a very good horse. I would never allow any harm to come to you."

"Nevertheless, sir. I will not be moved in this. I shall either walk beside you or wait right here for the carriage to return."

Mr Darcy conceded with a short bow. She breathed a sigh of relief, exceedingly grateful he did not press her. The idea of revealing to him just how deep ran her fear of the animal greatly disturbed her, though she could not think why. She had shared her aversion with the Colonel with nary a hesitation. She knew only that she wished for Darcy to have the best opinion of her; which was only natural, of course. If she married Colonel Fitzwilliam, he would become her cousin and she certainly did not wish her new family to think ill of her.

"You are in good hands, madam," Colonel Fitzwilliam assured her. "There is no one in the world I trust more."

Just before Darcy turned away to tie his horse behind the carriage beside his cousin's, she was dismayed to see his face set in a stony scowl. It was unsettlingly knowing she was the cause of his displeasure. She much preferred inspiring his breath-taking smiles and adorably awkward flirtations. He was a quiet, reticent man but she had seen glimpses of a passionate nature beneath his impeccably tied cravat and gentlemanly manners. There was a fire in his eyes when he looked at her that, she was quite certain, had the power to warm her on even the coldest of days.

When he had held her in his arms on Oakham Mount, he had made her to think of things a young maiden ought not; passionate embraces and deepening kisses, loving endearments whispered in the darkness, cold winter nights passed in a warm bed, wrapped in a pair of strong yet surprisingly gentle arms.

More than this, it made her think of forever. Of wedding flowers and bells, arguing with her mother over lace and bonnets, tearful goodbyes to her family, blissful wedding trips, quiet, domestic evenings reading in a vast library before a roaring fire, beautiful curly-headed children with dark eyes and the most adorable dimples.

But for the day he had asked for a courtship, Elizabeth had never thought of Colonel Fitzwilliam in such a way. She had never imagined him as her husband, never dreamily pictured how he might propose or what their life together might be like. She had never even thought to use his Christian name, even in her thoughts! It was not as though the Colonel did not engender any feelings within her. She liked him; she did! He would, in all likelihood, make a marvellous husband. He was kind and amiable, funny and intelligent. If she had never met his cousin, she would probably think of him as the very best of men.

The carriage pulled away, though Elizabeth hardly noticed. Somewhere in the periphery of her consciousness, she heard the goodbyes and clattering of the wheels. Vaguely, she noted a look on the Colonel's face which she might have described as smug satisfaction at any other time but was most likely stoic determination not to display weakness before so many ladies. But this was all happening somewhere outside of her. Within, all her attention was for Darcy. When he had ceased to be *Mr* Darcy to her, she could not say, but she could no longer bear to think of him with such formality.

The point was, she *had* met him. He had come into her life and neatly discarded her every preconceived notion of what she would wish for in a husband. Gone were the garrulous, amiable Colonel Fitzwilliams or Mr Bingleys of the world, and in their place stood only quiet, steady Darcy. He was not only the standard of her heart, she feared he was the one and only. Could there possibly be another such man?

Oh, dear. Though she had not meant to do it, though she had no idea as to how it had even come about, she had fallen in love with the Colonel's cousin.

Chapter Twenty-Two

"There is no one in the world I trust more."

Could there be words better designed to torture and shame him? If only his cousin knew the thoughts rolling around in Darcy's head at this very moment, or the thrill he felt at being alone in the company of this woman, Richard would be well within his rights to call him out.

Only years of gentlemanly training and practise had made him accept Richard's request to accompany Elizabeth. Years of training and his damned desperate need to remain near her. For the first time in his life, he cursed his privileged upbringing. Whether he begrudged his deeply ingrained sense of honour more for his current torturous situation or for not being the sort of man who could encroach on another man's territory, he could not immediately say.

Even still, he felt as the vilest of cads. Nothing but Miss Mary's timely—or horridly untimely, depending on how one was inclined to look at it—arrival had stopped him from kissing his cousin's lady. He wished he could claim that all sense and consideration had vanished in that moment, leaving nothing but Elizabeth and her tempting perfection. But that would be the grossest of lies. When he had pulled off his glove to caress her bare cheek, he had known he ought not. But his body seemed to have a will of its own, ignoring the warnings screaming in his head and acting upon those desires he most wished to heed.

He ought to be grateful for Miss Mary's blasted interruption—and in so many ways, he was. Yet, he could not help but feel that one kiss from Elizabeth might have compensated for any consequences which might have fallen from his actions. He would certainly have lived to regret it someday, but he would forever have known the taste of Elizabeth Bennet's lips.

Walking down the road beside her now was certainly not helping matters any. The light breeze danced with her skirts and her hems frequently brushed against his legs. It was entirely innocent, yet felt deeply intimate. That same breeze brought her intoxicating floral scent to his nose. It was devastatingly heavenly. He considered moving to her other side to end the delicious torture, but could not think of a valid reason for doing so. He certainly could not tell her that he was dangerously close to pulling her into the hedgerows that he might kiss her senseless.

"I believe we must have some conversation, Mr Darcy, else I fear this walk shall feel interminable." Her melodic voice washed over him and he was inordinately grateful she could not read his thoughts and desperately hoped he did not appear as flushed as he felt. "Perhaps I could comment on the fineness of the weather, then you might remark on evenness of the road."

Swallowing down his last lust-filled thoughts, Darcy searched his brain for a response that was not about how he would carry her off to Gretna Green at this very moment if he thought her amenable. He glanced back the way they had come in a bid to stall for time and was surprised to see that, though it felt as if they had been walking for ages, they could not be more than half a mile from the castle ruins. When no topic presented itself to his muddled brain, Darcy felt it safest to default the choice of topic to her.

"If you will tell me what you most wish to hear, I shall happily oblige." Elizabeth's steps faltered slightly and he remembered too late their earlier flirtatious conversation. When he heard his words as she must have, he brought them to a complete stop. "I meant only...I did not mean..." Forcing the air from his lungs with a noisy exhale, Darcy wondered how on earth he had managed to make the situation more awkward. Truly, he must have a talent for it.

Before he could think of anything to say which would not make matters worse, the tinkling sound of her bright laughter broke through the tension. He looked down and was nearly knocked off his feet by the enchanting sight of her laughing eyes and beaming smile. What she found so diverting, he could not say, but her mirth tickled the corners of his lips until a deep chuckle escaped despite his efforts to contain it.

"Mr Wickham is not as clever as he believes. No one could ever believe you to be a rake," said Elizabeth, the teasing curve of her lips softening her words.

"Thank you, I think."

"Oh, it is assuredly a compliment, sir." She tilted her head at an enchanting angle, twisting her lips in a way that made him feel he was about to be thoroughly teased. "'Tis interesting considering the company you keep. The manner in which Mr Bingley and Colonel Fitzwilliam flirt with abandon, one would think you ought to be a proficient."

"Are you saying I am a poor flirt?" Gesturing with his arm, he signalled that they ought to continue. He certainly had no wish to remain still whilst having this particular conversation.

Darcy was sure she made a valiant effort to temper her laughter but he could hear the smile in her voice. "Only that you are very clearly not practised at the art. Of course,"—she raised one finger to her lips as if she had only just come upon an idea. This had the added effect of drawing his notice to her exquisite mouth and it required great effort to pull his gaze away and listen to her words—"perhaps 'tis all an act. Perhaps you only affect being a clumsy lover to set yourself apart from your competitors."

"And is it effective?"

"Mr Darcy, you must know a lady would never confess such a thing. Even if I do find it rather charming."

The blush which coloured Elizabeth's cheeks at this coy hint rendered her so incredibly beautiful, Darcy knew at once the battle had been lost. In vain had he struggled, it simply would not do. No longer could he deny, to himself at least, that he was completely, ardently, and irrevocably in love with this woman. The power of this discovery was such that his hands shook with a great need to reach out and take her in his arms. With determination, he clenched his fists and swallowed down the words he desperately wished he could say and forced out the ones which needed to be said, though it may kill him.

"I am leaving Hertfordshire."

As if the heavens themselves were angered by his words, a deafening clap of thunder exploded around them. Elizabeth jumped at the sound and looked up to the sky. Unbeknownst to them both, dark clouds had gathered above them, choking out the bright afternoon sun. Within moments, a torrential rain had begun to fall upon them.

Quickly looking about, Darcy spotted a lone oak tree standing in the adjacent field. Without a second thought, he grabbed her hand and they began running towards it. With his hands around her waist, he helped her to climb over the stile and quickly followed, praying he would soon forget the delicious feeling of her body in his hands—while simultaneously hoping he never would. Hand in hand, they dashed across the field to the relative protection of the ancient tree.

Chests heaving from the exertion—or possibly the emotion—they turned to look upon one another, paying the rain no more heed than if it had been but a trifling sprinkle.

"You are leaving?" she asked, her voice trembling.

"I must. I cannot stay here and watch...I cannot."

"I cannot marry him."

The joy he felt at these words was quickly snuffed by his cousin's words echoing about in his head. *There is no one in the world I trust more.* He released what was left of his hope in a long, slow breath.

"And I cannot marry you."

He watched her eyes cloud over with hurt and cursed himself for being the author of it. Yet, what else could he do?

"I see." She swallowed and looked away, swiping furiously at the tear that fell onto her cheek. "It *was* just an act. Nothing more. I ought to have known a man such as you would never stoop to marry a woman such as I. I did know it! But I...I...I need to go."

She quickly turned and made to run away despite the torrential rain pouring around them, but he reached out and grabbed her by the wrist, pulling her back and wrapping his arms around her, holding her tightly to his chest. She gave a feeble struggle but quickly gave up the fight and sagged against his chest.

"No, Elizabeth," he murmured urgently into her ear. "It was no act. You mistake me, entirely. I ceased to care for society's expectations and familial obligations some weeks ago. I had not known you a fortnight before I knew you to be special beyond measure. But, still, I was too late. Richard had already laid claim to you."

Elizabeth pressed her hands against his chest and attempted to extricate herself from his embrace, but he held tight. "'Laid claim to me?' I am a woman, Mr Darcy, not some common horseflesh a man can simply take ownership of."

"Forgive me, Elizabeth. Forgive me. I did not mean to be crass. I simply meant..." He released her then, growling his frustration as he turned away, pounding his fist into the trunk of the tree. "He is my dearest friend," he all but shouted. "The nearest thing I have ever had to a brother. But for my sister, there is no one I love better." Slowly, he turned back to face her, making no attempt to disguise the affection and the anguish which was tearing him apart. "I cannot hope to marry the woman he had meant to make his wife."

She was silent for several moments, gazing upon him with those glorious eyes. What she sought, he knew not, but soon, her face softened.

"I understand," she said so quietly he barely heard her over the sound of the driving rain.

"You do?"

A tiny huff of a laugh escaped her lips as she wiped at the tears that mingled with the raindrops which fell from the brim of her bonnet. "I do. Jane is my dearest sister. If Mr Bingley were to offer for me, I could never accept, even were it my dearest wish. I could never be happy if it would bring her pain."

"Elizabeth." Darcy stepped forward and took her face in his hands, desperate to make her see. "You must understand, if there was no Richard, if it were a matter only of my heart, I would beg for your hand here and now. Nay, would have begged you to accept me weeks ago. You are everything I could have ever wished for in a wife and so much more."

"That, I suppose, will have to sustain me all my life."

The war raged within him once again, but this time he knew there would be no winning. If he must leave, never to set eyes upon her again, he would, for once in his life, indulge his own whims. For her words rang true within his heart, as well. If he could not have Elizabeth, he knew with every fibre of his being he would never marry. There could never be another to fill the place in his heart she now occupied.

"All my life, I have been a man of honour and principle, bending my wishes to meet duty and obligation," said he, his voice thick with emotion as he lowered his face to hers, stopping only a hair's breadth away. "One moment of weakness will neither destroy nor define me."

Hungrily, he pressed his lips to hers and the world around them shattered into oblivion. A voice in the back of his head told him he must be gentle; cautious of her maidenly sensibilities. But he heeded it not. If this was to be his one and only taste of Elizabeth, he would ensure it would be a moment he would never forget for as long as he lived.

Again and again, he attacked her lips with increasing fervour. He wrapped his arms around her and spread his hands across her back, holding her tightly to him as he devoured her lips, flavoured with the salt of her tears. He was master enough of himself to be alert for any signs of protest from Elizabeth, but she gave none. Her small hands clutched desperately to the lapels of his coat as she seemed to be trying to pull him even closer.

When her lips parted and her hot breath caressed his skin in invitation, his knees very nearly gave out.

Deepening the kiss, he committed every sensation to memory. The warmth of her hands against his chest. The velvety softness of her tongue. The taste of her lips. The floral scent that clung to her skin and left him feeling more intoxicated than an entire bottle of his finest brandy. The sound of her soft whimpers in his mouth. This would be a moment he would relive every day for the rest of his life.

A muffled cry was the first reminder that there was a world beyond Elizabeth Bennet. It had been so faint, Darcy was sure it had been nothing more than the call of a bird or the creaking of the old oak tree. When he heard it a second time, Elizabeth stiffened against him and pulled her head back. He tried to follow her, keenly feeling the loss of her lips against his and wishing the kiss never to end, but she stayed him with her hand against his chest.

"Did you hear...?" she began to ask.

"Lizzy! Mr Darcy!" drifted softly across the field on the wind.

They both looked towards the source of the sound. With the pounding of the driving rain and their passionate distraction, neither had heard the approach of the carriage on the road. Standing beside it under a large umbrella was Elizabeth's sister, Miss Mary, waving her arm at them.

Elizabeth gasped and stepped out of his embrace, reaching up to straighten her drooping bonnet. He knew it was only proper, but the loss of her nearness nearly gutted him all the same. This perfect moment was at an end, and he was not at all prepared for it.

"Wait here," he said and ran out into the rain across the field. Taking the umbrella from Miss Mary, he handed her into the carriage and went back for Elizabeth. Not a word passed between them as they made their—rather slower than was necessary—way to the road. What was to be said? These were to be their last moments together, and nothing that came to his mind seemed to capture the significance of the occasion. Under the pretence of sharing the shelter of the umbrella, he wrapped his arm around her shoulders and held her tightly to him. Elizabeth's hand laid against his side as if she, too, was reluctant to break the connection with him. It was all that was available to them and said volumes more than any words ever could.

"We went all the way to the castle," Miss Mary informed them when they had seated themselves inside the carriage. She passed them both thick rugs to dry off and warm themselves with. "When we did not find you, we turned back. That was when I spotted you, um...beneath the tree."

"It began to rain," said Elizabeth, sheepishly and rather unnecessarily. "So, we took shelter."

Pretending to adjust his long legs, Darcy reached out across the carriage under the rugs and tapped Elizabeth's foot, but did not pull it away. He was immensely gratified when she rested her ankle across his boot.

Miss Mary informed them that Richard had been delivered safely to Netherfield and had recovered so much as to enter the house under his own power, with the aid of his stick, of course.

"Would you like to go see him, Lizzy?" Darcy thought he detected a hint of censure in her tone but chose to ignore it. He turned his gaze out the window and stared moodily at the passing scenery as he awaited Elizabeth's answer.

"Oh, surely if there is no real danger to the Colonel, I had best return to Longbourn and change. I will be of no use to anyone if I catch a chill from remaining in wet clothes too long."

Nothing else was said as the carriage carried them to the Bennet's home. When they arrived, Darcy climbed down and first handed out Miss Mary. When Elizabeth laid her hand in his, he gently squeezed her fingers, the chasm which had erupted in his heart widening with each passing second that brought them closer to their final separation.

She turned to him but seemed unable to meet his gaze. She spoke to his cravat. "Thank you, Mr Darcy, for...for everything. I will never...never forget your kindness." She glanced to where her sister had stepped away, most assuredly to give them a mote of privacy. Taking the smallest of steps forward, she spoke in a low voice. "I know you will wish to speak to your cousin. If you would be so kind as to wait. He deserves to learn of my decision from me."

The honourable, gentlemanly thing to do would be to walk straight to his cousin and confess all that had happened beneath the oak tree. To confess having fallen in love with his lady. But Elizabeth was right. It was her prerogative to end their courtship as she saw fit and Richard deserved to hear her explanation. Darcy felt his admiration for this spectacular woman grow and he could do nought but agree.

Swallowing down the despair that was creeping up his throat, Darcy bowed over her hand. Glancing around to ensure no one watched, he turned over her hand and pressed his lips to her soft palm. Hearing her breath hitch was nearly his undoing. Before he could lose his head—and any more of his heart—he nodded his farewell to Miss Mary, sent one final, longing look to Elizabeth, then boarded the carriage and left without a look back.

Chapter Twenty-Three

Jane arrived at Longbourn shortly after Darcy had quitted it with a radiant smile on her face which brightened upon seeing Elizabeth safely at home. She brought with her news that Colonel Fitzwilliam seemed to have suffered no lasting damage to his leg and had professed his eagerness for the ball two days hence.

It was, perhaps, Elizabeth's good fortune that her family had the upcoming ball to occupy their thoughts and discussion over dinner that night; in their noisy exuberance, no one noticed her uncharacteristic melancholy. Kitty and, most especially, Lydia loudly bemoaned not being allowed to attend, begging their parents to reconsider. Mr Bennet took a good deal of entertainment from goading them along, teasing that they might be allowed to attend an assembly in ten years or so if they had learnt to show a little common sense by then.

For once, Mrs Bennet paid her youngest daughters little heed, but waxed long of her expectations of having two daughters soon to be married to such fine, wealthy gentlemen—

and one the son of an earl! Jane said little but stared distractedly into nothingness with a blissful smile on her face.

Mr Collins babbled on endlessly of his love of dancing and the great enjoyment he anticipated in standing up not only with his excellent betrothed, but all of his fair elder cousins. As no one listened to him, he chose to interpret their lack of response as eager acceptance of his hand for a set each.

No one noticed that Elizabeth spoke not at all, but sat pushing her food around her plate, stifling sorrowful sighs and quietly sniffling. No one, of course, but Mary who watched her sister with concern throughout the meal.

When Elizabeth claimed fatigue from the long day, no one questioned her wish to retire early. She was sitting before her dressing table mirror, lost in decidedly heart-breaking, if delicious, memories when a soft knock sounded on her door. Pulling her dressing gown tightly about her, she called out for her visitor to enter expecting Jane who was a frequent evening visitor to her chambers. She was, therefore, surprised when Mary slipped into her room.

She did not say anything, only leant against the door, chewing on her lip as she looked expectantly at her sister.

"Do stop looking at me like that, Mary," Elizabeth sighed to her sister's reflection in the mirror. She was struggling to keep her emotions in check at the moment. "I am in no humour for lectures at present."

"I did not come to lecture you, dear Sister. I came to see that you are well."

"Well?" Elizabeth gave a little laugh, though there was no humour at all to be found in the matter. "No, Mary. I am not well."

Mary looked for a moment as if she knew not what to say or do to comfort her sister. Then her eyes grew wide and she gave a small gasp. "Mr Darcy. Did he...did he...*impose* upon you?"

Spinning around in her seat, Elizabeth quickly set Mary's mind at ease. "No! No, not at all. Mr Darcy's attentions were,"—she took a deep breath and released it slowly as she remembered the heavenly feel of his lips caressing hers—"they were very much welcomed."

Realising too late what she had said and how inappropriate was such an admission, she looked contritely towards Mary, expecting a rebuke at the very least if not a stern lecture on proper ladylike behaviour. But her sister appeared neither disapproving nor as if she were preparing to pontificate. Rather, she looked concernedly confused.

"Are you torn?"

"Torn?" It took a moment for Elizabeth to understand her meaning, having been caught off-guard by the unexpected response. "Oh, you mean between the Colonel and Mr Darcy? No, I am not torn."

"Then you are not in love with Colonel Fitzwilliam?"

"Sadly, no," Elizabeth sighed.

"You are sure?" Mary asked, a strange expression dancing across her features as she crossed the room to sit on the bed. Elizabeth knew not what to make of it.

"I am sure. If I loved the Colonel, truly loved him as I ought to love the man I would marry, no other would have the power to touch my heart, or even to come near it."

"And, Mr Darcy?"

Elizabeth sighed long and deep. "And Mr Darcy has laid claim to my heart, my mind, and my soul."

It was strange. Though she had baulked at the words earlier, she now felt she understood what it meant to be a woman claimed. Even if they could never be together, even if she never again laid eyes upon him for as long as she lived, she knew she would forever belong to Fitzwilliam Darcy. With very little effort, he had imprinted himself upon her heart and entwined himself into the very make-up of her being.

"I do not understand," said Mary. "Does Mr Darcy not return your feelings? Because, I must say, if he does not after what I witnessed this afternoon, then I have a decidedly poor opinion of the gentleman."

Elizabeth could not help a small chuckle at her sister's righteous indignation on her behalf. "I agree he would be a very undeserving young man if he had kissed me as he did and did not return my feelings. But,"—Elizabeth turned to gaze dejectedly into the mirror—"he loves me."

"Oh, well. Um, yes. Yes, I can see why this would be upsetting to you. I rather tire of rich, handsome men falling in love with me, as well."

"Oh, Mary!" cried Elizabeth with a watery laugh, marvelling at this sarcastic side of her sister she had never seen. She quickly sobered as the first of her tears began to fall. "He loves me, but he cannot marry me when I have been courted by his dearest cousin and friend. It would be tantamount to my accepting Mr Bingley's hand knowing of Jane's feelings."

Before anything more could be said, another knock was heard and Jane entered. Elizabeth swiped at her wet cheeks as Mary jumped from the bed to greet her eldest sister. Jane showed only the slightest surprise at finding her middle sister in the room but she smiled brightly at them both. Having no desire to dampen her most deserving sister's happiness, Elizabeth sent a plea for Mary's silence, which received an acknowledging nod.

"Oh, what a day it has been!" Jane exclaimed, falling back onto Elizabeth's bed. "So much excitement to be had! Oh!" She quickly sat up and looked apologetically at Elizabeth. "Though I am sorry the Colonel was injured. And that you were made to walk so far with Mr Darcy. That must have been awkward."

"Not at all. He is a very fine gentleman," Elizabeth said evasively. Then she turned the subject. "But you seem to be in high spirits, dear Jane. Do you have something to tell us? Has Mr Bingley spoken?"

Jane pulled her lips in between her teeth in an attempt to temper her smile. "No, he has not spoken. But I believe he soon will. I have been reluctant to allow myself to hope, he is such a fine gentleman and could have any woman he wished. I was sure his feelings did not go beyond friendship."

"And now? What has changed your mind?" Mary asked.

Looking nervously between her two sisters, lingering especially on Mary, Jane seemed reluctant to speak. At last, after being assured of their secrecy, she looked about the room as if afraid someone might be hiding in the corners and whispered, "He kissed me."

As soon as the words left her mouth, her hands clamped tightly over her lips. Shocked that her very prim and proper sister would allow any gentleman to so much as kiss her hand without an understanding, Elizabeth stared in amazement. Even as she marvelled at Jane's daring, she felt Mary's eyes boring into the side of her face. Deliberately ignoring her own discomfort, she pressed Jane for the details.

"After we arrived at Netherfield and the Colonel was situated and Mary had left to fetch you and Mr Darcy, there was little enough to do. Mr Jones had already arrived and was looking after the patient. Miss Bingley went off with Mrs Hurst to discuss some matters over the ball and Mr Hurst was nowhere to be seen. So, Mr Bingley asked if I should like to walk in the garden."

"A walk in the garden?" cried Mary. "Jane, you had been walking with him all afternoon!"

"Yes, I know. But we had been with Miss Bingley the whole time and I was so far from objecting, that I accepted at once. It was so very sweet, walking side by side. He spoke to me of his home in York and balls and parties he had attended in London. He is looking forward to hosting Christmas in his own home for the first time and he told me of the festivities at fine homes in London he has attended.

"We soon found ourselves under a sweet little arbour and he looked into my eyes and told me I was the most beautiful creature he had ever beheld. I thought he was going to propose to me right at that very moment but he leant down and pressed his lips to mine. He pulled away so quickly, it was over almost before I knew what he was about, but it was so lovely!"

Elizabeth and Mary exchanged looks. Elizabeth wondered if her sister was thinking the same as she. She hoped Jane had left out some of the more salacious details for it seemed a rather lacklustre tale, especially as compared with her own experience with first kisses. But she could not seem to find the words to ask in a way which would not cause Jane offence.

"What happened next?" she asked carefully. "Did Mr Bingley say anything?"

"Oh, well then it began to rain. When we returned to the house, Mr Jones had finished his exam of Colonel Fitzwilliam and wished to speak with Mr Bingley. I waited in a parlour until Mr Darcy arrived and I was able to return home in the carriage." Jane lowered her eyes to her hands playing with the fringe of her shawl. Quietly she admitted, "You know I should never like to be an imposition, but I confess I harboured hopes that the rain would keep me at Netherfield as it did last time."

For a moment, none of the sisters spoke, each lost in her own thoughts. Jane sat on the bed beside Mary, hugging the bedpost, a most blissfully contented look on her face. Mary had pulled her legs to her chest under her billowy nightgown and was resting her head in her crossed arms on top of her knees. If either of her sisters had been able to discern her thoughts, they might have been surprised to find that she was considering neither of her sisters' improper behaviour with gentlemen to whom they were not betrothed. Rather her thoughts danced around her own secret hopes which she had not, until this moment, dared to give wings.

Elizabeth's thoughts dwelt, quite naturally, on Darcy and that earth-shattering kiss they had shared. She knew she ought to put it from her mind rather than torture herself with that which could never be. Yet, she could not. There was a strange sort of comfort in knowing to the deepest depths of her soul that she would never be kissed again, and certainly not like she had been kissed today. Darcy's lips would be the last ever to touch her own, and she was not sorry for it. The memory of that kiss would remain with her for the rest of her life, warming her on lonely nights and reminding her that she had been loved, however briefly, by the very best of men.

"Just think, Lizzy," Jane's voice pulled her from her sweet contemplations, "we shall both soon be married! And our husbands are such good friends. It is everything I could have wished for. And I am sure you will soon meet a wonderful gentleman, Mary. Perhaps you could stay with Lizzy or me and we could introduce you to friends of Mr Bingley or the Colonel. How lovely that would be if we could all remain close! Oh, but, Lizzy. You look so tired. You have had such a long day and we ought to go and let you rest."

She stood and gave each of her sisters a kiss on the cheek then turned to the door. When she had opened it, she looked expectantly towards Mary who had not moved. "Are you coming, Mary?"

"In a moment. I need to speak to Lizzy about our riding lessons."

"Oh, I see. Goodnight, my dear sisters."

Elizabeth and Mary bid Jane goodnight as she closed the door behind her. Then Elizabeth turned to Mary.

"I hardly think there is any need to proceed with the lessons, Mary. I had only thought to do so when I still imagined I might marry the Colonel."

"Yes, I know. Though I still believe it would be a good idea. I think you would enjoy the activity and it might offer some distraction from your current troubles. I only wished to know that you will be well."

Would she be well? Elizabeth hardly knew. How did one recover from such heartache? Was it even possible? She would never forget Darcy and was sure she would never cease loving him. Did she even wish to? Of course, she did not. But she also had no desire to cause her sister any further concern, so she lied.

"I am certain, in time, I will have gotten over it tolerably well."

"And you will think about the riding lessons?" Mary asked as she stood from the bed.

Elizabeth smiled. "I will think about it. Thank you, Mary."

Mary crossed the room and threw her arm around her sister, pressing a kiss to her cheek. It was as unexpected as it was sweet and very nearly reduced Elizabeth to tears again. Mary pulled away and quickly turned to leave. When she had pulled the door open, she leant against the jamb and gave Elizabeth a saucy look she had never seen before.

"Who would ever have thought it would be left to *me* to set the example of proper, ladylike behaviour for our youngest sisters! Kissing gentlemen, indeed!"

She swept from the room, leaving her sister behind her, indulging in a much needed laugh.

Chapter Twenty-Four

Rain continued throughout the night and into the next day, keeping the Netherfield and Longbourn parties apart. Darcy both cursed and blessed the weather. Had it been fine, he might have seen Elizabeth. Richard would surely wish to call upon Longbourn and insist his cousin accompany him. Knowing their final separation was imminent, he could not help but feel that he needed to soak up every last moment in her company he could steal. Desperately did he wish to memorise her every look, smile, and mannerism. He wanted to gaze into the depths of her magnificent eyes until they were imprinted upon his memory and were all he saw when he closed his own.

However, had the weather been fine, he might have seen Elizabeth.

Being trapped within Netherfield was an acute misery all of its own. Not only did Miss Bingley pester them all endlessly with her complaints at being made to throw a ball for savages whilst simultaneously scrutinising every last detail, becoming irate if anything should be even slightly out of place, but she also made it perfectly clear that her efforts were designed to showcase her eminent suitability to be Darcy's wife. She never missed an opportunity to hint that she expected to open the ball with him. She was to be disappointed and Darcy could not bring himself to care.

When he was not being beleaguered by Miss Bingley, he was faced with Richard. His cousin seemed determined to remain at Darcy's side like a bur. If he was not waxing poetic about Elizabeth's many perfections—of which Darcy certainly needed no reminding—he was rattling away about his plans for the Grünerberg estate and how grateful he was that Darcy would not be far off should he ever be in need of assistance. When he could stand it no longer, Darcy made a weak excuse about having a letter to write and fled to his chambers. He needed neither the reminder that Richard had been the one so fortunate as to court Elizabeth nor the guilt of knowing his cousin's hopes would never see fruition, yet being bound to silence.

As the morning of the ball dawned bright and promising for an evening of gay festivities, Darcy greeted it with no less conflicting feelings than he had felt the day previous. He hated balls at the best of times and this one was sure to be nothing short of torturous. Elizabeth would certainly be dressed to her finest advantage and he was not certain his equanimity could countenance that. Of course, he was of the opinion that she could arrive dressed in sackcloth and still easily be the most beautiful woman in the room, but did he need to see just how stunning she could be when given the proper incentive? To imagine how fine she would look in the wardrobe he could provide her and the Darcy jewels? No doubt the vision would haunt him at every ball, party, and dinner he attended in future.

Yet, how could he not wish to see her in her finery? To possess the ability to envision walking into a party with Elizabeth on his arm, being the envy of every man in the room?

So, he dressed with the utmost care, determined to leave her with the very best memories of himself. If he was to be haunted by her spectre the rest of his life, why ought she not suffer the same as he?

With a final look in the mirror, he thanked his valet for his excellence and left to face the music.

Downstairs, Darcy found an out of the way chamber and placed himself before a window overlooking the drive. It was foolishness, he knew, but he did not wish to miss a moment of Elizabeth's presence. Carriage after carriage arrived in a long, slow processional, spewing their occupants out on the walk before the entrance. He paid each one only enough mind to confirm that it did not belong to the Bennets.

After a quarter of an hour, he, at last, spied a familiar carriage some three vehicles from the door. In an instant, the beating of his heart picked up pace and his palms began to sweat. She was here. He did not move a muscle, only watched as the carriage crept closer, finally coming to a stop where a footman waited to open the door. First, Mr Bennet stepped down, shaking out his cloak and donning his hat. He turned and made a remark to the footman; some dry, sarcastic comment about the evening, no doubt. Mr Bennet laughed while the footman merely nodded, looking acutely uncomfortable.

Turning away from the servant, Mr Bennet reached in and procured his wife from the confines of the vehicle, then his eldest daughter followed by his middle. Darcy's heart plummeted to his feet when no one followed. Had she not come? Was she unwell? Dear God, had she taken ill effects from having stood so long in the rain? He was ready to race down to the carriage to demand answers when Miss Bennet turned back expectantly.

He watched, transfixed, as Elizabeth emerged from the carriage, moving with a grace that held him spellbound. Taking in a deep breath to calm his racing heart, he held a lungful as she turned to say something to her sister but caught sight of him in the window. Time came to a full stop as they stood, separated by glass, mortar, and circumstance, and gazed upon one another. She sent him a small, doleful smile with an almost imperceptible nod. He returned the gesture, knowing he would stand like this all evening if it was all he might be granted of her.

Miss Bennet nudged her sister and Elizabeth pulled her gaze away and Darcy instantly mourned its loss. Never had a woman held such command over him, and never would again.

His eyes followed her form until she disappeared under the portico, savouring the thrill he felt when she glanced back up at him just before she stepped from his sight. Only then did he turn away from the window. He was treading a very fine line and felt the danger of giving her too much attention. If he did not regulate himself, he feared he would soon be beyond caring for the consequences of his actions.

Knowing he could not allow this to happen, he avoided the great hall where Bingley and his sisters were greeting their guests and made his way straight to the ballroom. As was his custom, Darcy played the part of the observer, keeping to secluded corners and alcoves where he might watch without being noticed. Still, Elizabeth seemed attuned to his presence. The way she never looked at him, but often turned her head in his direction over her shoulder; the way she meandered through the crowd, speaking with her neighbours and granting smiles which refused to reach her eyes, yet never venturing near to where he stood.

After two sets, neither of which Elizabeth danced, Darcy could stand it no longer. His entire being screamed to do that which he detested—dance. His legs shook with the effort it required to prevent them from carrying him to her to beg a set, his hands itched to take possession of hers, his brain was desperate for just a hint of her intoxicating scent and the melodic sound of her voice. It was too much and he was not strong enough to stand here, watching her every graceful move, and not go to her. So, he did that which gave him the greatest pain. He left.

Pushing off from the column he had been leaning against, he strode purposefully towards the doors of the ballroom. Looking back, he granted himself one last look at the greatest object of his desire. He would leave on the morrow and never see her again. Elizabeth stood amongst a small group of people which included her sisters, Bingley, Miss Lucas, and Richard, but she was not attending to the conversation. Instead, she was looking about the ballroom, almost frantically, clearly seeking someone out. When her eyes met his, her lips parted as her chest rose in a small gasp. His resolve nearly crumbled as he saw painful understanding dawning in her beautiful eyes. This was goodbye, and they would not even be afforded the opportunity to speak.

Swallowing down the tightness in his throat, Darcy bowed his head to her, sending his prayers and best wishes, then turned and fled the ballroom.

✌

Over the sound of the fine musicians Miss Bingley had hired from London, over the shuffling of a hundred pairs of feet, over the murmur of gossiping, laughing, and conversation, Elizabeth heard that door close with heart-breaking finality. Or, perhaps she had only imagined hearing the deafening click of the latch over the din of the room, but the pain of it was as real as if her heart had been caught in the jamb and splintered by the heavy oak.

It had been foolish, but she had held on to the tiniest sliver of hope; hope that their love might be strong enough to overcome any obstacle which stood in their way. That hope had given her the strength to step out of the carriage that evening when she had felt entirely unequal to the task. Then it had taken wings when she looked up at Netherfield and saw Darcy standing in the window, watching for her arrival, she was sure of it.

All evening, she had been excessively aware of his presence, even as she feigned ignorance. She dared not approach him nor even look at him, knowing in her head there could be nothing between them. Her heart, however, had not heeded the message and prayed every moment that he would come to her and beg a set then promise he would stay.

Then she had lost track of him. Colonel Fitzwilliam had asked her a question and she had turned her attention to him for but a moment. When she glanced back, Darcy was not where he had been standing an instant before, watching her as he had all night. Panic gripped her heart as a feeling of agony pressed in on her from all sides.

When her eyes found him, she knew. There was an anguish in his gaze that pierced her soul and tamped down the last embers of hope that had remained. She understood his reasons well enough. But understanding could not ease the stabbing ache in her chest.

"Would you care to dance, Miss Elizabeth?" Colonel Fitzwilliam asked beside her, tearing her gaze away from the door that had sealed her fate. "I understand the next to be a more sedate figure and I believe I might manage well enough."

For a moment, she only looked upon him, his words having failed to breach her understanding at first. In his eyes, she thought she saw disappointment and felt the time had come to put an end to their doomed courtship. It would be cruel to string him along any further.

"I am sorry, Colonel. I am afraid I am in no humour for dancing this evening."

"'Tis a pity you should be at a ball then."

"A great pity." She tried to smile, but was sure her execution was lacking. "Perhaps we might talk?"

"Of course."

He gestured to a secluded corner where they took seats. Elizabeth took a deep breath, as much to fortify her strength as to beg time to find the words she must speak. Before they came to her, however, the Colonel preceded her.

"It has been an incomparable pleasure getting to know you these past weeks, Miss Elizabeth," he said and she felt her eyes widen in alarm. Surely, he did not think she had made her suggestion in order to create an opportunity for him to make his declarations! She was not at all prepared to entertain a proposal and even less so to accept one. She searched her mind desperately for the words to forestall him when he spoke again. "But I do not believe I am mistaken when I suppose I have not touched your heart?"

The breath she had been holding left her in a great whoosh of relief she hoped did not show too blatantly. "I am sorry, Colonel." What else could she say?

"It would be the grossest of falsehoods if I said I was not disappointed that things have not turned out as I had hoped."

Colonel Fitzwilliam glanced away. She thought she saw his eyes flicker ever so briefly to the door where his cousin had disappeared only moments ago. It was so fleeting, however, she was sure she was mistaken. Likely, she was projecting her own preoccupation with that spot and her foolish, disappointed hopes for every moment the door did not fly back open to reveal Darcy, prepared to fight for her.

"You are a good man, Colonel. You deserve a woman who can give you not only her deepest respect, but her unwavering love, as well."

"Thank you, Miss Elizabeth. I suppose I never stood a chance, in any case. You and I are far too similar, I fear. I suspect we might have driven one another to Bedlam within a fortnight of the wedding had things ended differently."

"I think you may be correct," she laughed, feeling the need for it to her very core.

"I meant what I said, Elizabeth. You are a remarkable young woman and any man worthy enough to win your heart must consider himself the most blessed amongst men."

"You are too kind, sir," she said, fighting to keep her voice even. He could not know the pain those words caused her. "What will you do now?"

"Bingley has business in Town on the morrow and Darcy is to accompany him. There is little use in me hanging around Meryton, though I have thoroughly enjoyed my stay. I do not relish the thought of being left at Netherfield with nought but Bingley's sisters for company. One can hardly count on Hurst for entertainment. I might as well tag along and see what trouble I can get into in London."

"Tomorrow?" she gasped. She knew Darcy would leave; he had told her as much. It had seemed so much more bearable when she did not know when it was to occur. So long as he remained in the county, she could pretend there was still a chance. "So soon?"

"Aye. Bingley wishes to be done with his business and return as quickly as possible and Darcy is impatient to see his sister. I confess, I miss the scamp a good deal myself." He continued in this vein for a short while, though Elizabeth hardly heard two words in ten.

"I hope we shall always be good friends," he said at last, squeezing her hand.

Elizabeth smiled as best as she was able and lied. "I am sure we shall."

Chapter Twenty-Five

*ondon was the last place Darcy wished to be. The streets were crowded and noisy and everyone seemed to want something of him. Almost immediately, invitations poured in for everything from teas and dinners to balls and musicales. Nearly all were met with immediate polite refusal, but there were some obligations which could not be avoided; until Georgiana was wed, he was required to maintain a certain presence in Town.

One could not accuse Fitzwilliam Darcy, however, of not learning from his mistakes. When an engagement could not be avoided, he was a polite and civil guest. Making conversation was never a pleasant or easy task, but he made a greater effort than ever before. The reactions he garnered were almost amusing and he received a great deal of pleasure pondering Elizabeth's bright smiles were she to witness it.

Richard was a constant presence. Since selling his commission and giving up soldiering, Darcy's cousin seemed at a loss for what he was meant to do with himself. He had grand plans for Grünerberg and the horse breeding program he intended to implement there, but the estate was not yet equipped for such a venture and ground would not break for the new stables until spring.

So, he was decided to wait out the winter at Darcy House where his mother could not pester him so incessantly to marry. Though it had not been successful, his recent courtship had given her hope and she was now relentless in her mission to see her second son to the altar.

Darcy had ever welcomed his cousin in his home, Richard being one of few men whose company he could tolerate with equanimity. But lately, Darcy found himself setting about to tasks of dubious necessity in order to have reason to avoid the man he loved like a brother. He could scarcely look upon Richard without thinking of Elizabeth. Not that it truly mattered; that wondrous woman was rarely far from Darcy's thoughts. Yet, his cousin's constant presence only served to remind him of why he was not with the woman he loved.

Soon, he would retire to Pemberley with Georgiana for the Christmas season. His home had ever been a place of peace and comfort to him, a place he loved most to be. Yet, since meeting Elizabeth Bennet—no, since leaving Elizabeth, it held few charms for him. Pemberley, he now knew, was designed for her. That she would never see it, that its halls would never know the sound of her voice, her bright laughter, her natural radiance and refreshing joie de vivre, seemed to rob the home he had ever loved of a good deal of its allure.

Nearly a week after his return to Town, Darcy was ensconced in his study reviewing some correspondence from his steward when a rapping at the door pulled his attention from his letter. He bid the visitor enter and Jeffries, the Darcy's efficient and exceedingly capable townhouse butler stepped in with a bow.

"I beg your pardon, sir. I thought you would like to know that Miss Bingley and Mrs Hurst have come to call on Miss Darcy."

Only the best education and years of practise prevented the groan from escaping Darcy's throat. He had not the fortitude to face these ladies, yet knew he must. Georgiana was often overwhelmed by Miss Bingley's relentless ingratiating manners and endless fawning.

"Thank you, Jeffries. I will join them shortly." It would not do to allow Miss Bingley to believe he had rushed to greet her the moment he had learnt of her arrival. His sister could manage five minutes on her own.

"Very good, sir. They are in the blue parlour. Miss Darcy has called for tea."

Jeffries bowed and left to attend to other duties while Darcy tucked his letters away and replaced his pen in its holder and capped his inkwell. Belatedly, he wondered at the peculiarity of these particular ladies calling at Darcy House. Last he had known, they were meant to remain at Netherfield to await Bingley's return. What could they possibly be doing here?

After five minutes had passed—and not a second sooner—Darcy stood from his desk and made his way to offer his support to his sister.

He found the ladies in the parlour Jeffries had indicated and was unsurprised by what he saw when he stepped through the door. Georgiana was cowering on a sofa between Miss Bingley and Mrs Hurst as the former pelted her with words and the latter nodded along, occasionally parroting something her sister had said. Mrs Annesley, Georgiana's companion, was in an adjacent chair, but neither sister paid her any attention. When he cleared his throat to announce his presence, both ladies stood, Georgiana all but forgotten, and Miss Bingley rushed forward to greet him.

"Oh, Mr Darcy! It seems an age since we have seen one another. How good of you to put aside all your important business to come visit with us."

At this, Darcy nearly scoffed. They had been in company less than a week ago at Netherfield, and he ought to have known that Miss Bingley would consider his presence a compliment to her, regardless of the delay—had it been five minutes or an hour.

"Yes, well...I am surprised to see you. I had thought you were to remain in Hertfordshire."

"Oh, there was nothing and no one of consequence to keep us there," she said with a dismissive wave of her hand. "Surely, you recall the vulgar society of that savage county. Louisa and I agreed we had best shut up the house and follow you to Town."

After this speech, Miss Bingley gave her sister a pointed look with a glance towards Georgiana. Mrs Hurst instantly placed herself on the sofa beside his sister and engaged her in conversation.

In a low voice, she addressed Darcy again as she took a step nearer. "I am pleased you have joined us, sir, for I had hoped to speak with you. We are sorely in need of your help."

"Whatever the problem, I am certain your brother is more than capable of assisting you."

"Yes, well. You see, Mr Darcy, it is Charles who is in need of your help, though he is in denial. He is set on returning to Netherfield and Jane Bennet. You know how my brother depends upon your wisdom and guidance. You must make him see that an alliance with such a horrid family would surely be a grave mistake. You would not deny your dearest friend the same kindness you bestowed upon your cousin?"

"I have not the pleasure of understanding you, Miss Bingley. To what kindness are you referring?"

"Come now, sir. You must not think me ignorant of the part you played in extracting the good Colonel from such a distasteful alliance."

Darcy swallowed down his reaction to this statement. Surely, Miss Bingley had not noticed his attraction to Elizabeth? Even Richard, who knew him so well, had not discerned his feelings. "And what part is that?"

"There is no need to be coy with me. You are to be commended for persuading your cousin of the folly of his choice. I would now ask that you extend the same kindness to my hapless brother."

"Miss Bingley," said Darcy, resisting the urge to sigh his relief, "you are quite mistaken, I assure you. Even had I plied my cousin with such opinions, you overestimate the importance my cousin would place on such advice. Had Colonel Fitzwilliam been determined to marry Miss Elizabeth, no one could have swayed him from that course but the lady herself."

As he thought of her, something Elizabeth had said when they had stood together under the great oak in the pouring rain, buried by other far more powerfully pleasant memories, surfaced. *"Jane is my dearest sister. If Mr Bingley were to offer for me, I could never accept, even were it my dearest wish. I could never be happy if it would bring her pain."*

He thought back to his beloved's eldest sister. He had warned Bingley of raising her expectations but Miss Bennet had been so complacent, so serene, he had been convinced that her heart was in no danger of being touched by his flirtatious friend. She had received Bingley's attentions with pleasure, certainly, but without any outward symptom of peculiar regard. If that had been the case, why would Elizabeth have spoken so? Could he have misjudged Miss Bennet's tranquil demeanour as indifference? Had she sought to disguise her feelings for Bingley as Darcy had striven to hide his for her sister?

"However," he said, "Upon further consideration, perhaps it would be prudent to speak with Bingley."

"Oh, thank you, sir! Thank you! You are too good to our family." Miss Bingley looked up at him with such open admiration, Darcy was forced to repress a shudder. "I daresay, Charles has ever looked upon you as a brother. Perhaps, soon, he might be granted his dearest wish?"

"Unlikely," he said dully. "As I have but one sister, and she is far too young yet to consider marriage, I fail to see how such a thing might be accomplished."

"There are other ways just such a reality might be brought to pass, Mr Darcy," hinted Miss Bingley, trailing a bony finger down his jacket sleeve.

"None which I would consider, Miss Bingley," he said, fighting down the bile which had risen in his throat. Thinking quickly and ignoring the venomous look on the lady's face, he turned to his sister. "Georgiana, is it not time for your music lesson?"

"Oh, um," Georgiana stammered. As it was Wednesday and her music master came on Tuesday and Friday, her confusion was justified. Darcy hoped she would not give away his ruse.

"Indeed." Mrs Annesley stood and gave his sister and pointed look. "We must not be late, Miss Darcy. Come."

With a quick curtsey and mumbled thanks for their visit, Georgiana bid farewell to their visitors. Darcy, likewise, made his excuses and tasked his housekeeper with seeing the ladies out.

*S*itting at a table in a secluded corner of his club, Darcy contemplated the conversation he was soon to engage in and his reasons for having it. His motives were, almost entirely, altruistic. He had no wish to witness two good people trapped in a loveless, miserable marriage. Though Bingley had shown a greater regard for Miss Bennet than Darcy had ever seen him bestow upon any other woman—his affections lasting more than a month—there had also been little enough feminine charm to turn his head from one lady to the next in Meryton. If he married her, would his constancy remain when faced with larger London society? He owed it to Miss Bennet to ensure his friend knew what he was about.

Still, a little voice in the back of his head that he could not quiet would not let him forget his more selfish motivations. If Bingley married Miss Bennet, their friendship would by necessity come to an end. His good friend's union with Elizabeth's dearest sister would certainly bring them often into company and he was certain he was not strong enough to endure it.

But, most of all, if her sister was unhappy, Elizabeth would be unhappy. And that, he could not countenance.

"Darcy!" The gentleman looked up to see his friend walking towards him, led by a White's footman. "I am glad I got your note. Another day and it would have been too late. I return to Netherfield on the morrow."

"Indeed," was all Darcy could bring himself to say. He signalled to the footman for a couple of brandies then turned to his friend. "Have you had a pleasant time in Town?"

"You know me, Darce. I always have a pleasant time in Town. I did not see you at the Haversham's ball, though I know you to have been invited." Displaying one of the few traits he shared with his sister, Bingley did not wait for a reply but ploughed on. "You missed a devil of a time."

He went on to describe an evening Darcy could only be grateful to have missed, naming no less than half a dozen beautiful women he had danced with, or wished he could have danced with, and firming Darcy's resolve to speak his piece.

"So," said Bingley at last, "to what do I owe the pleasure?"

"I am glad you asked. Your sisters called on Georgiana the other day."

"Oh, blazes! Do not tell me. Caroline wants you to convince me not to return to Hertfordshire, does she not?"

"That is exactly what she wanted," Darcy answered honestly.

"And so, what?" asked Bingley in a petulant whine. "Do you agree with Caroline? Will you also tell me that Miss Bennet is a despicable fortune hunter from a family far beneath me?"

"Not at all." Darcy enjoyed the look of surprise on his friend's face for a moment before he continued. "I think Miss Bennet is a very fine lady without a mercenary bone in her body. And the Bennets, while somewhat unconventional and unrefined, are a respectable family with strong roots amongst the gentry. If you are serious about your intentions, you have my full support."

"Oh. Um. Thank you, Darcy. Thank you very much." Bingley gazed distractedly into his glass before taking a deep swig of the amber liquid. "Then...then what did you wish to speak to me about?"

"I would ask you to consider delaying your return to Netherfield."

"Blast, Darcy! You just said—"

Darcy held up his hands in a placating gesture. "Only a short delay."

"But, but, why?"

"Bingley, you are among my oldest and dearest of friends. So, please, do not take offence from what I am about to say." He waited for Bingley to acknowledge his words before continuing. "I have known you a long time, my friend. Over the years, I have seen you fall in love more times than I can count."

"I admit, I have been as fond of a pretty face as any man might, but I have never felt before as I feel for Miss Bennet!"

"Have you not?"

"No...no, I...of course, not." It did not go unnoticed that Bingley would not meet Darcy's eyes.

"Miss Granger."

"Oh, come now! She was—"

"Miss Hartwell."

"You cannot hold that—"

"Lady Arabella. Miss Dinton. Miss Haddy. Miss Constance Pyke. Lady Tr—"

"Alright!" cried Bingley. "I see your point. I am a deplorable rake!"

"You are not a deplorable rake, Bingley," Darcy reassured his friend. "You are young and possess an enviable zest for life. You want only for a little experience and maturing. But you are, at your core, a good and honourable man."

Bingley blushed at this praise and Darcy chuckled. "Thank you, Darcy. That means a great deal to me."

"Humour me. Remain in Town another week complete. If, at the end, you still feel that Miss Bennet is the key to your everlasting happiness, by all means, return to Hertfordshire with my best wishes. But Miss Bennet is a good woman who deserves nothing short of your full devotion. If you are not yet prepared to give it, it would be kinder to let her go."

For several minutes, Bingley sat in quiet contemplation of his friend's words. Darcy had never seen his friend so reflective. If asked at that moment what lay in the man's future, Darcy would not have bet a farthing either way. This moment had just as much of a chance to be the defining scene for the rest of Bingley's life as being brushed off, forgotten in the haze of fine brandy.

"Very well, Darcy. One week. Then I *will* make for Meryton and my sweet Jane!"

Chapter Twenty-Six

December 1811

Christmastide at Longbourn was always a noisy, festive affair. Each year, the ladies of the house gaily strung together berries, pinecones, and greenery to hang about the family rooms. The bannisters, doorways, and mantels were adorned in fragrant bows of pine and holly and Lydia took great delight in hiding kissing boughs in the most surprising places in hopes of catching unsuspecting couples unawares—or perhaps being caught *unawares* herself by an unsuspecting gentleman. Together, the sisters would sit, preparing boxes and gifts for the household servants and their father's tenants, an unspoken truce from the daily squabbles and quarrels ruling the day.

If they were so fortunate as to receive snow, Elizabeth would press her reluctant sisters to join her out of doors where fierce snowball wars were waged, snow angels created, and the peace and beauty of the winter season admired. Afterwards, a cosy evening before the fire, steaming cups of chocolate in hand, was shared.

When their dearest relations from London came to spend the holidays in Hertfordshire, their joy was multiplied. The two eldest sisters, especially, enjoyed the youthful enthusiasm of their young cousins and took care to entertain and spoil them to the best of their abilities.

It was, therefore, a surprise to the Gardiners when their carriage came to a stop before a rather subdued welcoming party. The family was received with pleasure, of course, and greeted with smiles and warm embraces. Yet, there seemed to be a shadow cast over the whole party.

Mrs Gardiner, a great favourite with her nieces and particularly close with the two eldest, was a regular correspondent with Jane and Elizabeth. She was consequently aware of the recent goings-on at Longbourn. The reports she had received did not seem to line up with what she was witnessing.

Mrs Bennet's displeasure she had anticipated, and Jane's melancholy she could well account for, having heard all the particulars of their disappointments from Elizabeth. She knew of Mr Bingley's having gone to Town on some brief business only to fail to return. Miss Bingley's subsequent letters, expressing not only their intent to quit Netherfield entirely and her rather disparaging comments against Elizabeth, but also a stunning revelation regarding her brother and his apparent attachment to Miss Darcy, had put paid to all of Jane's hopes. Still, Mrs Gardiner had not expected so brief an attachment to cast sweet, optimistic Jane so far down.

Kitty and Lydia, she had been informed, had prevailed upon their parents to lift their banishment to the schoolroom in the wake of Elizabeth's failed courtship. Mrs Gardiner had held every expectation of finding her youngest nieces as exuberant and silly as ever they had been. Kitty seemed happy enough, though rather dull, but Lydia was downright petulant.

It was Elizabeth who gave her aunt the greatest pause. Though her pen had declared herself not at all heartbroken over the dissolution of her courtship and that she and the Colonel had parted on the best of terms, Mrs Gardiner had detected a distinct lack of spirits in her niece's letters. There was a pitiful dearth of the witticisms and the light-hearted gaiety for which Elizabeth was known. Looking now upon the girl, it was clear to the lady who knew her well that her smile lacked its customary brightness and there was a disconcerting dullness in her lovely eyes.

Only Mr Bennet and Mary seemed unaltered to their relations—but for Mary's looks, which were greatly improved. Though, if they had looked closely, they might have noticed her ennui was not her customary piousness. But they had never been as close to the middle Bennet daughter as they had her elder sisters.

After the children had been settled into the nursery and a short rest from their journey—and patiently listening to all of her sister-in-law's complaints—Mrs Gardiner sought out her second niece to see what truths she could uncover. She found Elizabeth alone in a back parlour, tending to some sewing.

"Well, this is a surprise. I have never known you to be so diligent in your needlework," teased the lady.

"That is because I never have been, Aunt. But I wish to finish this before Christmas. 'Tis for Mary." She held up the handkerchief upon which she was embroidering a rearing stallion, prancing in a field of wildflowers.

"You have certainly never lacked talent."

"No. Only patience!" Elizabeth laughed, and it did her aunt good to hear it. "But I have learnt that my sister dearly loves horses so I will persevere for her."

"She is a fortunate girl to have such a sister."

"Oh, no, Aunt. It is I who is the fortunate one, to have such wonderful sisters. Though Kitty and Lydia have been sorely trying on everyone's nerves of late."

"Yes, I noticed they seem displeased. I had thought they would be unbearably exuberant, having reversed your parent's restrictions."

"At first, they were. But you will recall my having written and told you of a certain officer of whom they were exceedingly fond? An officer against who we were warned?" Mrs Gardiner acknowledged these words with a curious nod, remembering Elizabeth's having told her of her former suitor's childhood friend. "In the wake of Mr Wickham's arrest for outstanding debts and conduct unbefitting an officer,"—she gave her Aunt a decidedly pointed look—"Colonel Forster has implemented several restrictions upon his officers. Such as severe punishments for improper behaviour towards any female." Elizabeth leant in conspiratorially and whispered, "It was discovered that Mr Wickham had meddled with several of the merchant's daughters and he was flogged in the middle of camp as an example before he was sent away to London. It seems to have had its desired effect as the other officers will not come within ten yards of my silly sisters." Sitting up, she concluded, "Lydia declares her heart is broken and will never mend. Kitty seems to understand, at least a little, that if the officers want nothing to do with them if they cannot trifle with them, then perhaps they never had honourable intentions towards them at all."

"Oh, dear. But I must say, I am glad to hear it."

"What is more, Mrs Forster, the Colonel's very young, very silly wife, had meant to invite Lydia to join them at Brighton when the regiment decamps for the summer. But, what do you think, Colonel Forster would not hear of it. Lydia has determined that everyone is out to ruin her fun forever. Kitty is at least pleased by this as she was not to be included in the invitation."

"I daresay it is for the best. I do not like to think what mischief might be got into if Lydia were let loose upon a camp full of soldiers." The two ladies spent a moment considering this horror, then Mrs Gardiner turned the topic. "And, what about you, my dear? Are you well? You do not seem yourself?"

"I am very well, Aunt" Elizabeth answered after an almost imperceptible hesitation, though it did not go unnoticed that she did not take her eyes off her motionless needle.

Certain she would get nothing more from her niece, Mrs Gardiner pressed no further. Whilst Jane hid much of her feelings behind a serene mask, and Elizabeth's expressive face often gave away her every emotion, the second Bennet daughter was no less protective of her private sentiments. If she wished to disclose her feelings, she would do so when she was ready. Mrs Gardiner was, therefore, surprised when Elizabeth spoke again.

"I am concerned for my sisters. Jane and Mary, anyway."

"Jane, I understand. But what is the matter with Mary?"

"Mama is relentless in her opinion that Mary is at fault for not securing Mr Collins. She abuses Mary most abominably."

"No more so than she abuses you for having allowed the son of an earl to escape, I daresay."

"True. But I am better able to withstand Mama's tirades, having heard them all my life. Mary has ever been invisible to Mama and does not know how to handle it." Elizabeth put her sewing down and looked imploringly at her aunt. "I wondered if you and my uncle might be persuaded to take Jane and Mary back to Gracechurch Street with you after Christmas? Mama does not know how she injures Jane with her wailings about Mr Bingley's desertion, and Mary sorely needs a break."

"I think we could arrange that very well. Would you not like to join them? Could you not also use a respite?"

There was again a slight hesitation before Elizabeth answered. "Thank you, dear Aunt. But I do not think Papa would countenance losing all of his most sensible daughters all at once. Besides, Charlotte has invited me to visit her in Kent in the spring. I will have my holiday then."

10 February 1812
Gracechurch Street

Dearest Lizzy,

I am pleased to hear that all is well at Longbourn and that Mama is not giving you too much grief. I am sure Papa is vastly pleased that you remained at home to lend him company, though your company would be greatly appreciated here, as well.

You will remember that I called upon Miss Bingley and Mrs Hurst some weeks ago when our aunt went into that part of Town, and that Miss Bingley did not return my call for several weeks. I have already admitted to being entirely deceived by their displays of friendship, but it has been made abundantly clear that none of that family ever held any true regard for me.

We were recently invited to a ball by an associate of our uncle's. It was a lovely affair in a respectable part of town but I confess, I can scarcely recall many details.

Mr Bingley was in attendance.

I am now convinced that all the attraction was entirely on my side. He was very kind and greeted Mary and myself with his usual ease and friendliness but gave no indication that he holds me in any higher regard than that of a friend. I must conclude that Mr Bingley now no longer cares for me.

Let me hear from you soon. I should like it, however, if we did not speak of him again. I will be well soon enough and am happy in my family.

Yours &etc,
Jane

✦

12 February 1812
Gracechurch Street

Dear Lizzy,

I thank you for your last letter, and most especially for your suggestion that I accompany Jane to London. I have had such a pleasant visit with our aunt and uncle and our dear cousins. I wonder sometimes that Uncle and Mama could be related.

By now you have heard of our meeting with Mr B. From Jane's manner, I am convinced she did not enlighten you to all that occurred that evening. I will inform you now, for you ought to know how ill our sister has been used.

When we came upon Mr B at the ball, he was as he ever had been; kind and amiable, though obviously surprised at seeing Jane in Town, though she had written to Miss B twice and called upon his sisters in Grosvenor Street. Miss B had even returned the call, though made it very evident she took no pleasure in our sister's company. The gentleman spoke with us for a few minutes of the happy times he spent in Hertfordshire but gave no hint that he would return to Netherfield in future.

A moment later, a very pretty lady very much of Jane's likeness approached and took rapid possession of Mr B's arm. One might have thought we had vanished into thin air for the vague leave he immediately took of us. His sisters acknowledged Jane with only the slightest of nods and myself not at all.

I am of the opinion Mr B is a most undeserving young man and our sister has had a lucky escape. Jane does not let on, but I fear she is deeply injured. I will do all in my power to raise her spirits. Aunt is my accomplice in this endeavour.

I hope you are not pained by my mentioning having also seen Colonel Fitzwilliam. He was at the same ball and even asked me for a dance. Forgive me for saying, dear sister, I think him a fine gentleman. His cousin, he told me, has been in Derbyshire since shortly before Christmas.

I do hope all is well and that Mama is not giving you too much trouble about the Colonel.

Your sister,
Mary

Chapter Twenty-Seven

March 1812

Spring brought with it to Hertfordshire a renewal of warmth and life and also much of Elizabeth's former good spirits. Her feelings for Darcy had not diminished in the slightest. Rather, she was determined to be grateful for having known so great a love than to be cast down by disappointment. Too few people, she reasoned with herself, ever even tasted such affection; she would cherish the gift that it was.

She was not a creature made for melancholy so Elizabeth allowed herself to take all the enjoyment from her forthcoming trip to Kent there was to be had. She did not expect a good deal of excitement, residing under the roof of her cousin Mr Collins; but she had travelled so little, every new place was of interest to her. That she was to be in proximity of—and might even meet—family of the gentleman she most longed for was to be pushed aside and not dwelt upon.

After a night spent in Gracechurch Street, which gave Elizabeth the satisfaction of seeing her dear sisters in as good of health and heart as she could have hoped for, the journey southward began. Her companions, Sir William and Maria Lucas, chattered excitedly the whole way, speculating as to the delights to be found at Rosings. But as the palings of Rosing came into view, they both grew quiet in wide-eyed awe at the sheer vastness of the property.

They were greeted at the parsonage with great courtesy and a good deal of pleasure. Mr Collins was as entirely unchanged; all formal civility and self-importance. They were promptly invited into the house, but delayed on multiple occasions by her cousin's need to point out the evenness of his drive, the practicality of the garden, the neatness of the entrance, and every dull thing they were called upon to admire and acknowledge Lady Catherine's hand in.

At length, the guests were shown into a parlour where Charlotte offered refreshments, only for the offer to be immediately repeated by her husband. As they sat and took tea, their attention was, again and again, called upon to take notice of some small feature of the house of which Mr Collins was chiefly proud—which seemed to be nearly everything. He seemed particularly intent on gaining Elizabeth's notice on the comfort and suitability of his situation. She gathered by his manner—and the letter sent to her father complaining of having been ill-used when neither of his eldest daughters had yet married, as he had been given to expect—that he wished to make her feel what might have been hers had circumstances been different. Though the house was comfortable and well-situated, she could not bring herself to repine having accepted the Colonel's offer of courtship; not for her silly cousin's sake, anyway.

Through all this, Elizabeth surreptitiously watched her friend. But for a faint blush when her husband said something especially ridiculous or that might have bordered on spiteful, Charlotte appeared curiously deaf to his absurd babble.

When the tea had been drunk and the guests shown to their rooms, Mr Collins prevailed upon his father-in-law to accompany him to his gardens. Maria remained in her room to rest and Elizabeth followed Charlotte to a small parlour at the back of the house. There, she learnt enough to be perfectly at ease for her friend. Though not ignorant as to the faults of her husband, Charlotte had not yet learnt to regret her choice. They lived separate enough lives under the same roof as to make for a very pleasant arrangement and she was ever so pleased to have the management of her own home at last. Elizabeth was sensible enough of Charlotte's disposition that, though she could never have been content with such a man, she was happy for her friend.

On the following day, such a commotion was heard whilst Elizabeth was in her room writing a letter to her sisters of her initial impressions of the Collinses situation, that she quickly threw aside her pen and rushed downstairs, fully expecting that some great calamity had occurred. She was very nearly put out to discover nothing even so disastrous as the pigs having got into the garden was afoot; only the occasion of a small phaeton pulled by a smart pair of matching ponies having stopped in the drive carrying two ladies.

When Elizabeth surmised the visitors to be Lady Catherine de Bourgh and her daughter, Maria corrected her mistake by informing her that the elder of the two ladies was Mrs Jenkinson while the other was, in fact, Miss Anne de Bourgh. Elizabeth watched the young lady with some fascination, searching for any resemblance to her cousin, though she was hardly aware of it.

Miss de Bourgh was a thin, frail thing scarcely visible under piles of shawls and blankets. She spoke hardly a word to Charlotte, who had stepped out to greet her visitor, but seemed content to allow her companion carry the conversation. They spoke for several minutes and Elizabeth was growing weary of the scene when suddenly, Miss de Bourgh turned her head towards the house, gazing through the window to where Elizabeth stood.

Moments later, Miss de Bourgh turned away and, with a flick of her wrists, set the ponies in motion and they were gone. Mr Collins hastened into the house, Charlotte following at a more dignified pace, to inform his guests of their excellent fortune; the whole house had been invited to dine at Rosings Park on the morrow.

❦

"This young lady, I suppose," Lady Catherine asked when she had finished instructing Charlotte as to the precise manner in which she ought to instruct her maid how to best starch Mr Collins' cravats, "is Miss Elizabeth Bennet?"

Though certain her ladyship's question was rhetorical, Elizabeth answered in the affirmative nonetheless.

"The same Miss Bennet who was engaged in a courtship with my nephew?"

"Yes, your ladyship."

After scrutinising Elizabeth from head to toe, Lady Catherine tilted her head towards her daughter and addressed Miss de Bourgh. "She *is* a genteel, pretty sort of girl."

Bemused, Elizabeth looked to Miss de Bourgh to see how she would respond to this statement. The lady said nothing, only stared back with an inscrutable expression.

"'Tis a shame," Lady Catherine continued. "Fitzwilliam could use a good wife. Why did you not marry him?"

"I am afraid we did not suit, your ladyship."

"Did not suit? He is the son of an earl from an old and respected family. He is a decorated colonel in the king's army with an excellent education and everything to recommend him. I understand your father's estate is entailed upon Mr Collins and you, your mother, and your sisters will have nothing when your father is gone. The advantage was entirely on your side."

For a brief moment, Elizabeth considered employing evasion in her response but then thought better of it. Though she had only just met the lady, she suspected her ladyship would not cease her interrogation until she was satisfied. Besides, Elizabeth was not ashamed of her principles.

"You are in the right, Lady Catherine. If one is concerned only with the material advantages of marriage, it might seem foolhardy to have spurned such an opportunity. However," she pressed on with confidence, "I have long determined to marry only a man whom I can both love and respect and who will love and respect me in turn. While I have nothing but the deepest respect for Colonel Fitzwilliam, I cannot love him and I am convinced he could not love me. Not in the manner I require."

Silence descended upon the parlour while her words hung in the air. Sir William and Maria stared, slack-jaw and wide-eyed at her. They knew her propensity to speak her mind well enough but seemed stunned that she would dare to speak so within such exalted company. Sir William had hardly spoken since their arrival but to directly answer Lady Catherine's questions and Maria had yet to say anything at all.

Mr Collins sat rigidly beside his patroness, wringing his hands and looking very much as though he might faint. Charlotte appeared to be torn between exasperation and admiration for her friend's boldness. Everyone seemed to be holding their breath as they awaited her ladyship's reply.

Everyone, that is, but Miss de Bourgh. When Elizabeth glanced at that lady, she could have sworn she saw her lips quirk up in an almost imperceptible smile.

"My, but you do give your opinion rather decidedly for so young a person."

"I always have, your ladyship. My mother quite despairs of me."

"Yes, well." Lady Catherine then turned to Charlotte and inquired after the welfare of one of her parishioners. She did not address her young, impertinent guest again, but very often Elizabeth felt her ladyship's appraising eye upon her and, though she could not readily interpret the looks, she did not perceive any apparent disapproval from the great lady.

After this first evening, the residents of the parsonage were invited often to dine at the great house. Mr Collins was absolutely beside himself with rapturous delight. He was perfectly happy to accept the credit for the boon in their intimacy at Rosings and no one was of a mind to contradict him.

Sir William remained in Kent only a fortnight. He went away well satisfied with his daughter's situation and convinced of his family's having made a very fortunate alliance.

Each morning, Elizabeth ventured out into the park surrounding the estate. Beyond the well-cultivated formal gardens at the edge of the main grounds was a beautiful grove that had been left almost entirely untouched. Hours were spent exploring its paths and glades. In a very few days, she came to feel that had the situation not included a lifetime of subjection to her ridiculous cousin—and her heart not been entirely devoted to another—she might have envied the mistress of Hunsford parsonage at least a little.

One evening, when the party had been dining at Rosings, Elizabeth took the opportunity of complimenting her ladyship on her beautiful estate. She was not at all prepared for what she learnt in response.

"Of course," agreed Lady Catherine. "Rosings is one of the finest estates in the country. Oh, Pemberley is grander, to be sure, but when Anne is mistress of that estate, she will not be at all unprepared."

"Pemberley?" Elizabeth asked, wondering if she might have heard wrong.

"Indeed. My Anne was born for the role."

Unsatisfied with this response, Elizabeth sought clarification. "Pemberley in Derbyshire? Mr Darcy's estate?"

"Of course," her ladyship replied and Elizabeth felt her heart shatter to pieces. "When Anne and her cousin are wed, she will take the place my honoured sister held. And why should she not?"

"No, forgive me," said Elizabeth quickly. Lady Catherine was eyeing her with suspicion. "I only...did not know that Miss de Bourgh was engaged, is all. My...my congratulations."

"Yes. The arrangement was made whilst Anne was yet in her cradle. It was the greatest wish of his mother as well as mine to see our two estates joined. It is a terrible tragedy my dear sister did not live to see our careful planning come to fruition."

The lady went on to rhapsodise long on the eminent suitability of the match and many benefits which would result from such a union, but Elizabeth hardly heard a word of it. Darcy was engaged to be married. Had been so when he came to Hertfordshire and made her fall in love with him. The kiss he had given her that had shaken her very soul had been bestowed whilst he was promised to another.

Had this been part of his reasoning for insisting there could be no future for them? He had been clear that he could not betray his cousin, but he had never even hinted as to being engaged. Had he lied to her? Had he used his cousin as a convenient excuse? Had he used her?

Hardly aware that she did so, Elizabeth watched Miss de Bourgh. But for a very slight rolling of her eyes, the lady had barely reacted to her mother's announcement. There was no blushing at the mention of her intended, no eager smiles or displays of anticipation. She appeared rather unimpressed at the prospect of marrying the best man Elizabeth had ever known, almost bored. Did Darcy love her? Had he thought of his betrothed when he had so passionately kissed another woman? Did Miss de Bourgh love Darcy as Elizabeth did? Would she be a good wife to him?

Elizabeth could hardly think so. The lady was thin, frail, and cross-looking. Had she been in better health she might have been pretty but, as it was, she could only be considered tolerable at best.

Stifling a gasp at these uncharitable thoughts, Elizabeth fought back the tears that threatened. She could not explain why she was affected so deeply. There had never been any hope for them; she had long known there was no future and had believed herself reconciled to that reality. One day he would marry, she knew. But she had never imagined it would be so soon, or that she would be on hand when it was announced—or that she would ever meet the lady who would hold the position she so coveted.

Chapter Twenty-Eight

18 March 1812
Rosings Park

Dear Cousin,

I thank you for your last letter and every other pleasant nothing I am meant to include when writing a letter to those who are of interest to me.

Now, for that which truly matters. Mr and Mrs Collins have a visitor. I do wonder at your letting Miss Elizabeth Bennet get away. She is everything delightful and such a refreshing addition to our dull party here at Rosings. Mother would never confess as much, but she likes the lady rather well. It is quite the shame you could not, as Miss Bennet put it, love her the way she required. I confess myself surprised. I had thought you were considered as universally charming.

She is to remain in Kent several more weeks and will likely still be here when Darcy comes for his yearly visit. Why am I telling you this? No

reason. None at all. I will only say, I should very much like to have just such a
lady as a relation. I believe her to be just what this family needs.

Yours &etc,
AdB

*R*ichard read the letter from his cousin three times over before he was decided as to what he wanted to do about it. Darcy would set out for Rosings within the week. It would not be impossible to join him. He was not needed at Grünerberg until next month and already he had secured the purchase of two excellent mares for his stables. He still needed to find a few good stable hands, but he had spoken with both Matlock and Darcy's head grooms regarding the matter. They could send him word in Kent as easily as in Town.

Besides, this was important. He had known almost as soon as he had met her that Miss Elizabeth Bennet was special, and he still believed so with all his heart. For the last four months since leaving Hertfordshire, he had pondered what had gone wrong. Had it been a matter of timing, location, or both? Had he been too audacious? Or not audacious enough? Whatever the case, he had been granted a second chance and this time, he was determined to succeed.

*S*pring planting was complete. All the tenant cottages had been inspected and, but for a few minor repairs his steward was more than capable of seeing to, were found to be in good order. His investments in Town were sound and profiting nicely. Richard had everything well in hand at Grünerberg. Georgiana's lessons were going well and her companion was a good, sensible lady who had brought his sister a long way since her disappointment last summer. In short, everything was as it should be and there was very little to occupy Darcy's time or thoughts. Once upon a time, this might have been a welcome development. As it was now, he was halfway to Bedlam.

Every day had become a futile exercise in seeking employment; or rather, distraction. At Pemberley, he had summoned Mrs Reynolds and Mr Hays to his study so oft to inquire if there was aught which required his attention, he was sure his housekeeper and butler were quite relieved to see the back of the carriage as it pulled away from the house.

On the journey south, he had opted to ride within the carriage with his sister with the hopes of engaging in conversation; even the most banal chitchat on fashion or whatever occupied a sixteen-year-old girl's head would have been welcomed. Being alone astride Sleipnir would have afforded him far too much time alone with his thoughts. He had not counted on the latest in a series of novels having just been published and Georgiana's enthusiasm for the story. Hardly a word had been spoken on the three-day trek.

Each morning in his London study, he sorted through the same correspondence he had sorted through the day before, looking for some matter of business which might have been overlooked. A visit to his solicitor's and the bank reassured him of the efficiency of those he employed to look after the Darcy holdings, but frustratingly left him with nought to do.

There was only so much time he could spend at Angelo's or Gentleman Jack's. Adams was beside himself with excitement at the need to order new jackets as his master's arms had grown too large for his old ones.

Having never been in love before, Darcy had naïvely believed he would simply get over the feelings like any other ailment. Time, space, and a hearty diet would surely cure him of this heartache. Yet, he missed Elizabeth as desperately now as he had the day he rode away from her. Everything seemed to serve as a reminder of her. Every book he read left him wondering what she would have thought of it. When he could not avoid a dance, he could not help but recall how light she had been on her feet and the saucy looks she threw over her shoulder when she would tease him. Every lady he encountered was, rather unfavourably, compared to his Elizabeth. The colour yellow made him think of the Netherfield ball and how beautiful she had looked in her butter-coloured gown; and the sadness in her eyes when he left.

He was seated in a parlour at Darcy House one morning, thinking of Elizabeth and paying little heed to his surroundings or the comings and goings of others, having given up on fruitlessly seeking a more productive use of his time, when a hauntingly familiar scent assaulted his senses. Startled out of his reverie, half expecting to turn and find his estranged love standing in the room, he looked up to see Georgiana crossing the floor carrying a vase filled with beautiful flowers in full bloom.

"Georgiana, what are those?" he asked. He had not meant to sound so harsh and had little idea of having done so. Every thought was for that heavenly scent and from whence it came.

His bemused sister looked from the vase in her hands to Darcy, her brows knit in concern. "They are flowers, William. Do you not like them?"

Ignoring her question which he hardly heard, he stood and quickly came to stand before her, his eyes locked on the arrangement she held. "But what kind are they specifically?"

"Oh, um. Well, these are roses, which you ought to know." He leant down and inhaled the fragrant rose.

"No. That is not it."

"These are chrysanthemums." She pointed to a soft pink bloom which he sniffed, shaking his head when it, too, was not the scent he sought. "Um...the lily, perhaps?"

One by one, Darcy lifted the colourful flowers to his nose, no longer hearing what his sister called them as he breathed in their unique scents. One by one, he dismissed each as deficient. At last, he pulled out a long, spiky stalk with tiny purple flowers. When he inhaled that scent that he knew so well, his eyes closed and he was transported thirty miles away to a sodden field in the pouring rain, standing beneath the shelter of a large oak tree. Elizabeth was in his arms, her sweet lips pressed against his own as that scent enveloped and bewitched him.

"This one," he whispered, his voice hoarse with emotion. "What is this?"

"That is lavender," Georgiana replied quietly, picking up on her brother's reverence, though she hardly understood the need; Darcy had never particularly cared for flowers before. Then she looked down at the bouquet she held and cried out. "Oh, William! Look what you have done to my arrangement."

"My apologies, dearest," said he distractedly. "Might I beg an arrangement of these—only these—for my study? And my private chambers?"

"Yes, I suppose. But why? There are much lovelier, more impressive flowers I might arrange for you."

"I am sure you could, Georgie. But it must be these. I have...I have grown fond of the scent," he said as he gazed tenderly on the soft purple sprig and raised it to his nose once more.

"What scent is that?" Richard's voice pierced the moment as its owner limped into the room.

Darcy quickly lowered the flower and enclosed it within his fist, but Georgiana outed him.

"William has taken a liking to lavender. And now my arrangement is ruined."

"Lavender?" He looked questioningly between the siblings. "Which is that?"

With a resigned sigh, Georgiana pulled another spring of the small, delicate blossoms from her vase. "This."

Taking the flower and lifting it to his nose, Richard inhaled deeply. "Lovely. And familiar. Is this your scent Georgie-girl?"

"No. I prefer rose. It reminds me of Mama."

The gentlemen smiled tenderly on their charge. She had been only four when Lady Anne Darcy had died, yet she had ever felt an affinity with her mother through roses, which had been that lady's favourite.

Richard took another whiff of the flower. "Yet, I know I know this scent. 'Tis not my mother's. Darcy? Where do I know this scent from?"

"How am I to know?" answered Darcy somewhat churlishly. He had no wish to discuss Elizabeth with her former suitor.

"Well, how do you know it?"

Swallowing down his panic, Darcy shrugged his shoulders and lied. "I caught the scent in the park and found it reminded me of something, though I could not say what, just as you."

His cousin and sister exchanged dubious glances. Such a vague explanation could hardly account for his almost worshipful adoration of the flower only moments ago. Before they could tear apart his answer, however, he changed the topic.

"Did you need something, Richard? Or had you only come in to admire Georgie's handiwork?" He gestured to the haphazardly arranged vase his sister had placed on a nearby table and was attempting to correct. He was forced to smother a smile at the scowl she sent his way.

"I did, indeed, have a purpose for seeking you out."

"Then let us adjourn to my study. Georgie? For my debasement of your beautiful work, might you accept a trip to the modiste on the morrow in restitution?"

Georgiana squealed her delight and launched herself into his arms. "Oh, William! Yes! You are quite forgiven! But you must not grumble or complain even once and I shall order as much as I like."

"Very well. But I expect the flowers I requested before I retire for the night."

"I promise!" She kissed him quickly on the cheek then turned and swept from the room, the ruined arrangement forgotten in her haste to acquiesce to his request.

"Well," Richard scoffed. "I might have taken her shopping, just as well."

"Do not be bitter. I am her only brother. You are one of many cousins. Come."

Darcy led his cousin through the house to his study on the first floor, slowing his pace so that Richard might keep up. He had gained strength enough that he no longer need rely on a walking stick, but he would never be as quick as he once was and would ever possess an uneven gait.

Once the gentlemen had been supplied with a glass of Darcy's fine brandy and seated in his comfortable leather armchairs, Darcy turned expectantly to his companion.

Without any ado, Richard stated his purpose plainly. "I wish to accompany you to Rosings."

"Accompany me to Rosings?" Darcy repeated.

It would not be the first time Richard had joined him on his annual sojourn to Kent, but each time previous he had been required to part with a bottle of his finest brandy to persuade his cousin to come along. None of the family ventured voluntarily to his aunt's home. Darcy had inherited the task of seeing after Rosing's business each year when his father had died. The elder Darcy had taken on the duty as his sister-in-law could not bully and browbeat him as she did her brother, the earl. Darcy was of a similar constitution. Why the lady felt she could harangue him into marrying her daughter when she had never succeeded in persuading him to anything he did not wish before was beyond him.

"Why?"

"Why not? You attend to the business each year, and now that I am no longer a soldier, but a gentleman of leisure, I can do my part."

It did not escape Darcy's notice that Richard did not meet his eyes and jabbered on without stopping to take breath. But he was so far from objecting to the company on this journey and in dealing with his irascible aunt, that he made no further inquiries, only informed Richard as to the date of his departure.

Chapter Twenty-Nine

r Darcy is to be married. Elizabeth repeated this thought to herself over and over, like a mantra. As though the shattered pieces of her heart might magically piece themselves back together if only she could accept this truth. It was not working, however. With each repetition, the tiny shards splintered further until all that was left was a fine dust that was good for nothing.

It all brought on a terrible headache, but she was grateful for the excuse to cry off dining at Rosings for the evening. Where she had first looked upon Miss de Bourgh as an interesting character study, she was now nothing more than the woman who would be Darcy's wife.

Much to Elizabeth's chagrin, the manor house sent over tinctures, powders, and a basket of the lemon biscuits she had so enjoyed at tea. Even included was the receipt with a note on the back from Miss de Bourgh which she might have found diverting had she not viewed the lady as competition.

Except that she was not. Miss de Bourgh had already won.

No. That was not correct. There was no competition to be won. Even had there been no Colonel Fitzwilliam, Elizabeth never stood a chance. Miss de Bourgh was engaged to Darcy and had been all her life.

This thought turned Elizabeth's indignation to its proper course. Miss de Bourgh was not the enemy; Fitzwilliam Darcy was. He had had the audacity to come into her county all handsome and tall, charming her with his intelligent conversation about literature and the Scandinavian cultures and lore and ruining her courtship. For, surely, had she not had Darcy with whom to compare her suitor, there would have been no impediment to her falling in love with the Colonel. That she truly believed they did not suit was ignored in her anger. This was about blaming Darcy for his deceit.

However, blaming Darcy did little to cure her broken heart. She was no less in love with him now than she had been before. Only she now felt foolish for loving such a man.

"Eliza?" Charlotte called to her, drawing her from her tumultuous thoughts. "Are you well, dear? You look rather flushed." Charlotte leant forward in her chair in the small parlour to reach across and feel Elizabeth's forehead. "You do not feel warm. Would you like some tea? Or a biscuit?"

Elizabeth pushed her friend's hand away. "I am well, Charlotte. Perhaps I have stayed indoors too long. Fresh air and exercise are all I need. I think I shall go for walk."

"I am sure it will do you good."

Doing her best to hide her malaise behind a smile, Elizabeth stood to gather her outdoor things. She had hardly taken two steps, however, when the maid entered and announced visitors.

"Mr Fitzwilliam, Mr Darcy, and Miss de Bourgh, ma'am."

Incognisant of the gasp which escaped her lips, every ounce of Elizabeth's being begged her to flee but her feet would not obey. She was rooted to the spot as the callers entered. Vaguely, she noted the Colonel's entrance with his customary jovial grin, but the greater part of her attention was for Darcy. He was leaning down tenderly towards his other cousin when he looked up and their eyes met.

She could not have believed it possible, but he was even more handsome than she remembered. His dark, wavy hair was shorter than it had been in Hertfordshire, and his deep, coffee-coloured eyes seemed darker. He was a tall man, but he seemed...bigger somehow, manlier. It was terribly unfair of him to appear here, looking so fine and catching her entirely unaware. Yet, when she looked on his face, it was clear that her presence was just as great a surprise to him as his was to her.

Then she looked down and her eyes homed in on that spot on his arm where Miss de Bourgh's small hand rested—and Darcy's placed affectionately atop—screaming out confirmation of that which she had not realised she still held hope of being some terrible misunderstanding.

This, at last, jarred her from the spell Darcy's sudden appearance had cast upon her and she turned with determination to the Colonel, plastering a wide, if brittle, smile on her face and greeted him with all the enthusiasm she could muster.

"What is your hurry, Richard?" Darcy called to his cousin who was leading the charge towards the parsonage. "You do recall that we have met Mr Collins, do you not? One would think you would not be in a hurry to have the experience repeated." He chuckled at his own joke with a glance down at Anne on his arm.

"He is rather absurd, is he not?" she agreed. "But I confess, I have been amused by the ridiculous manner in which he desperately tries to please Mother. Though, I do feel for poor Mrs Collins."

"I am sorry, cousins," Richard called back. "I cannot recall a happier time than the weeks we spent in Hertfordshire. I suppose I am eager to have any connection with such pleasant memories."

"You will curse having been so eager for such poor recompense as Mr Collins' company when your leg is aching later."

"I am sure you are correct, Cousin, as usual," Richard laughed. "But, still, I am determined."

"Then, by all means, lead the way."

Richard did just that, leading his cousins across the park to the lane which would take them to Hunsford parsonage. He did slow, however, when Anne began to tire. She rarely ventured out so far on foot and had only been granted leave to do so by her mother because Darcy had promised most faithfully not to leave her side.

Though she could never let on as such, Anne greatly anticipated her cousin's yearly visits. Under Darcy's persuasion, Lady Catherine was apt to allow her far more freedoms than she ever enjoyed throughout the rest of the year. The only other exertions her mother allowed were her daily phaeton drives and only with her companion, Mrs Jenkinson, and an accompanying footman. They always ensured she did not venture beyond what Lady Catherine felt was too far for her daughter.

When the parsonage came into view, Darcy could have sworn Richard acquired a slight skip in his step. He simply could not account for his cousin's eagerness to visit with a man such as Mr Collins. Even if it did bring to mind pleasant memories of Elizabeth, he could hardly consider it worth the headache. There were a thousand other far pleasanter things which brought to mind his estranged love that did not require being forced to listen to the obsequious parson's incessant jabbering.

The party presented themselves at the parsonage door and asked to see the master of the house. Upon being told that the master was from home but Mrs Collins was within with her guests, Darcy breathed a sigh of relief. He remembered Mrs Collins, née Lucas, as a quiet, sensible young lady. She had been a dear friend to Elizabeth; he would be pleased by her company for no other reason than that.

Darcy paid scant attention to his surroundings as they were led through the house. Anne was leaning heavily on his arm—as heavily as was possible with her slight frame. He laid a comforting hand over hers as he lent her his strength.

Preoccupied with ensuring his cousin's welfare, Darcy scarcely heard the maid announce their presence and was entirely ignorant of others within the room until he heard someone gasp and instinctively knew who it would be. Frozen in place, he could do no more than look up and gaze into those exquisite, deep green eyes he adored so ardently.

For a moment that seemed to stretch on for ages, those eyes took in his person, from his hair to his boots. They lingered a moment where Anne's hand rested on his arm and something flashed across her face he could not read. Did she still hold him in affection? Had she found him lacking? Was her heart desperately attempting to escape its confines to reach him as his was only moments from bursting from his chest? All he could see was a sadness in the lines of her face that he was sure mirrored his own.

In an instant, it was over and she turned a radiant smile on Richard. All the detestable envy and resentment he had experienced in Meryton came flooding back. What he would not give to have her smile upon him in that manner. He watched, helpless, as Elizabeth and his cousin struck up their former comradery, putting awkwardness and hesitancy behind them in only a few moments.

Anne left his side to sit with Mrs Collins and he was left with familiar feelings of inadequacy when in company. Only now he carried the added burden of desperately wanting to speak with Elizabeth, but knowing not what to say. Was she angry with him? Did she resent his departure? Or, God forbid, was she indifferent? Had time healed within her heart that which still plagued his every waking moment?

She was more beautiful even than she appeared in his dreams each night. Her voice, more musical. He might have thought time would have diminished her effect on him, but no. He was more under her spell than ever before.

Rendered incapable of inserting himself into any conversation by the shock of seeing Elizabeth so unexpectedly and uncertain as to his welcome, Darcy moved to stand before the window and gazed unseeingly at the garden without. Far from inattentive, his ears clung to every melodious sound that rang forth from her delicious mouth.

His fists clenched at his sides as he listened to Elizabeth and Richard laugh over shared memories. Turning only enough to catch sight of her from the corner of his vision, his heart sank to his toes as she brazenly flirted with his cousin, reaching out to touch his sleeve and giggling absurdly at something he had said. But as he watched, he caught her eyes flickering to where he stood at the window. The longer he listened, the more hollow and forced sounded her coquetry. He had no explanation for her behaviour, but he was buoyed by the smallest spark of hope.

The requisite time for visiting soon passed; whether he was more relieved or vexed, Darcy could not say. When he made his farewells, he made a point of taking up her hand and bowing slowly over it, gazing into her eyes with all the love and affection he possessed. He felt a shudder course down her arm and knew her to be affected, but she quickly pulled her hand from his grasp and turned away.

The rest of the evening passed in much of a blur for Darcy. He heard none of Richard's recital of the afternoon's events, nor his aunt's endless chatter throughout the evening meal. Climbing into bed, he could hardly recall Adams having dressed him in his nightclothes. His every thought, his every care was for Elizabeth.

He lay in bed for hours, picturing her lovely figure, her pert nose, her flawless lips, her expressive brows. Everything about her was perfection. He recalled their every conversation in Hertfordshire; her every witty and intelligent argument, charming response, and titillating tease. She was like air to him and he was in desperate want of breath.

Even knowing it to be folly, he would seek her out on the morrow. Knowing her love of the out of doors and her preference for the wild and uncultivated, he felt a certainty she would gravitate to the groves surrounding Rosings. He had to see her one last time, then he would let her go forever.

Chapter Thirty

*ow dare he?! How *dare* he?!*

Elizabeth stormed through the grove, paying not the slightest heed to the lovely scenery she had so admired on mornings previous. She had never been so angry in all her life. Angry, hurt, confused. And it was entirely Darcy's doing.

She had stayed up much of the night trying to decipher just what he was about. He had simply appeared, looking far more handsome than any man had any right to be, stirring up feelings and longings within her. With his betrothed on his arm and not one word for herself.

Oh, what a fool she had made of herself, flirting with Mr Fitzwilliam in an ill-advised attempt to make Darcy see how little he affected her. But he did affect her; very much so. For one brief, delicious moment when he had held her hand yesterday and gazed into her eyes, she had forgotten everything; forgotten former suitors and current intendeds; forgotten her broken heart and dashed hopes. Forgotten all but the feel of her body pressed against his solid chest, the strength of his arms holding her up when her knees grew weak, the taste of his kiss on her lips. Forgotten all but that she loved him still, with every fibre of her being.

How dare he look at her *like that*?! She swiped the bonnet she had been too agitated to put on her head at some unsuspecting low hanging leaves, their only crime having been being unfortunate enough to be in her path.

Perhaps she had best leave Kent, put Darcy and his enticing looks and handsome face far behind her. It was what he had done, was it not? Oh, but she was loath to give up Charlotte's company. There could be no telling when they might meet again.

What was more, to leave would require her to give reason for her sudden desire to be gone. Admitting that she had fallen in love with an unavailable man was far too humiliating a prospect than she was willing to face. What else could she claim? Jane's letters of late had been cheerful and Mary's confirmed that their eldest sister was coping with Mr Bingley's inconstancy with a good deal of grace and had even allowed a gentleman to call on her recently.

She knew not what other excuse she might give. She knew only she never wanted to see Darcy again. Never again did she want to look upon his fine figure or hear his deep, calm, soothing voice speaking her name—

"Elizabeth."

She stopped short and looked up. There, standing mere feet from her, the low, early morning sun behind him casting a halo of golden light about his person, making him to appear as a heavenly being, was the very subject of her agonised thoughts.

He gazed upon her as a starving man might look upon a bountiful feast and she felt the stirrings of longing burning within her once again. Oh, what she would not give to feel the strength of his arms wrapped around her, to hear him promise that he would never let her go? Her legs shook with the desire to run to him, her heart cried out to his. Yet, she stifled it. She would not give in to these useless wishes. Her bruised heart could take no more.

"I had to see you," he said in a low voice and her resolve nearly crumbled.

Gathering her courage, she lifted her chin in defiance.

"This is a favourite path of mine, sir. Perhaps you would do well to avoid it. Good day." With a very clipped curtsey, she turned with a swish of her skirts and stormed off in the opposite direction.

"Elizabeth!" Darcy cried out to her.

"Pray, do not address me so familiarly, sir," she threw over her shoulder. "I am not certain your *betrothed* would appreciate it."

"My betroth—? Elizabe—Miss Bennet!" Darcy called after her, hurrying to catch her up. When he reached her, he took hold of her wrist to stay her steps and turned her to face him. "I am not engaged."

"Is that so, Mr Darcy? Then you ought to inform your aunt, for she seems to think you are. And your cousin did not correct her."

"No, Anne would not."

"I see. Well, please accept my best wishes for your future health and happiness, and that of your bride." She spun on her heel and stomped away.

"Miss Bennet. Elizabeth! May I please explain?" he begged though she did not slow her retreat.

"What is there to explain, sir? Either you are engaged or you are not. 'Tis as simple as that."

"I am not!" Darcy adamantly declared. Whether she was moved by the volume of his voice or the conviction of his words, he could not say, but Elizabeth finally halted her steps, though she did not turn to look at him. She stood resolutely with her back to him, arms folded across her chest and chin raised.

"Explain yourself," she said over her shoulder again.

"As I am in no doubt of your having heard Lady Catherine's claims, allow me to confess that she and my mother did plan a union betwixt my cousin and myself when we were but young children. But," he hastened to add when she looked as if she would flee again, "for my mother's part it was nothing more than a hope, a possibility for the future. She told me many times that she wished for my happiness in marriage above all other considerations. My father was adamantly against the scheme from the first and refused to sign any contract binding me to my cousin.

"After my mother died, my aunt began asserting that it had been her sister's greatest wish to see the match made, but my father continued to deny his consent. When he died, there was none left to contradict her but for myself. My uncle was of no use, having rarely stood up to his sister besides believing it to be a suitable match.

"Anne and I have discussed the matter, of course. It would be an advantageous union as far as fortune and status are concerned. But we are, neither of us, inclined to the other. I am fond of my cousin, but only as far as she is family. Anne wishes never to marry at all. So, we allow Lady Catherine to believe there is a possibility that we will wed to prevent her from pressing Anne towards marriage to any others."

Finally, Elizabeth turned slowly to face him. Her beautiful eyes were swimming with unshed tears. "Then...there is no engagement?"

"None. You may apply to both of my cousins if you doubt my word."

Slowly, she shook her head as a single tear trailed down her cheek. "I am sorry. I misjudged you."

Stepping forward, Darcy reached for his handkerchief in his breast pocket. "Think nothing of it. What else were you to think?" Tenderly, he reached up and wiped her eyes.

A silence fell between them, neither certain what ought to be said. Seemingly for distraction, Elizabeth took the piece of linen from him.

"This is beautiful," she said, studying the handkerchief Georgiana had embroidered with posies of lavender for him.

"My sister made it for me when I informed her I had grown fond of the scent."

When she looked up into his face, Darcy saw all the tenderness, hope, and love he felt for her reflected back at him. But it dimmed as quickly as it had appeared.

"Yet, it changes nothing," she said in a strained whisper, pressing the linen back into his hands as though it might bring harm upon her and stepping back. It was a moment before he understood her meaning. "We cannot erase the past. I was still courted by a man whom you respect. Unless...do you...do you feel any differently than you did in Hertfordshire?"

How did he feel? His love for Elizabeth was stronger than ever, yet he still owed his loyalty to his cousin. Richard had been there for Darcy during his darkest times. In every one of his worst memories, Richard was there offering strength, devotion, and distraction. When Wickham had taunted and teased him then laid the blame for his misdeeds at Darcy's feet, when his mother had died and then his father, when Wickham had once again forced himself on their notice and had nearly taken his dearest sister from him. Ever present had been Richard. Covering for his awkwardness at balls and parties; taking the focus from him when it became too much to bear. What did he not owe to that dear man?

"No," he said and hated himself as he watched the light extinguish behind her eyes. "I feel...I feel...trapped, Elizabeth. And torn. How am I to choose between two people whom I love best in the world? If I follow my heart, I may very well lose the dearest friend I have ever had. If I stand by duty and loyalty, I will lose the only woman I will ever love."

Elizabeth nodded her understanding even as a steady stream of tears tracked down her lovely cheeks. "Then, perhaps it is best that we say goodbye now. What use can there be in delaying the inevitable?"

A frustrated growl boiled forth from his chest and he stalked several steps away from her. "I am not ready!"

"Nor I."

This could not be the end. Not again.

"Could we...would you..." He looked imploringly at her. "Perhaps we might cherish this time we have been given. Steal up every moment possible until there is not one more moment left to take."

"Is that wise? Will that not make it all the more difficult when it must inevitably end?"

"Living without you was never going to be easy, Elizabeth. If I am to spend the rest of my life alone, at least I will have memories of you to ease the loneliness. Allow me to indulge this fantasy while I may. Unless...unless you would rather not." What was he thinking? "Dear God. Forgive me, Elizabeth. I ought not even to have suggested it. Of course, we cannot..." He raked a shaking hand through his hair.

She took a step towards him, followed by another and another until she stood directly before him, the swell of her bosom brushing against his coat. She lifted herself on her toes until their lips were a mere breath apart.

"We have no power over tomorrow. If today is all we have, let us embrace it," she whispered against his lips before closing the distance and pressing her mouth to his.

Of their own volition, Darcy's hands gripped the fabric of her gown at her waist and pulled her flush against his body. He felt as though he could not get near enough to her. He wanted to soak her into his clothing, into his very skin and make her a part of him. Already she was lodged deep within his heart; why ought she not possess the entirety of his being?

True to his words, he cherished every moment. The deepening of the kiss. The heat of her hands as they blazed a trail up his chest, over his shoulders, and around his neck. The tickling of the curl that escaped her pins and brushed his cheek. It was all burnt into his memory. Not one moment did he wish to forget; each was precious and would stay with him the rest of his life.

Eventually, the demand for air became crucial and Darcy detached himself from her lips only so far as to rest his forehead against hers. They stood this way for they knew not how long, their chests heaving in unison. When Darcy felt he would not be physically devastated by the loss of her touch, he pulled back.

Searching her eyes, he sought any sign of regret or sorrow but, to his immense relief, saw only love beaming at him.

Tucking her hand possessively around his arm, they silently turned and slowly meandered through the grove. Elizabeth's natural playfulness eventually came to the fore and she teased him into laughter. They spent several, all too short, hours walking through the grove, talking, laughing, and stealing kisses and touches. For a time, there were no impediments, no cousins, no former suitors. There was no past and no future. There was only the here and now and they were determined to take advantage of it.

Succeeding days passed in a like manner. The lovers met each morning, and any other moment they could steal, in the grove, blocking out any thoughts of his looming departure and the end of their beautiful love affair. They spoke of everything and nothing. He described his beloved home to her, in as loving detail as if he fully expected it to one day be her home, as well. He told her of his sister, and the worries he harboured whilst caring for a young girl who would be a young woman much too soon for Darcy's liking. He shared his entire history with Wickham, from childhood disputes to the reprobate's attempted elopement with Georgiana last summer in a thwarted grasp for her fortune.

In turn, Elizabeth shared stories of her childhood, of being raised in a home with so many siblings so close in age. She graciously gave advice and insight into a young girl's mind. Elizabeth confided her indignation on Jane's behalf for Mr Bingley's trifling with her affections and subsequent defection. Though initially hurt that it had been none other than the man before her who had urged his friend to refrain from returning to Netherfield, she soon saw, by his explanation, the kindness in that act and agreed her sister would, in the long term, be better off for it.

They took it in turns to ask one another questions; everything from how they took their tea to their deepest fears. That they would be torn apart in only a few short days was never mentioned or alluded to, though it was ever hovering in the background, easy to ignore if impossible to forget.

Chapter Thirty-One

"You have been avoiding Richard," Anne accused from the doorway, pulling Darcy from his heavenly reflections. Since parting from Elizabeth that afternoon, he had retired to his chambers and was currently nursing a glass of brandy in his shirtsleeves in front of the fire, reliving recent events.

Walking the grove that morning, he and his beloved had found a shady spot to sit beneath an old beech tree. Darcy had laid in the grass with his head resting in Elizabeth's lap as she gently ran her fingers through his hair. Never had he known such contentedness. He could happily live out his life in just that attitude.

"Nonsense." In a bid for time to master his expressions, he tossed back what remained of his drink. When the burn in his throat had cooled, he turned to his cousin. "What reason could I have to avoid him?"

Anne stepped into the room and slumped into the chair across from him in a manner her mother would surely have scolded her for. "I am sure I could not say. But we have hardly seen hide nor hair of you in ages, despite your having delayed your departure for some inexplicable reason. I am certain it is not on my account."

Avoiding her gaze, Darcy stood and walked to the sideboard to refill his glass. He despised deception. "I have been busy."

"Bollocks." Anne laughed at his shocked expression at hearing his quiet, diminutive, proper cousin utter an imprecation. Looking not the slightest contrite, she added with a smirk, "As Richard would say. You have not been haunting the library, Davison says Rosings is in good order and he has not met with you in nearly a week, and the stables informed me that you have not been on Sleipnir in days."

"You have been checking up on me."

"No. Richard has. Where have you been hiding yourself?"

"I have not been hiding," Darcy answered, though it was not entirely true. He did not sneak away with Elizabeth to abandoned sheds or secret away in haylofts, but they did keep to the unfrequented paths of the groves and woods. Already they were flouting the rules of propriety; if anyone discovered their assignations, Elizabeth's reputation would be tarnished. Of course, then he would have no choice but to marry her regardless of his cousin's disapprobation and Richard could not blame him. The idea had merit and he tucked it away to consider at another time—likely only for his own amusement. He could never risk Elizabeth's reputation in such a manner nor so flippantly betray Richard.

"Oh? Then where have you been?"

"I have been...exploring the estate." It was near enough a truthful answer. "There are many paths about the place I have not ventured down in years."

"Exploring the estate?"

"Yes."

"You had best stick to the truth, Darcy. You are a terrible liar. Well, I will not press you any further if you have no wish to confide in me. Before I go, however, I have but two things to say to you and they are thus—Richard loves you, Darcy. There is *nothing* in this world he would not give for your happiness. And the second—" She stood and stepped right up to him, leaning down to whisper in his ear, "What is she worth to you?"

Straightening, Anne turned away and tossed a blithe farewell over her shoulder before slipping out as quietly as she had come.

Astonished, Darcy did not even think to stand as she left, but remained seated, considering her words. His cousin had obviously noticed his attraction to Elizabeth, and hers for him. Had they been so transparent? Looking over their interactions amongst company, perhaps he ought not to be so surprised. He could hardly keep his eyes off her and took every opportunity to be near her. And Elizabeth was often sending tender glances his way. They had thought themselves rather clever, carrying on under his aunt's watchful gaze. Perhaps they had not been as sly as they had imagined. Dear God! Had Richard noticed?

"Richard loves you, Darcy. There is nothing *in this world he would not sacrifice for your happiness."* Belatedly, her words hit him with great force. He had been so preoccupied with his own feelings of loyalty and love for his cousin, he had failed to consider Richard's brotherly affection for himself. Was it possible? Would Richard give his blessing for their union out of

cousinly love? Did Darcy dare ask? How could he? Yet, how could he not?

In answer to Anne's question, there could be only one answer: everything. Elizabeth was worth everything to him. Even, he thought with a nervous exhale, risking his relationship with his dearest cousin. Not that he truly believed it would come to that, Richard would understand. He had to. Darcy would make him understand.

Determination flooded him along with a surprising sense of clarity. He knew what he must do; perhaps he had always known.

Tossing back the last of his liquid courage, Darcy unceremoniously slammed the glass down on the table before jumping from his seat. He grabbed his jacket as he verily ran from the room, shoving his arms through the sleeves as he crossed over the threshold.

Taking them two at a time, he bounded down the stairs and across the hall to his aunt's favourite parlour. He was grateful to find his aunt and both of his cousins within.

With little preamble, he began. "Aunt, you will forgive me but I will never marry my cousin Anne." Turning his gaze to his male cousin, he felt a wave of uncertainty course through him. Nevertheless, he forged onward. "I am in love with Miss Elizabeth Bennet. She alone will I marry."

Several things happened at once. Lady Catherine rapped her gilded walking stick against the marble floors with a force that belied her advanced years, shouting her indignation. Anne clapped her hands together in delight, laughing gaily. It was Richard's response, however, which Darcy watched with bated breath.

That man burst from his seat, pumping a fist in the air, and shouted, "Ah ha! I knew it!"

"Darcy! What is the meaning of this?" Lady Catherine cried.

"Congratulations, Cousin," Anne beamed at him.

"I knew it! I knew it! I knew it!" repeated Richard. "Did I not tell you, Anne?"

"You did, indeed."

"Of course, you will marry Anne! I demand on being satisfied!"

"No, Mother. He will not."

"What do you mean?" Darcy asked Richard. "What did you know?"

"I knew you were not indifferent to Miss Bennet! I knew you loved her!"

"Of course, he is indifferent to that country nobody! He certainly is not in love with her! He is to marry Anne!"

Ignoring his aunt's imperious indignation, Darcy continued to question his cousin. "But, how did you know? When did you know?"

"Good God, Darcy, from the very beginning! Why do you think I courted her in the first place? I could see almost from the very moment I met her that she was perfectly suited to you. But I also knew you would likely not consider her on the fact of her meagre fortune alone. So, I courted her in your stead!"

"You believed, from the first, Elizabeth to be perfectly suited to me?" Darcy asked slowly and deliberately.

"I did," Richard answered proudly.

"You believed I would not see her excellent merits for myself?"

"I did not."

"So, you courted her, without any intentions of marrying her?"

"We are of too similar a disposition. I was quite certain I could not touch her heart. Indeed, I did not even try. Why do you think I was ever foisting her company upon you?! Feigning difficulty dismounting. Faking falls so you could walk eight miles in her company. Pressing you to dance with her? You know what they say; dancing is the food of love!"

Darcy pinched the bridge of his nose, hardly believing what he was hearing. "Poetry, you idiot. Poetry is the food of love."

"Oh, well. The principle is the same. I only wished to throw the two of you together so that you might see the remarkable lady that she is."

"Wait. Did you say faking falls? What happened at the ruins? That was an act?"

The ladies observed this exchange with interest, their heads turning from one gentleman to the other as if they were watching a riveting game of shuttlecock. A few footmen and maids watching eagerly from an adjoining parlour took a good deal of amusement from the scene.

"But of course! One of my more brilliant ideas, if I do say so myself. Though I had thought my scheme unsuccessful until this very moment. When Anne wrote to tell me Miss Bennet was here at Rosings I—"

"You imbecile!" Before even Darcy knew what he did, his fist was clenched and drawn back. The force of the facer he planted on his cousin sent Richard stumbling back and across Anne's lap.

"Whad da hell, Darcy?!" cried Richard, clutching at his bleeding nose while Anne struggled to help him to rise. "Whad was dad for?"

"You imbecile!" Darcy repeated as he paced back and forth before his relations, one hand shaking on his hip whilst the other was raked through his hair again and again.

"I do nod udderstan'!"

"If you had not meddled, Elizabeth and I might already be married!"

"Will somebody tell me what in heaven's name is going on?!" shouted Lady Catherine, though she might as well have remained silent for all the attention paid her.

"Did you truly believe I would not see the worth of that magnificent creature?" He threw a hand towards the door to the great beyond where he imagined his love to be. "I had not known Elizabeth a fortnight before I felt she was the only woman I could ever marry! But you had already gone and engaged her in a courtship."

"Whij ended mon's ago!"

"And what was I to do then? Hope to marry the woman I had believed my cousin, whom I respect and love above almost all others, had hoped to marry? What do you take me for?"

"Oh." Richard lowered the crimson-soaked handkerchief from his still profusely bleeding face. "I had nod considered dad."

"I have gathered as much."

Lady Catherine looked between her two nephews, her interest in the intriguing rivalry undisguised. "What has changed?" At the questioning looks she received, her ladyship elaborated. "You said you would not marry the lady Richard seemingly had designs upon. But you have blown in here, presumably to announce your intentions to marry Miss Bennet. Which I still object to," she added hastily. "But what has changed?"

He looked gratefully upon Anne, a smile overtaking his features. "Elizabeth is worth everything. Even should Richard hate me and refuse to acknowledge me from this moment onwards, we are still bound by blood. But Elizabeth...I will never meet another woman like her."

"I cood never hade you, Darcy. Eved 'ad I wijhed do agdually marry da girl, you 'ad odly do dell me—"

"Enough, Richard," Anne interrupted. "You sound like a fool. Go on, Cousin. Go get your lady."

"Thank you, Anne. Aunt, I am sorry if you are disappointed but I will not be swayed. Richard, forgive me. I am terribly sorry about your nose."

Richard waved this away with his blood-soaked handkerchief. "I waz dever az ha'dsome az you, adyway."

Darcy conceded with a cheeky shrug before turning away and hastening out the door. Before he had gone too far, he heard his aunt call after him.

"Wait! No, Darcy! What about Anne?!"

"All will be well, Mother," he heard Anne reassure his aunt. "Darcy is far too dull for my liking, anyway."

Chuckling to himself, Darcy ran from the house. He was carried on light feet across the park and down the lane to the parsonage where his beloved awaited him, unbeknownst to herself. He stopped before the door and forced a few deep breaths before banging on the solid oak which separated him from Elizabeth. A wide-eyed maid answered with a clumsy curtsey.

"I must speak with Miss Bennet," he demanded. It was hardly proper, but they would be engaged soon and he was too excited to care.

"Oh, um, beggin' yer pardon, sir, but Miss Bennet isn't here."

Chapter Thirty-Two

"I beg your pardon?" Darcy asked, feeling as though it had been he rather than his cousin who had been cuffed.

Where had she gone? And why had she not spoken to him before she left? Had she returned to London early? Had the sneaking and secrecy become too great a burden for her? She had seemed to be as happy as he when they were together, despite the improper, clandestine nature of their relationship. Though she had expressed a good deal of anxiety at his departure which had been scheduled for the morrow. Was the prospect of saying goodbye yet again too arduous even for his brave Elizabeth?

"Oh, um. Yeah, she lef', sir."

"But, why? Has she returned to London? When?" Wild thoughts of racing down the road on Sleipnir to catch her up rushed through his head. Dramatically demanding the coach to pull over so that he might declare his love to his lady. It would certainly be romantic.

"That will be all, Sally." Mrs Collins appeared at the door and dismissed the maid to her chores. "Forgive the confusion, Mr Darcy. Eliza has gone for a walk. She was, well, she has been in rather subdued spirits. Something is bothering her, but she will not confide in me. I surmised it was a matter of the heart, but I had rather believed it was inspired by your cousin. I gather I am mistaken?"

Darcy swallowed. He knew not what to say. He had never enjoyed having his private affairs laid open for the world to see and he would like to speak to Elizabeth before any more people became acquainted with his feelings. However, this was Elizabeth's dear and trusted friend.

"Forgive me, sir," she said before he had made any decision. "I forget sometimes that I am no longer amongst those I have known all my life. Elizabeth walked in the direction of the grove. But if you have sad tidings to deliver, I beg you would reconsider seeking her out. She is already greatly disheartened, though she tries to hide it."

"Thank you, Mrs Collins. For your assistance and for being so devoted a friend to Miss Bennet. I assure you, I have no intentions of distressing her. Quite the opposite, in fact."

"Then go to it, sir."

"What is going on, Mrs Collins?" Mr Collins' voice sounded from the depth of the house. "Who is here?"

"For your own sake, go quickly," Mrs Collins recommended before shutting the door in his face.

Darcy needed no further prompting. Spinning on his heel, he ran down the path and through the parsonage gate, turning his feet towards the place where they most often met. He would search the entire grove until he found her; he would follow her to the ends of the earth if necessary.

When he did not find her at their usual meeting place, he walked a few of the trails they had frequented, but to no avail. Inspiration struck then, and he turned to follow the stream to a small glade they had discovered some days ago. It was quiet and secluded and had utterly charmed Elizabeth. He had been utterly charmed by Elizabeth being charmed by the glade. It had become his favourite place to be with her. He took an inordinate amount of joy in watching the delight in her beautiful eyes and kissing the smile on her lovely face surrounded by a carpet of wildflowers. It would certainly be the ideal place for a proposal.

As he approached the glade, his heart was in his throat. Never had he imagined being in such a state over a woman! But here he was, and gladly!

Passing through the slight parting in the brush which served as something of an entry to the glade, Darcy looked around eagerly—but she was not here. His shoulders slumped and his frustration voiced itself in a low growl.

Where could she be? Had he missed her on another trail? Ought he retrace his steps and revisit some of the places he had already looked? Or had he best remain here, in hopes she would wish to visit this place and revel in the same memories as he?

Then doubts began to set in. Had she thought he would seek her out and was avoiding him? Had she, perhaps, gone to another part of the estate altogether, feeling it safest to avoid the grove where he would of a certainty look for her? Mrs Collins had spoken of her friend being disheartened. Was that of his doing? Had it been foolish to suggest they indulge in their desires when they had no notion of there ever being any hope for a future? Or was she simply dreading the morrow when he was meant to leave? Surely, they would not be granted another opportunity to be together again. Especially not with such freedoms as they had enjoyed here. In trying to capture what little time they had left, had he inadvertently broken her heart further? By God, what a fool he was!

If only he could find her, all would be made right.

"William?"

The sound of her voice drifted across the meadow and wrapped around his entire being, rendering him stunned and frozen in place. He was not entirely convinced it had been real; that his wishful heart had not interpreted the gentle breeze as Elizabeth's most beloved voice.

All doubt fled when she called out to him again and he spun around, an indescribable joy giving flight to his feet. He could not reach her fast enough, and when she was within reach, his arms wrapped around her waist and lifted her clear off the ground. His lips crashed into hers as he twirled them both in circles, the world around them nought but a hazy swirl of colour and light.

"Marry me," he said between kisses. "Marry me, my darling, lovely Elizabeth!"

"Oh!" she cried, pulling back just enough to look up into his face, a look of astonishment upon her own. "I...but what about your cousin?"

"My cousin! Oh, my cousin!" He shook his head in annoyance for that beloved man and his well-intended, if misguided, scheming. "I will tell you all about him in a moment, but for now it is enough to say that he has given us his blessing. Even had he not, my love, my resolve would be the same. There is no reason in this world good enough to keep us apart. I love you, Elizabeth Bennet, most ardently. I would risk everything in the world if only you would consent to be my wife."

"Oh!" she cried again, a radiant smile stretching across her lips. "Yes! Yes! Yes! A thousand times, yes! I love you!"

He pulled her close again for another heart-thundering kiss, punctuated by exultant smiles, joyful laughter, and fervent declarations of their love. They each believed themselves to be the most fortunate creature on the earth and were utterly convinced of their future felicity. Already they had endured much apart; there was nothing they could not weather side by side.

"Oh, forgive me, my darling," said Darcy when they had expressed much of what was in their hearts. "Are you well? Have I upset you in any way?"

Elizabeth looked up at him in confusion? "Upset me? Why should I be upset with you? You have rather undone the upset!"

"I am unsure. Only Mrs Collins had said you were of low spirits when you left the parsonage. I feared...Lord, I do not know what I feared. I knew only I would do anything to make it right again."

"Spending any length time under the same roof as Mr Collins will upset anyone, I am sure. I am in awe of my friend's forbearance."

"Then I have not offended you with my selfish suggestion to continue as we have?"

"Offended me? Not at all," she assured him with a loving smile and gentle kiss on his cheek. "I confess, I have at times wondered at the wisdom of our decisions, knowing they could only end in further heartbreak. But I would not have given up this time with you for all the world." She placed a hand on his cheek as she gazed lovingly into his eyes. "There are few in this world who will ever experience true love, and even fewer who will be fortunate enough to be with the one they hold in their heart. Had our arrangement remained temporary, I should have been grateful to have known what it is to love, and be truly loved in return. If you were to leave me on the morrow—oh! Are you leaving?"

"Certainly not. Eager though I am to obtain your father's consent, I am in no hurry to leave you when I am at last secured of your hand and heart. I will speak with Richard and put off our departure once again. He will not object. It is the least he can do after his actions in the autumn."

"Oh, yes. Will you tell me now what has happened? What has the poor man done?"

"You will not think him so poor when you have heard what I have to tell you." Darcy then relayed his cousin's dubiously brilliant plan to bring them together which, of course, resulted only in tearing them apart.

"You mean to tell me that he never intended to marry me at all? Had not even wished to truly court me?" She had a strangely detached look on her face that made Darcy a little uneasy.

"Are you...well, my love?"

Starting slightly at his words, Elizabeth fixed a thin smile on her face. "Perfectly, my darling. May we return to Rosings? I should like to have a word with *Mr Fitzwilliam*."

There was such a fire in her eyes, Darcy dared not deny her. He offered his arm and they walked away from the glade together in silence. Looking down at the tiny, angry woman at his side, he vowed never to cross his beautifully fierce wife. At least, not too oft. There was something undeniably alluring about a passionately indignant Elizabeth.

Not a word passed between them as they made their way back to Rosings; Darcy for fear of attracting her ire towards himself and Elizabeth for thinking over what Darcy had told her and rehearsing what she wished to say to his cousin. They climbed the steps of the great house and entered together. After checking with his aunt's butler, Darcy led her to the drawing room. Richard and Anne stood when they appeared at the door while Lady Catherine sniffed and turned her nose up. Darcy considered it a win that she did not immediately begin to harangue and abuse Elizabeth.

"Mizz Elizabet'!" Richard addressed her, stepping forward eagerly to greet her. Before he could utter another word, however, the slip of a woman at Darcy's side who stood barely to the top of his shoulder drew back and slapped his cousin squarely across the cheek. Then she pointed one angrily shaking finger right under Richard's nose.

"If I ever, *ever* hear of your toying with another lady's affections ever again, even for a noble cause, I swear to you, Mr Fitzwilliam, you *will* regret it, sir. Do I make myself perfectly clear?"

Richard visibly swallowed as he looked down into her marvellously flaming eyes and nodded vigorously.

"Say it."

"Y-yes. Yes, ma'am. I do apologise most profusely."

"Good."

An oppressive silence fell over the occupants of the room as Elizabeth continued to stare daggers at Richard. Darcy was torn between wishing to laugh at his cousin's having been so thoroughly set down, while Anne looked upon Elizabeth with something akin to awe.

"Well," said Lady Catherine, breaking the tension hanging thick in the air. "I suppose you will do after all. Welcome to the family, Miss Elizabeth."

The young people all exchanged incredulous looks and then burst into astonished laughter. Darcy had held every expectation of having to go to battle with his stubborn, irascible aunt over his right to choose his own bride. She would never have persuaded him away from Elizabeth, but he had never believed she would ever accept any choice but her daughter, and certainly not quietly. It appeared, however, that Elizabeth had won the lady over by her own merit. He ought never to have doubted. His beloved was utterly magnificent.

"Your ladyship! Your ladyship!" Mr Collins' strident tones brought an instant death to all their merriment and Elizabeth drew nearer to Darcy. The corpulent parson stumbled into the parlour, clutching his chest as he heaved for breath and swiped at his sweaty brow. "Your ladyship!"

"What on earth is the matter, Mr Collins?" Lady Catherine asked her bothersome clergyman, distaste writ clearly on her countenance. "This is most irregular."

"Oh, do forgive me, your ladyship. I have just learnt the most disturbing, the most distressing news. I felt it was my duty to make haste to your esteemed presence to acquaint you to the dangers lurking in your very own—you!" His eyes had drifted to where Darcy stood, Elizabeth standing close to his side, holding tight to his arm. With a speed no one might have believed him capable of, Mr Collins marched across to the couple, grabbed Elizabeth by the arm and wrenched her from Darcy's grasp. "I invite you into my home, expose you to such society as you may never again have the privilege of associating with, and *this* is how you repay my notice of you?! Lady Catherine's notice of you? Coming here and imposing yourself upon persons who are far above you?! I assure you, my lady, I will have a very stern conversation with my wayward cousin regarding her brazen, improper, wholly desper—"

"Mr Collins!" Darcy shouted over the absurd, voluble man. "Unhand my betrothed at once!" He stepped forward and rescued Elizabeth from her cousin's clammy hands. Quietly, and most solicitously, he asked after her well-being as she massaged her wrist where her cousin had gripped her so tightly.

"Your...oh, no! You have fallen under her spell! My dear Lady Catherine, I offer my most humble and fervent apologies for inflicting this plight upon your most august, revered, respected, noble, estee—"

"Mr Collins!" Lady Catherine stopped the parson this time. "I will not tolerate insults upon members of my family. As Miss Bennet is to be my niece, she is now to be considered as under my influence and protection."

"Your niece?" cried Mr Collins in a scandalised screech. "But, but, but, but...but, what of the incomparable Miss de Bourgh? Of the engagement between your most excellent daughter and your illustrious nephew? Had it not been the greatest wish of her mother as well and his? Have they not been intended since Miss de Bourgh was in her cradle? Are they not descended from the same noble line on their mothers' side and equally respected and great families on their fathers'? Are the shades of Pemberley to be thus polluted?!"

"Mr Collins!" the entire group cried as one. Lady Catherine gave them all a look that clearly stated she would handle this. Though Darcy bristled at not being the one to defend his beloved, he nonetheless gave way for his far more experienced aunt to deal with her parson.

"Mr Collins, all that you say was, indeed, the hope of my dearly departed sister and myself. We did as much as we could in planning the union. Its completion depended upon others. My nephew is confined neither by honour nor inclination to my daughter. Why may he not make another choice? If Miss Bennet is that choice, why may she not accept him?"

"But what of her deplorable connections? Though my cousin may be a gentleman's daughter and not *all* her connections are so very bad,"—he gripped his lapels and puffed out his chest proudly—"her mother's brother is in trade!"

Darcy held his breath after this pronouncement. He knew his aunt's opinion on those who worked for their living. It did not lessen Elizabeth's worth in his estimation one jot, but he would not have her offended by his family. Indeed, Lady Catherine's lips pursed and she looked to be fighting valiantly for composure.

"Whatever Miss Bennet's connections, if my nephew has no objections, they can be nothing to you." She swallowed thickly and closed her eyes in forbearance. "Or to me.

"It is in decidedly poor taste to denigrate a worthy young lady, particularly one within your own family. Now, you will kindly look to your own affairs and cease imposing upon mine."

At this obvious dismissal, Mr Collins turned a sickly shade of green. He stammered a good deal and made several ridiculously low bows to everyone. "Ma-ma-ma-my m-m-m-most hum-m-ba-ble ap-ap-apol-apologies, ma-m-m-my l-l-ady. I, I, I—"

"Enough, Mr Collins! Go!"

With a rather unmanly squeak, the clergyman performed an undignified leaping twirl and ran from the room, still mumbling obsequious apologies.

"Thank you, Lady Catherine," said Elizabeth, her eyes brightened by unshed tears.

"Yes, well. See that I do not regret it," Lady Catherine replied, though there was the faintest smile tugging at the corner of her lips. "Now, off with you, as well. I am sure you have much to discuss."

The young couple each thanked her ladyship, Darcy stepping forward to kiss his aunt on her blushing cheek, then did as they were told. Arm in arm, they left his relations behind to stroll in the gardens.

"When should you like to be married, my love?" Darcy asked his bride, praying her wishes aligned with his.

"Soon," she answered with feeling. "We have been apart long enough."

"I have no engagements on the morrow," he said with a wry twist of his lips. "What say you?"

"William! You have not even sought my father's consent."

"Very well. But I agree. I am impatient to make you my wife. Besides, you might decide you prefer Richard, after all."

"William!" She laughing cried as she swatted his arm. "You have nothing to fear on that score. It has been many months now since I have been ardently and irrevocably in love with the Colonel's cousin."

Finis

Epilogue

Spring, 1814

Richard took a deep, fortifying breath and looked his opponent square in the eye. He would need every ounce of his battle-hardened fortitude to see him through this interview. In truth, the idea of facing the entirety of the French army did not frighten him half so much as the formidable foe seated across the large cherry wood desk from him.

"I have come to ask for your blessing to wed Ma—Miss Mary," he corrected himself at the sight of that sharply raised brow. *It must be a family trait,* he thought to himself. When Mary turned that look on him, it made his heart race. He had not understood his cousin's strange fascination with purposefully vexing his wife until he had fallen in love with her younger sister.

Grünerberg—the name had rather grown on him—was doing well. He had begun to make a name for himself all over the country for his fine horseflesh and had felt for some time now that he was ready for the next adventure. When he had, at last, acknowledged his growing envy for Darcy and his nearly sickening felicity with his charming wife, there was only one woman Richard could imagine being by his side.

He had been impressed with the steady, sensible young woman when he had first met her in Hertfordshire. But when Mary had come to live at Pemberley last year, he had been instantly struck. She was everything lovely, kind, intelligent, and, most importantly, had a love for horses which rivalled his own. Never had he been so grateful for the short distance which separated his estate from Pemberley.

"Ahem."

With some force, Richard pulled his thoughts away from his beloved Mary and back to the matter at hand. Too much was at stake to lose focus now.

"I beg your pardon. As you are well aware, I can readily afford to take a wife. As my wife, Miss Mary will want for nothing."

An interminable silence followed this statement.

"You will understand my hesitancy," was the eventual answer. "You have courted a member of my family before."

Richard swallowed, then nodded shamefacedly. Would he never live that down? If he had known what trouble his well-intended plans to bring his cousin together with his wife would bring upon his own head, he may never have bothered—never mind that he need not to have bothered in any case. "Yes, I have. But you know I acted with only the very best of intentions. It was never my intent to deceive anyone, least of all you."

The only reply was that damnable accusing brow.

"Oh, come now, Elizabeth! Your father was not this troublesome!"

"My father is as of yet unaware of the part you played in William and my courtship."

"How many times must I apologise for that? I am sorry, I am sorry, a thousand times over, I am sorry!"

"Not bad. A few more times and I might be satisfied."

"Darling," Darcy softly chided her from the corner where he had taken himself to bask in his cousin's discomfort.

"Very well," Elizabeth conceded. "State your case, sir."

"My case? I…" He vented his frustration in a great huff of breath as he ran both hands through his hair. "As I have already stated, Grünerberg is thriving. I can well afford to take a wife. I have a good income and can settle a respectable amount on Miss Mary and provide amply for any children. Your sister will want for nothing."

A short silence followed these words as if she expected him to say more. "I have no doubts that she will."

"But that is not good enough for you? Good God, Elizabeth!" He jumped from his chair and paced to the window. Spinning back to face Elizabeth, he threw his hands in the air. "What do you want from me? Mary has already accepted my hand and your father has given his consent, though it is unnecessary. Mary is of age, you know."

"I wonder why you would bother with me, in that case."

Looking away, Richard sniffed. "Mary will not set a date until I have your blessing," he admitted grudgingly. "You were courted by me."

"I was."

"Then you know that this is entirely different!" Breathing deeply, Richard sat back down, lowering his head into his hands. "I love her, Elizabeth. She is as essential to me as air, as food and water. As essential to me as my horses. Her kind and gentle nature calms my battle-weary soul and brings me a peace I had despaired of ever finding again. I cannot imagine walking through this life without her. I...I love her."

"That," said Elizabeth gently, "was all I needed to hear." Slowly, Richard lifted his head to peer at her. "Mary deserves to be loved for the special young woman that she is. She has been invisible at Longbourn for far too long. If you can see the beautiful and unique soul that resides within my sister and promise to cherish her for it, then you have my blessing."

"I promise, Elizabeth. With all my heart. There will not be a more cherished wife in all of England."

"Now," Darcy cut in, "do not get carried away." He flashed that look at his wife that Richard had seen far too many times before and knew it meant he had best make himself scarce before they became insufferable.

"Thank you, Elizabeth. Thank you, dear sister! Darce! We shall be brothers, after all!"

"Congratulations, old boy," said Darcy, standing to salute his cousin. "I daresay, she will be the making of you."

"She already has been."

With a fierce embrace and a kiss on his future sister's cheek, a hearty handshake from his cousin, and a leaping shout of joy for himself, Richard hurried from the study to seek out his beloved Mary and share with her the good news.

Darcy closed and locked the door behind him, leaving only he and Elizabeth alone in the study—the way he preferred it. Crossing to her, he held out a hand to help her out of his large leather master's chair. When she had vacated it, he swiftly sat himself in it and pulled her onto his lap, wrapping his long arms around her.

"Did you have to make it so difficult for him, my dear?"

"But, of course! Because of him, we were made to wait months of agony before we came to an understanding. He can suffer through a few minutes of my teasing very well. There was never any danger of denying my blessing. Mary has held a tendre for him since first you all came to Hertfordshire and has been desperately in love with him this past year at least. Besides, Papa gave him hardly any trouble at all."

"Yes, I believe he learnt his lesson when Harkin threatened to make off with your sister to Gretna Green after he could not discern whether or not your father had given his consent to marry Jane."

"Dear me, yes. Though I am rather proud of Jane. I had not thought it in her to deliver such a set down. And to Papa, of all people."

"She is a woman who has learnt what it is she wants. I am happy for her. Though I am fond of my friend, Bingley could not have made her happy." He leant in and began trailing kisses up his wife's neck.

"And how is Mr Bingley these days?" she asked, tilting her head to give him greater access.

"Same old Bingley." He nibbled her ear. "He may be ready to settle down by the time he is fifty, I should imagine."

"So young?"

"Ha!"

"At least he no longer has Miss Bingley to contend with. Excuse me, Lady Doring."

"I never thought I should ever feel sorry for the lady. She was sorely mistaken in the baron's consequence."

"Mistaken or misled?"

"Both, oh! William!"

"Enough. Others do not interest me right now. I am alone with my delectable wife and mean to make the most of it before the twins wake and lay claim on you."

Elizabeth turned her head to glance at the fine clock on the mantel, which gave her husband a new angle to explore and he took full advantage.

"William! We have not the time! Margaret and Wills will be up at any moment."

"Then we had best hurry."

"There is no such thing as hurry when one is made to wear stays and corsets."

"Turn around. I have become quite the skilled lady's maid. I will make quick work of it."

Elizabeth's shifted on her husband's knee and leant forward. Darcy trailed kisses down the back of her neck as his fingers worked the small buttons at the back of her gown. When he had opened her dress, he smiled at what he saw.

"You are wearing neither stays nor a corset, my dear."

"Am I not? Oh, my."

"Minx. You planned this."

"Are you calling me wanton?"

"I am calling you irresistible. Amazing. Utterly charming. Entirely delectable. Richard may believe himself the most fortunate man in the kingdom, but he is wrong. I would have waited a lifetime for you, my darling Elizabeth."

"I am pleased to hear it, my dear. But inordinately glad you did not have to. Now, enough talk. We have not much time."

She stood and took her husband by the hand, pulling him from his chair and across the room to the very large, very comfortable sofa where they tumbled into one another's arms.

"God, I love you, Elizabeth."

"I know. But show me again, my William."

Thank you for reading *The Colonel's Cousin*! I hope you enjoyed reading it as much as I enjoyed writing it. This was an idea that has been with me since the very beginning and it has been so much fun to see how this one turned out. It will never cease to amaze me how these stories can take on a life of their own.

I want to thank my family for their support and seemingly endless patience while I worked on this. Thank you for enduring late dinners when I just couldn't pull myself away from the story in time. For your ideas that were of no help at all but made me smile, nonetheless. And for indulging me when I went on and on about fictional characters as if they were real people. I love you!

Thank you to my mom for reading anything and everything I put to paper and telling me it's wonderful, even when I know it's not. And my western/mystery reading dad for reading a sweet, regency romance just to make me feel loved. It means the world to me.

And, of course, thank you, Jane Austen for writing such wonderful, lovable, timeless characters we can fall in love with over and over.

About the Author

Melissa first discovered Pride & Prejudice at the age of eleven when visiting family while her aunt was recording the BBC miniseries from TV to VHS and instantly fell in love. A voracious reader, this led her to the novel which, in turn, led to the discovery of Jane Austen's other excellent works, Persuasion being her favorite. She stumbled upon the genre of JAFF in 2019 and her heart was irrevocably gone. After reading so many variations and imaging storylines of her own, she began writing them down and, for the first time, discovered her passion in life.

Melissa lives in Alaska with her husband, a delightful combination of Mr. Darcy and Mr. Tilney, their five children, and their behemoth of dog, Knightley. When not reading or writing, which is not very often, Melissa enjoys camping in the wide Alaskan frontier, hiking, traveling, and watching all the adaptations of Jane Austen's works on DVD. And sleeping. Sleeping is the best.

Other works by Melissa Halcomb

 <u>Mr Darcy's Daughter</u>
An unfulfilled promise to his late wife has followed
Darcy to Hertfordshire. For three years, it has hung like
a dead weight about his neck, yet his first priority has
been and must continue to be his young daughter.
A rocky first encounter with the handsome friend of her new
neighbour leaves Elizabeth reeling. Meeting his adorable daughter
will change her life forever. But what about the tall, brooding man
she calls Papa?

Printed in Great Britain
by Amazon

40910029R00189